Worth The Effort

The words were cut off as he grabbed her upper arms and whirled her around, placing her back against the building.

"Why didn't you say any of your ideas today?" he asked. Growled.

"What?" she asked, confused. This was her rant. What was he blathering about?

"Today. In the meeting. You had it all down in your notes. Why didn't you speak up?"

"You were looking at my laptop?"

He shook her arms, stepped closer to her. The envelope under his arm rustled, but held. His breath came out in frozen clouds. She could see hers as well. Why was she breathing so hard?

"I even gave you the opening about the methane, but you let the others bring it up. Why?"

She tried to think back to the meeting, but her mind shut down. She couldn't think, she could only feel. Feel his strong hands on her arms, even through the thick wool of her coat. Feel his breath against her face. Feel the weight of his gaze as his eyes searched hers.

"I don't know…I… What do you mean?" she asked, her voice not sounding like her own.

His eyes dropped from hers to her mouth, and she bit her lip. In anticipation.

"Aw, hell," he whispered, then leaned forward and kissed her.

OTHER TITLES BY
MARA JACOBS

The Worth Series
(Contemporary Romance)
Worth The Weight
Worth The Drive
Worth The Fall
Worth The Effort
Totally Worth Christmas
Worth The Price
Worth The Lies
Worth The Flight

Freshman Roommates Trilogy
(New Adult Romance)
In Too Deep
In Too Fast
In Too Hard

Anna Dawson's Vegas Series
(Romantic Mystery)
Against The Odds
Against The Spread
Against The Rules
Against The Wall

Romantic Suspense
Broken Wings

Countdown To A Kiss
(A New Year's Eve Anthology)

WORTH the EFFORT

The Worth Series, Book Four

MARA JACOBS

Published by Mara Jacobs
©Copyright 2013 Mara Jacobs

ISBN: 978-0-9852586-4-1

For more information on the author and her works, please
see www.marajacobs.com

For Colleen

Prologue

~m~

Twenty years ago

"COME HERE, DENI, I WANT TO SHOW YOU SOMETHING," Denise Casparich's father, Barry, said to her.

Eight-year-old Deni walked across the dirt road at the top of Brockway Mountain to the side of the hill where her father stood.

"What is it?" she asked as she came to stand beside him. He slipped an arm around her shoulders, and she leaned into his hip, a practiced movement between them.

"When I was at Tech, we'd come here in the spring, after the snow had melted and the road up here was open. And if it was a clear day, like today, you could see Isle Royale in the distance." He knelt down to Deni's level and stuck out his arm, pointing in the direction of Lake Superior. "There. Can you see it?"

Deni wasn't sure that she did. It all seemed like a huge mass of water to her, with the sky and lake meeting at some indiscernible point. But she nodded to her father and squinted a little harder.

Her father chuckled, always able to read her. "It's out there. But it is kind of fuzzy." He stood back up, put his hands on his hips, and breathed in deeply as he surveyed the view. "Freshest air in the world."

Deni didn't think the air was that much fresher than back home in Farmington Hills, but again she nodded her agreement.

She'd endured the ten-hour drive in the back seat between her older brothers—who'd fought the entire time—with anticipation because her father was so excited to visit his "always mother." Or whatever it was that he kept calling the place he went to college.

But walking around campus looking at buildings was not her idea of a summer vacation. Her best friend Stephie was going to Cedar Point. She was probably riding on their newest roller coaster at this very minute.

Deni turned in a circle, taking in the view from the top of Brockway Mountain. They'd had to drive *another* hour and a half past the university to get there. It was pretty and all, and the curvy drive up was kind of cool, but it really wasn't much of a mountain. Certainly not compared to those of Colorado, where they'd gone to ski last Christmas.

"Some said you could see all the way to Canada, but I never did." Her father was going on again about the beauty of the place. And because she loved her father so fiercely, Deni stood by his side and continued to stare off into the distance.

She could hear her brothers goofing off on the other side of the large, circular lookout. Maybe they'd take their games too far and fall off the side of the mountain and she'd at least have the backseat to herself for the interminable ride home.

She didn't even need to look behind her to know her mother was still in the car, flipping through a magazine. Content to let her husband walk down memory lane but not desiring to take the walk with him.

"Boys, not too close to the edge now," her father said without even turning around to see what the cretins were doing. He didn't need to; he always had an innate sense of what her brothers— Caleb, twelve, and Josh, ten—were getting into.

"We're not," the boys called out together. Deni could hear the rustling of them obeying their father and presumably moving closer to safety.

So, it was to be a crowded drive home after all.

"But my favorite part of this trip was always trying to find the hermit."

Deni perked up at that. "What? What hermit?"

"Do you know what a hermit is?" Her father seemed surprised.

"Somebody who lives by himself. Away from everybody else." She was sure about that much, just a little hazy on the reasoning. "Because they did something bad?"

"Not necessarily. In fact, most of the time someone becomes a hermit because he wants to. Because he wants to be left alone." There was a sort of wistfulness in his voice at this, and Deni realized she wasn't the only one who might have wished for a brother-free car.

"And one lives here?" she asked, trying to get him back to the good stuff.

"That's the legend, anyway. The Brockway Mountain Hermit. They said he lived on this side, and that if you looked really hard you could see his hut. That he'd built it so wisely most people could never see it."

A thousand questions rushed through Deni's mind. How did he eat? Was there a shower in his hut? Did he have cable?

But most importantly: "Did you ever see him?"

Her father shook his head. "No. I don't think anyone ever has. Maybe the people who live in Copper Harbor, but they don't talk about him. I did think that I saw the hut once. I was standing in this very spot."

"Where? Where?" she cried, pulling on the leg of his khaki shorts.

He knelt down again, one knee sinking into the lush grass. "It was a lot of years ago, and we were all pretty hung—we were really tired." His eyes scanned the side of the mountain below them. (It had regained mountain status in Deni's eyes with the hermit announcement!)

"It seems to me it was about two hundred yards down and about fifty yards west from this spot. I remember because of the telescopes." He pointed to the two machines next to them and started fumbling in his pockets for coins, which he fed into one of the machines.

Deni scrambled up onto the cement slab and stood on her tiptoes to be able to see into the viewfinder. It reminded her of the thing that they looked into on submarines in movies she'd seen. Except there was no scope coming from the top of it. Kind of like her View-Master on a big metal pole.

"Can you reach?" her father asked, and she nodded. He moved the machine in the direction he'd mentioned and stepped back, moving to her side. "Okay. Take a good look, and see if you can find the hermit's hut." There was humor in his voice. The kind of tone that told her he was most likely teasing her. She chose to ignore it and searched through the trees and landscape of the mountain below her looking for signs. When her viewing time on the machine ran out, she asked for another quarter. And another. She asked her father to reset the viewer to the original spot he'd remembered. Her little hands fiercely clutched the sides of the view magnifier.

"Deni, honey, it's time to leave," her father said sometime later.

"Not yet," she said, afraid to take her eyes from the machine. As if in the split second it would take to look back at her father to plead for more time, she'd miss the movement that would alert her to the hermit leaving his hut. The view had grown much darker than when she'd started looking, and it was then she realized she needed to use the bathroom.

Did the hermit have a toilet?

Thoughts of a bucket in the corner of the hut—

Wait. What was that? She moved closer to the machine, her nose pressed against the warm metal. Was that it? Could that be a roof, cleverly disguised to look like a bunch of fallen trees? Perhaps even a log cabin, not a hut at all?

She heard her mother approaching with an exasperated "Really, Barry, how long are you going to let her stare out of that thing? I can only imagine how many germs she's picking up."

Deni knew that tone of voice. Her time was up no matter how much interference her father was willing to run for her. And, given that he hadn't piped up yet, Deni supposed he wasn't going to run any this time.

She took one last squint, now seeing how easily the hermit could have made the fallen brush into a covering for his home. She was still not sure if it was a small cabin or a hut, so she decided to just go with "home." The brilliance of it astounded her; the hermit used his natural surroundings and used it to hide his home from everyone.

Everyone but her.

"I found it, Daddy," she said as she stepped back off the cement and into the grass.

"Did you?" her father said. There was that spark in his voice again, and she knew he was just humoring her. It didn't matter. She knew she'd seen the architectural masterpiece that was the hermit's hut.

Her mother was upon them now. Her brothers were coming out of the gift shop with suckers in their mouths.

Darn, had she missed out on candy?

"Here, baby," her mother said, holding out a sucker for her. She quickly took the treat, unwrapped it, and stuck it in her mouth. Cathy Casparich herded her daughter and husband toward the car and the rest of the family—a not-uncommon task.

Deni ran a few steps ahead, but not so far that she couldn't hear her parents speaking softly behind her.

"What on earth were you two looking at for so long? I mean, yes, it's pretty and all, but…."

"Oh, nothing. Just trying to see Canada."

"And did you?"

Deni turned around at this. Her father had been watching her, and when she looked at him he winked. "Oh, we found what we were looking for, all right."

Deni turned back around and ran for the car, not even minding having to squeeze in between her stupid brothers.

The ride down the mountain was filled with twists and curves. Deni kept expecting to see the hermit in the middle of the road with a goat or something under his arm with every curve they turned.

At home she had a lot of storybooks, most of them vividly illustrated with lots of pictures. But the one she liked best had only a simple line drawing at the beginning of each chapter. Her father would read to her from that one on the nights when he would tuck her in.

There was one story in it, "Rumplestiltskin," that Deni thought of now. In one of the drawings, Rumplestiltskin was dancing as the maiden sat at the spinning wheel. He was small, scrawny really, with a scraggly beard and madness in his eyes.

That image was what Deni saw when she thought about the Brockway Mountain Hermit.

They made their way into Copper Harbor, stopping at an old-fashioned general store (more candy!) and then driving on to Fort Wilkins, which the boys loved. Caleb was almost kicked out for climbing on the cannon when their parents weren't looking.

And it was all neat and kind of cool. But the memory Deni took away from that particular family trip—which would turn out to be their last as a complete family—was that of a little, bearded man dancing around his hidden hut.

One

—ᴡᴡᴡ—

DENI TURNED ON THE LIGHT BOX AND SAT DOWN AT her kitchen table. Never much of a breakfast person, she now consumed a bowl of oatmeal each morning as she awaited the light therapy's magic.

At first, she'd tried getting a jumpstart on the day's emails with her laptop on the table, but it tended to block most of the light. Angling the light box didn't work because while you weren't supposed to look straight at it, you were supposed to face it.

And Deni knew if it had gotten this bad—bad enough to break down and order the light box—then she might as well go by the book with the treatment.

Treatment. God, she hated that word. Therapy was just as bad. Although she did enjoy her sessions with her therapist, Alison.

She just hated that she needed them.

But, after two weeks of the daily half-hour light therapy sessions, she was beginning to feel a change, albeit a slight one.

At least she didn't spend half her workday wishing she were home in bed with the comforter wrapped tightly around her. Now it was only like a quarter of the day.

Progress.

She slowly ate her oatmeal while looking at—but not *at*—the special box. It kind of reminded her of the Lite-Brite she'd had as a kid, only it was completely white, and you couldn't make cool designs on it.

After she finished the oatmeal, she still had fifteen minutes left, so she flipped through yesterday's *Copper Ingot*—the small area's daily newspaper—for any story she might have missed last night.

With ten minutes left, she pulled her laptop over and positioned it as best she could while still soaking in the magic rays. She pulled up her personal email account first, prepared for at least one message from her mother.

There were three.

Deni had put her foot down with her mother two weeks ago—about the same time she had broken down and ordered the light box—about calling so frequently.

Her mother had seemed to take the edict well—but after a day, the emails had started. Thank God the woman didn't know how to text.

Sighing, Deni prepared to open her mother's emails, expecting to find links to articles about the newest wonder vitamin or online dating site. Perhaps today there would be a link to an engineering position in Detroit, closer to her hometown of Farmington Hills.

But another email caught her eye—one from her boss and owner of the firm, Andy Summers.

Odd. She didn't think she'd ever received an email from Andy to her personal account. Deni wasn't even sure how Andy knew this email address. Oh right, it would have been on her résumé. But that was nearly seven years ago. Really odd.

The subject line read "If you check your email before you come to work—READ THIS." The message asked that everyone report right to the conference room at eight and if they'd planned to work at home or be on a site to come in for a short meeting instead.

Really, really odd.

Summers and Beck was a small engineering firm. Some might even call it a boutique shop, though all the men cringed at that term.

And it was all men, except for Deni and Sue Haapala, their office administrator. Sue basically had the task of corralling the minds of engineers and making the day-to-day business work.

Sue—a mother to six, grandmother to nine—ran the office well, allowing the engineers to do their thing while still keeping them focused.

It was a pretty laid-back place to work. The staff was allowed to work from home on any two days of the week if they wanted. Except Mondays, when they had their all-staff status meetings that took up most of the morning.

So why was Andy calling another meeting two days later?

Deni called up her work email and saw the same message from Andy. He'd done it as a blind CC, so Deni wasn't sure if everyone got it in both their work and personal accounts.

Oh God, it wasn't just to her, was it?

There was absolutely no reason for Deni to think she was getting "called into the boss' office," but a shiver of panic ran through her body. She started to take deep breaths as she thought it through with the analytical part of her mind that made her an asset to Summers and Beck. And that was just exactly the phrase she'd use too, if she *were* in some kind of trouble!

But no. Andy would have put a personal salutation on an email meant just for her. And there'd be no need to do a blind CC. Right? She pushed the laptop away and turned her face fully to the light box, as if the glow would ease her sudden anxiousness.

And another thing—Andy knew she never worked from home, so there would be no reason to put that in there.

Deni would have loved to work from home on these cold mornings. To stay in her warm fleece pajamas and wool socks, sipping hot chocolate all day as she sat at the computer in her home office—the unused third bedroom.

But she knew that staying home, not *leaving* home, could be dangerous to her at this point. She needed to take a shower, get dressed, drive to the office, greet Sue and her other coworkers and interact with humans face to face throughout the day.

Because if she didn't, it would surely soon get to a point where she *couldn't.*

Her mother's emails left unopened, Deni put her laptop in her messenger bag, turned the light box off, grabbed her keys, and started off to work, curiosity and still some anxiety coursing through her.

Somewhere in the back of her brain, she acknowledged that she liked the rush of emotions.

At least it was better than the numbness she'd been feeling.

"I SEE EVERYBODY CHECKS their emails in the morning. That's good to know," Andy said to the group when they'd all assembled in the conference room at eight. The coffee was brewing, and there were packages of Danish and Finnish nissu from Jim's Foodmart on the table.

No Dunkin' Donuts or Tim Hortons in the Copper Country.

"I saw it when it came in last night," Charlie Simpson, one of the younger engineers, said.

Charlie and Deni were the only two on staff under thirty. Andy was a young owner, probably in his late thirties or early forties. There were two older men, Jim and Bob, whom Andy had wooed away from Tech to work for him when he first started the firm. The other five men in the room were a few years younger than Andy, hired fresh out of Tech while Andy was building his company.

"Really? You're up at 2am on a Tuesday night?" Andy asked, his eyes narrowing, studying Charlie.

Charlie shrugged. "I don't need much sleep."

God, that must be nice, Deni thought. She couldn't get enough sleep these days, sometimes crawling into bed by eight. "Besides," Charlie added, "*you* were up at 2am."

A smile came over Andy's face, and he took his seat at the head of the long conference table. "And I'll tell you why." He took a sip from his coffee, in what felt to Deni like a planned dramatic pause. He then scanned both sides of the table, making eye contact with all the engineers. Sue, who had her head down ready to take notes, didn't even notice.

"I was up at two because I was still putting together some preliminary research on something we're hopefully going to take on."

A new project? That was what the all-hands-on-deck meeting was about?

They were a small firm, but not small enough that every new project was worth an all-staff meeting.

"And it's more than just a new project," Andy said, reading her mind—probably reading everyone's mind. "Hopefully, it will be the beginning of a new economic growth period for the Copper Country."

That would be good. The three-county area in the Upper Peninsula's northwestern tip had been hit hard by the economic downturn. Oh, not as badly as other Michigan cities, but the Copper Country was a tourist destination—for snowmobilers in the winter and families in the summer—and when times were tough and gas prices high, people took fewer vacations.

"I ran into Petey Ryan last night," Andy said, and again took a sip of coffee as that news sank in. Which it seemed to do with everyone in the room but her. They all leaned a little closer to Andy, as if he was about to impart a secret. Even Sue poked her head up from her tablet, interest showing on her wrinkled face.

"Who's Petey Ryan?" Deni asked, then wished she hadn't when everyone at the table turned to her with looks of disbelief, or scorn, on their faces.

"Petey Ryan is a local boy who plays for the Detroit Red Wings," Andy said in a non-patronizing but understanding tone. She really did like her boss.

"I keep forgetting you're not from around here," Mac, one of her colleagues, said. She smiled at him because it was meant as a compliment, or at least she took it that way. Mac's smile in return confirmed it.

"Or that you have zero interest in sports," Randy, another

coworker, said. There was no smile from his direction, and she didn't give him one.

Randy had never warmed up to her, for some reason, but Deni didn't let it bother her. Everyone else in the office had been very nice to her the seven years she'd been with Summers and Beck. She wasn't going to worry about Randy.

"Actually," Andy said, drawing her attention away from Randy, "I guess I should say Petey *used* to play for the Red Wings. He just retired about a month ago—knee injury."

"And he lives here?" Deni asked. There was surprise in her voice, but she supposed there shouldn't be. She'd fallen in love with the Copper Country and had chosen to stay here though her career would have been better served elsewhere. She probably shouldn't be surprised that a native son would return home. He probably felt the way that she did about the place.

"Yes. He has a house here. He's spent every summer here since he's been in the league. And is back for good now. Or so he told me last night. He was at the Cat's Meow having a beer with…" Another dramatic pause, another sip of coffee. Everyone leaned in. There was a reason Andy was the owner and the one who secured most of their projects—he was not only a good engineer, but he was also a good people person. Not skills that typically went together. Engineers tended to the geek side, with less-than-stellar social skills.

"Darío Luna," Andy finished. More nods from around the room. Deni kept her mouth shut this time. "He's a professional golfer. He married a local girl last fall," Andy said, obviously for her benefit though he addressed it to the whole group. "Apparently Ryan and Luna are in the same circle of friends. They were talking about a new business venture they want to undertake."

Now Deni perked up. She didn't care about hockey, or golf, or even local celebrities. But a new business in town—that had her full attention.

"They want to build an indoor driving range," Andy said. This time he was the one who leaned forward, his arms on the table, hands clasped in front of him. He seemed to know the reaction he was going to get, but Deni didn't.

All the other men, except Charlie, leaned back in their seats with looks of disappointment on their faces. Some even sighed.

"What'd I miss?" Charlie asked what she was thinking.

"It can't be done," Jim said. Bob reached for a Danish and added, "Not up here, with the snowfall we get."

"What about the Superior Dome in Marquette?" Charlie said. "Same concept. And they get as much snow as we do. Some winters, more."

"Let me put it a different way," Jim said. "It can't be done for the money that a driving range—charging a couple of bucks for a bucket of balls—could sustain."

"The Superior Dome has Northern's events and other stuff going on. They generate a hell of a lot more revenue to offset costs."

"Nope," Bob said. "Can't be done."

At that, several of the men began picking through the pastries, putting them on the little plates Sue had most likely provided and sitting back to enjoy the free breakfast.

Deni and Charlie looked at each other, then at Andy. "There's got to be a way to do this," Charlie said.

"There is," Andy said. "And you each have until three this afternoon to figure out how."

That had everyone looking away from their goodies and back to Andy. "We're meeting back here at three, and we're going to brainstorm on how we can make this viable."

"We wouldn't make any real money from it, anyway," Randy said.

"Maybe not. But if those two are teaming up, I want to make sure we're their go-to firm for any other projects they might have."

That quieted the room. Deni could sense the wheels turning in the minds of the staff.

She didn't know Darío Luna or Petey Ryan from Adam, but she did know that professional athletes made a lot of money.

Money that could be invested in the local economy.

"Why three o'clock? Why don't we brainstorm now?" Mac asked.

"I want you to do some research first. Maybe even some preliminary numbers, though it will be hard to come up with that so early." He looked at Gerry and Larry, who, besides having the unfortunate circumstance of rhyming names, were always thought of together as they handled most of the financials and costing on jobs. They nodded their heads in unison at Andy.

"And," Andy continued, "at three, we'll be joined by someone else who couldn't be here this morning."

"Who?" asked at least three people. Deni wasn't one of them, but she was thinking the same thing. It was too early to bring the client in. And you typically wouldn't do that for a brainstorming session. It was too risky that the client would latch onto something that wasn't feasible.

Andy stood, gathered his coffee cup and plate, and stepped away from the table. "We'll meet back here at three. Have some thoughts to share with each other, with me, and with…Sawyer Beck." Then he turned around and left the room.

The men all looked to Jim and Bob, the elder statesmen, who just shrugged. Then everyone turned to Sue, who looked at them all and shook her head.

"Who is Sawyer Beck?" Deni asked, unable to read the room. Was he yet another professional athlete who lived in the Copper Country? What were the odds of that?

"Beck. As in Summers and Beck?" Randy said, a bit of snideness in his voice.

"Oh. Right. Duh," Deni said, feeling like a fool. "It's just I've never met him. I guess I wasn't even sure there was a Beck." She tried remembering her long-ago orientation during her first week with the company. She vaguely remembered something being said about the co-founder of the firm, but it obviously wasn't important enough to stick. She was pretty sure it wasn't on the company website, either.

"None of us have met him," Randy said.

"I have," Sue said. Jim and Bob nodded their heads. "But it's been several years since he's been in the office. Probably not since most of you were hired."

"Probably a lot of time since he's even been out of his hut," Randy said, snideness again dripping from his voice.

"His hut?" Deni asked. Everyone was gathering up their laptops and coffee mugs and reaching for the remaining pastries before leaving the conference room.

"Well, of course he doesn't live in a hut," Charlie said, but there was uncertainty in his voice.

Deni was still seated, her mind fuzzy. She wondered what she was missing. Even Charlie seemed in on it, and he'd only been here a little while longer than she.

"Charlie, what's the deal?" she asked her closest coworker as he approached the door.

He turned around. "You mean you've really never heard the talk? Heard the legend?"

Something tingled at the back of Deni's neck at the word "legend." She shook her head.

"I mean, it's not true. It *can't* be true." Again there was uncertainty in his voice. "But Sawyer Beck—of Summers and Beck—is the legendary Brockway Mountain Hermit."

He left the room, leaving behind an open-mouthed, huge-eyed Deni picturing a small, bearded man dancing in front of his hut.

Two

—⚮—

SAWYER BECK RAN HIS HAND THROUGH HIS BEARD. Or rather, where his beard had been until three o'clock this morning. Now, nearly twelve hours later, there was already a pretty good amount of stubble, but they'd just have to deal with it.

At least he'd shaved off the thick beard after Andy had called him, apologizing for waking Sawyer up in the wee hours of the morning. Sawyer hadn't let Andy off the hook by admitting he wasn't asleep, nor was he likely to be any time soon.

Let his partner feel bad. Hell, he was making Sawyer come to town—and shave!—for a staff meeting when it had been part of their arrangement that he would never have to attend one.

Just the thought of it had him rubbing his non-beard again as he drove down Highway 41 toward Houghton.

Lucy yawned in the back seat, and he stuck his hand back to pet his yellow lab. "I know, Luce. I could use a nap, too."

He never did get to sleep after Andy called, and though going a day, or more, without sleep wasn't unusual for him, it was taking its toll lately.

He looked in the rearview mirror at his dog, who was looking back at him. Noticing the gray that took up most of her face, he said, "Guess we're both too old for all-nighters, eh?"

Lucy yawned again and burrowed into the blanket, which was her home when they were in his beat-up Bronco.

Quincy Hill was a little slick as he made his way into

Hancock, and he slowed the Bronco almost to a crawl as he made his way through town and to the bridge that would take him to Houghton and the offices of Summers and Beck.

How long had it been since he'd been in the office? He remembered the leaves were just starting to turn, so sometime last fall. As he did whenever he came in, he'd met Andy late after hours in the office to go over anything that needed Sawyer's attention or signature.

Sawyer had tried to get Andy to just mail or email anything for him to sign and return, but Andy held his ground on having Sawyer come in at least once a quarter. Since Sawyer got his way with most other things, he gave in to Andy on this one point. But he made sure it was either in the evening or over a weekend, so he wouldn't have to schmooze with the staff.

Not that he didn't like the staff. Truth be told, he only knew the old-timers in any way other than a polite nod. Sue, Jim, and Bob he knew well, but it'd been years since he'd had any kind of relationship with them.

With anyone.

Once across the bridge, Sawyer made an immediate right down to the Houghton waterfront, where the office was located in an old train depot.

Sawyer and Andy had renovated it themselves when they'd first started the company. They'd had lots of offers on the land as the waterfront area developed and could certainly have afforded more land and better digs by now—but they both felt a connection to the building, so Summers and Beck remained in the depot.

The small parking lot was full when he pulled in, and he felt a tiny sense of dread at the coming meeting. The coming display, really, as Andy would no doubt trot him out to the staff. God, he wasn't expected to speak to them all, was he?

He got out of the Bronco, let Lucy out of the back, and made his way in. Sue was at the front desk and—bless her—said a quick hello like she saw him every day.

He made his way to the back of the building to Andy's office,

Lucy at his heels. He felt the stares of people, noticed some stood from their work areas as if to speak to him, but he kept his eyes forward and didn't hesitate until he got to Andy's office where he shut the door behind him.

"Hey, Sawyer. Glad you made it. How were the roads down?" Andy said as he rose from behind his desk, made his way over to Sawyer, and shook his hand.

"Not great," Sawyer said. He released Andy's hand and sat down in one of the two guest chairs in front of the desk.

"I assumed you'd bring Lucy with you. I even put some water in a bowl for her," Andy said, pointing to a plastic bowl on the floor in the corner of the room.

Sawyer swiveled his head around, only now realizing he'd lost Lucy somewhere between the office and the front door.

Strange. Lucy typically never left his side, especially when there were other people around.

"She's here. I mean, she was," he explained, getting up from his chair and opening the door. He looked down the walkway he'd just come from and about halfway down lay Lucy, on her back, belly up, legs shaking with excitement as someone scratched her tummy.

Very strange.

What was stranger still was that the hand rubbing Lucy had shocking-pink fingernails.

That was all Sawyer could see. The rest of Lucy's pleasure administrator was hidden by the cubicles that populated the open floor. "Lucy, come," Sawyer called. When his dog still didn't move, he gave a sharp whistle, which caused the pink-nailed hand to disappear behind the wall of the cube. Which, in turn, caused his dog to finally get off her back and head toward him.

When his dog entered the office, Sawyer closed the door behind her and sat down in one of the chairs facing Andy. Lucy circled the area by Sawyer's feet twice and then sank down next to the chair, her chin on Sawyer's boot.

"I thought Sue was the only woman in the office," Sawyer

said.

Andy looked puzzled. "You mean Deni? Sawyer, she's been here for six or seven years. Don't you read any of the briefings I send you?"

"Yes, of course," Sawyer said, fudging. He did read them, but it was usually as a last-ditch effort to try to fall asleep. Who knew how much his mind had absorbed. "But I thought Deni was, you know, Denny."

"With an 'i'?"

"How the hell do I know how people spell their names? Besides, she's not mentioned often in your briefings." He was guessing on that one. For all Sawyer knew, she could have been mentioned in every paragraph of the succinct, bullet-pointed emails Andy sent him every month. Yeah, they were pretty much insomnia aids to him.

Wait. A thought was tickling his brain. "Wasn't she the lead on the restoration on the church in Calumet?"

Andy's face perked up, obviously pleased—and surprised— that Sawyer did read his emails.

"Yep. That was her."

"That was nice work. I checked it out once it was done."

"You did?" Surprise had turned to shock.

"Yeah."

"When?"

Sawyer shrugged. "I don't know. About a year ago, I guess."

"Why didn't you stop in at the site while the project was going on?"

Sawyer deflected the question by asking, "Has she worked on much else?"

"Not as lead, no."

"Why not? She any good?"

"She's very good. The restoration jobs seem to be her forte, and we haven't gotten a lot of those lately." He looked down at his desk, folded his hands together, and sighed. "The truth is we haven't gotten a lot of jobs lately, period."

"I know," Sawyer said quietly. He might not read the briefings with much interest, but he did look at the financial reports quite closely. He was a silent partner, but he wasn't a stupid partner.

"There should be enough in the reserves to get us through this economic downturn, though," Sawyer said with as much encouragement as he could muster. Which wasn't much.

Andy's head was bowed, but he was nodding. Then he seemed to gather himself, and his head came up, the nod more jaunty. "Yes. We do. But that's why getting this job, making this feasible for Pete Ryan and Darío Luna to do, could help weather the storm. Open up a whole new revenue stream for us. If this business can succeed for them, who knows what else they might do? It could really help the area."

"Whoa," Sawyer said, holding up his hands. "We're talking about one project that may not even be doable. And even if it is, it's only going to employ about three people."

"I know, but it's a start," Andy said, his enthusiasm back. Andy was never down for long. That was why Sawyer had become partners with him. At the time, they'd both been like that—so optimistic, ready to save the world by creating great buildings.

Somewhere along the years, Sawyer had lost that feeling, the ability to see what could be instead of what was.

He envied Andy's ability to hang on to that quality.

"Thanks for coming down, Sawyer. I think having you on the project might just be the edge we need."

"Are they looking at other firms?"

Andy rubbed his hands across his face. He looked tired. But then, if he'd been up at three when he'd called Sawyer, it was no wonder. Not everyone could exist on no sleep.

"He said he wanted to keep it all local."

"So, that's us and Three Sixty."

"Right. And he said he hadn't talked to them yet. I'm assuming he'd tell me the truth on that."

"He would, yes."

Andy got up from his chair and walked around to the front

of his desk, settling into the chair next to Sawyer. "See. That's why I called you. I know most of the business owners and decision makers in town, now. And, of course, I work with the Chamber of Commerce on courting new business to town. But I don't know these guys. Ryan has never been around for longer than a summer at a stretch, and he never showed any entrepreneurial interest that I'm aware of."

"But—"

Andy held up a hand. "I know. You said last night you didn't know him very well."

"And when I did, it was nearly twenty years ago."

"Right. But he remembers you. In fact, he asked about you last night. That's what gave me the idea to get you down here. To put the two of you together."

"Yeah, about that. Explain it to me again. You were a little excited on the phone."

"So, I'm at the rink with the girls. And there's Petey Ryan skating with a girl."

"Yeah, that sounds about right," Sawyer said.

"No, not that kind. I mean a little girl. She looked to be about Jessie's age."

At Sawyer's blank look, Andy added, "Around ten."

"Right," Sawyer said. He figured if he had to, he could guess the ages of Andy's daughters pretty closely.

The oldest, Heather, was born right around the time they'd completed their first really big job, an office park in Marquette. So she'd be close to fifteen.

Andy and Jane's second daughter, Megan, was born thirteen years ago. Probably right around this time of year, because Sawyer remembered Andy grabbing some leftover Valentine's candy from the drugstore to bring to Janie just before she was due.

And Jessie. Jessie had been born three days before….

"So, around ten," Sawyer said.

"Yeah, thereabouts."

"I didn't know Ryan had a kid," Sawyer said. And why would

he? He'd been out of the loop for that long. Why would he think he would have known if Pete Ryan had had a kid along the way?

And why did the thought of it piss him off so much?

"It's not his kid. I think she's a friend's kid or something. Jessie was telling me as I drove the girls home that this little girl—Annie, I guess—had been in a wheelchair until a couple of years ago." Andy snapped his fingers. "That's it. That's why I remembered her. She's the kid they had the benefit for a couple of years ago. The first Annie Aid?"

He was looking at Sawyer like this should all mean something. It rang some vague bells, but he just shook his head at Andy and motioned for him to go on.

"Right. Of course. Sorry. I forgot I was talking to the Brockway Mountain Hermit."

"Ha ha. Get back to the story."

Andy grinned. He obviously knew how much Sawyer hated that some people teasingly called him the hermit. Warmth spread through Sawyer as he joked with his old friend and talked shop. He started to match Andy's grin, and then a pang went through him and his face turned to a scowl.

"So, you saw Ryan at the rink?" He motioned to Andy again. "I don't have all day, you know."

"You don't? Really?"

And that just about summed it up. Sawyer *did* have all day to sit and listen to Andy's stories of taking his three daughters skating.

But there was no way he could endure it.

"Andy..." he warned.

"Okay. Okay. So, he and I start talking as the girls are all getting out of their skates. And he says that he'd been meaning to call me. That he and Darío Luna have an idea, and they wanted to run it past me."

"This Luna guy, the one you mentioned last night? He's a golfer, you said?"

Andy gave an exasperated sigh. "Yes. A very good one. He's

won three majors. I know at least one of them was a Masters." Andy looked away, his mind wandering. "I'd better look that up, eh? Might be good to pull out sometime in conversation."

That. That was why Andy ran the business and Sawyer stayed behind the scenes. It would never occur to Sawyer to look up someone's accolades so they could be dropped into a conversation. And yet, Andy did it in a very non-cheesy, non-used-car-salesman kind of way.

Sawyer sent up a silent thank you for sitting next to Andy Summers on his first day, in his first class, at Tech.

"So, you were at the rink…."

"Right. I said I could meet any time. He said he was actually meeting Darío in an hour at the Cat's Meow for a beer. Asked if I wanted to join them."

"Thus the 3am phone call."

"Yeah. We weren't there that late. Well, maybe they were. I left after we'd talked business and got the promise that you could take him to dinner tonight to talk about it more.

"They were celebrating. Darío and his wife had a baby a few weeks ago, and I think this was the first time the guys had been out to celebrate it. Petey was ordering shots when I left. I heard him tell Darío he'd call Al somebody to come pick them up, or I would have stuck around to make sure they got home okay. Must be a good buddy to come get two guys from a party he wasn't even invited to."

"So…."

"So then I spent a few hours looking at numbers and space and doing some preliminary research on indoor driving ranges." He sighed again, and looked Sawyer in the eye. "And then I called you."

"Yeah, explain that part to me again."

"Well, Petey asked specifically about you. How involved you were with the business. How you were…doing. You know."

Sawyer waved his hand in a "keep going" motion.

"I said you were good. Semi-retired but still involved."

Sawyer shot Andy a withering look, but Andy ignored it and kept going. "He seemed very interested in you. Said you played hockey against each other?"

"A thousand years ago. High school. He played at Tech with my brother."

"Well, whatever. I finally asked if we could get a meeting with them. Darío said he wouldn't be available much. I guess he's busy with the new baby, and then they're leaving in a few weeks for him to play the Florida swing of the tour."

"I don't know what that means."

"It's when the golf tour—never mind. It doesn't matter. What matters is Petey Ryan is doing the legwork on the project and checking in with Darío when needed."

"Okay. And…."

"And you, my partner, are having dinner with Petey Ryan tonight to extol the virtues of doing business with Summers and Beck."

"Well, shit."

"Exactly."

Three

—ɯɯ—

"FIRST OFF, I AM NOT THE BROCKWAY MOUNTAIN Hermit. That was Bill Mattila. He died nearly thirty years ago, and they've since torn down his shack."

There was a gasp from someone in the conference room. A very female gasp. Sawyer looked in Sue's direction, but her head was looking down at her tablet, hand poised to take notes. She hadn't deemed his icebreaker worthy enough to jot down, so the gasp probably hadn't come from her.

Sawyer didn't look in the direction of the other female in the room.

"I've met some of you. Most of you I haven't. I'm...looking forward to working with you on this...exciting new project." There. Just like Andy had told him to say.

He looked toward Andy, nodded, and then sat down in the seat directly to Andy's right. Like he was some mafia consigliere or something.

"Thanks, Sawyer. And a big thank you for becoming personally involved in this project."

Andy went on as Sawyer mentally snorted. Yeah, right. He *wanted* to be personally involved. Like Andy hadn't tried everything on the phone last night to try to get him to come. None of it had worked, and Sawyer had held firm until Andy had tried the one thing guaranteed to work on him.

Guilt.

He'd tried to hide it, so Andy wouldn't realize it was Sawyer's Kryptonite. He'd pretended that Andy had just finally worn him down. But no, it was the guilt.

And it hadn't even been a huge guilt trip. Just a mention about how things were tight at the firm, and they could really use this job to springboard this type of thing to other northern areas. And that if they didn't, they may have to look at layoffs.

That was what had done it. Sawyer honestly couldn't care less about the firm's bottom line. He didn't need much to live on and probably had enough to get by for the rest of his life if he so needed. But the company did support ten other employees and their families. Not to mention the contractors they worked with and all the subsidiary workers.

The realization that a decision he made could have that kind of ripple effect had had Sawyer's stomach in knots since he'd gotten off the phone with Andy.

The no sleep hadn't helped, either.

"So, let's start this off," Andy was now saying, Sawyer having missed his pep talk. Andy rose from his seat and went to the long wall in the room that was covered with a whiteboard. He opened a marker and stood, poised to write down greatness.

"Let's start with obstacles. Don't even throw out solutions yet. Just obstacles."

"Cost," someone said. Sawyer thought it was Jim, but it could have been Bob. Andy wrote.

"Support for the heavy snowfall," somebody else said. Andy wrote.

They were all adding ideas, some looking at their tablets or laptops in front of them, some eyes on Andy. Except her. She of the pink nails and small gasps.

She was looking right at Sawyer.

When he met her eye, she quickly looked away. First she looked at Andy. Then, as if sensing Sawyer was still watching her—which he was—she bowed her face to her laptop.

She was young. Younger than Sawyer would have thought.

He vaguely remembered their last full-time hire had been around six years ago. So, she was obviously older than the twenty-two, twenty-three, that she looked.

Her hair was a chestnut brown with some golden highlights and was pulled back into a low ponytail. A very thick ponytail that hung down between her shoulder blades. A few loose wisps fell in front of her as she gazed at the laptop screen, and she reached out and tucked them behind her ear, the hot pink of her nails flashing.

The nails seemed out of character. She was dressed in a black turtleneck with a gray cardigan over that.

Thwarted by the table in his effort to see more, Sawyer surreptitiously rolled his pen off the table and then leaned over to get it.

She was about halfway down the long table from him, but he could easily make out the long gray wool skirt and black tights. She wore comfortable looking clog-type shoes that had a fleecy lining peeking up against the black of her tights.

Sawyer sat back up in his chair and glanced at the whiteboard that Andy was filling up as the others had been speaking. But not her. She hadn't said a word. Hadn't typed anything into her laptop, either.

She glanced at Sawyer again, then quickly away. He couldn't tell her eye color from here, but he'd guess a deep brown. Maybe with gold flecks, like her hair. Her cheekbones were high and pronounced, and she had lips that movie stars paid for. In fact, she kind of reminded him of one. Sawyer couldn't recall the name, not much of a pop-culture person. The one who was married to Ben Affleck. Yeah. This girl reminded Sawyer of that actress. Strong but pretty, wholesome, all-American. And with a mouth that had men thinking about—

"Sawyer? Thoughts?"

Oh yeah, he had a few. But none that Andy could write on that board.

And that realization—that he'd had a sexual thought of *any* kind—had Sawyer reeling.

"Um…lots of thoughts, Andy," Sawyer said, covering. "But I'd like to hear more from the group." He looked at the board, scanned it quickly. "Does anybody want to extrapolate on the heating situation? How do we economically heat this huge thing enough that people can take their coats off and hit golf balls for an hour when it's ten below out?"

People started throwing out ideas, referring to notes and laptops. Andy kept scribbling on the board.

Sawyer rose and walked to the other side of the room, ostensibly to get a better look at Andy and the board. But where he stood happened to be directly behind the girl.

Woman. Intellectually he knew she was a woman, not a girl, but Sawyer had a hard time wrapping his mind around thinking of her as anything but the new girl.

Who had been here over six years.

He got close enough that he could see her laptop screen, but not too close that he was right on top of her. She had a couple of windows open. One was a web page that had a story about the collapsed Metrodome in Minneapolis. The other was a Word document with a bunch of bullet points. He could just make them out. They were nearly word for word the things that were on the board, though she hadn't had her hands on her keyboard once and had not offered up any of them.

But she had thought of them all already.

Maybe they all had. Sawyer had.

But no. Most of the others were taking notes or referring to things on their laptops and clicking away. Some of the ideas they voiced sounded like they'd just thought of them. Which was fine, this is what this was—a brainstorming session.

But she'd stormed her brain already, and Sawyer found he liked that about her.

There was one bullet point on her list under a heating subheading that wasn't on the board.

"Any others?" Andy asked, ready to move on to a bare spot of the board for another topic.

Sawyer waited to see if she'd mention anything, but she kept silent.

"What about methane?" Sawyer said, surprising himself.

The girl's already straight back stiffened; her ponytail softly swung with the movement.

"Could be a viable option," Sawyer continued. "Worth taking a look at, anyway. Could help keep ongoing costs down."

He could see her shoulders tense. *Come on. Let us know you thought of it, too.*

DENI KEPT HER mouth shut.

She wasn't sure if the reason was her fog-like attitude of the last couple of months, or the large man standing directly behind her.

"So? What about methane? *Would* that be viable?" Sawyer Beck said from behind her.

Was he looking at her laptop or just coming up with the same thoughts she had? She didn't dare turn around to see—he'd already caught her staring at him.

He was *definitely* not the small, bearded, Rumplestiltskin-like man she'd pictured as the hermit all these years.

Far from it. This guy had a total lumberjack vibe about him. Although he wasn't wearing flannel and Sorel boots, it kind of looked like maybe he'd changed out of them just in time for the meeting.

He wore a blue chambray work shirt and khakis, and though they fit his long, lanky body well, Deni thought he'd look more at home in jeans and…well…flannel.

His hair was dark brown, and he wore it a little long, but not hermit long. Just a little long for office life.

But then, he didn't do office life.

God, the idea of being a hermit appealed to her. To just lie in bed, warm covers wrapped around her—

Crap. She hadn't been listening, and they were discussing whether methane turned into energy would work for this project.

It wouldn't. Too costly for such a low-revenue-generating project, but she'd let them come to that conclusion.

It was an interesting venture, but it wasn't her thing. She took on the restoration projects. There were usually plenty of them in the historic area, but not so much lately with the economy tanking.

"Well, yes, it wouldn't be worth it for such a small-potatoes business," Beck was saying now. "But I don't think we should dismiss it out of hand. Something to think about, anyway."

He was behind her, but his rugged face was still in her mind. She'd guess his eyes were brown. His cheekbones were male-model quality, but there was nothing pretty about him. He had more of a haunted look.

But then, why bother being a hermit if you're not haunted?

"Okay. Good. That gives us a start. Sawyer is having dinner with Petey tonight, and he'll get some of the specifics," Andy said, pulling Deni back from her Sawyer Beck appreciation tour.

But, oh, there was much to appreciate.

He was older—probably forty. And he was technically her boss. And there was that hermit thing, which had to mean he had major issues.

Suddenly, the weight hit Deni. Sometimes it was constant, like a lead blanket wrapped around her shoulders.

Sometimes, like now, it snuck up on her. She'd be having a normal day, with normal, everyday thoughts—like how smoking hot the hermit was—when the weight of it all would just swarm around her, causing her brain to shift focus and shatter in a million directions at once.

"Mac and Charlie," Andy continued as Deni tried to swim out of the fog and concentrate on what he was saying. "Clear your schedules for the next couple of days. Once Sawyer gets the actual property information from Petey tonight, we'll want the two of you up on Quincy Hill surveying."

"Wear your long johns," someone said. There was some teasing and talk of how cold it would be on the hill. People were gathering their things, and Deni started to reach for her laptop.

"One last thing," Beck said. He'd moved from behind her back to the opposite side of the table—next to Andy, who had returned from the board. "Andy's right. This could be the start of other projects with these investors, so we'll want to make sure we get this one. The only way we'll do that is by working together." He looked at Andy for a second, but Deni couldn't make out the look Sawyer was giving him. Neither could Andy apparently, as he only gave back a questioning look and a shrug of his shoulders.

Sawyer looked down at the table, then kind of braced himself and looked up. Directly at her.

"You," he said to her.

"Me?" she said, pointing to herself.

"Yes. I want you there tonight. Meet me at the Commodore at six." He turned his back on her—on all of them—and left the room.

Everyone turned to stare at her, looks of confusion on their faces.

Which matched her own.

Four

—◊◊◊—

SAWYER TOOK A SWIG FROM HIS BEER BOTTLE AND looked at his watch. Five minutes to six. No sign of her yet, but it was still technically early. He'd gotten here a half-hour ago, wanting to make sure he got a table in the room that looked out onto the lake. The other room was fine, too, but it was mostly populated with large, circular booths. He wanted to be able to look across a table at Pete Ryan as they talked, and he didn't want Deni sandwiched between them. Besides, he wasn't even sure Ryan could fit behind one of those booths. Sawyer hadn't seen him in years, but the kid had been big in high school, and when Sawyer watched Red Wings games, Petey was one of the biggest players on the ice.

Just as he was about to bring the beer bottle back to his mouth, Deni walked in the room, looking around. She spotted him just as he gave a half-wave, and she walked across the restaurant, weaving around the tables.

She was still wearing her outfit from earlier, had probably come straight from the office. Sawyer had left shortly after his decree. But not before Andy told him it wasn't a good idea. That Deni Casparich was their restoration expert. That something like this would be better handled by Randy if Sawyer wanted back-up.

But Sawyer didn't want back-up. He wanted to hear Deni Casparich speak. He wanted to confirm whether her eyes were brown with gold flecks. And he wanted—desperately—to know if her toenails were also painted bright pink.

"Petey Ryan loves women. It wouldn't hurt to have her at the table," he'd said to Andy. Then he'd gotten the hell out of the office.

He'd run some errands around town, stuff he put off until he came to Houghton. Then he brought Lucy to his brother's house to stay while he was at dinner. He could have left the dog at the office, but he'd wanted to check up on his youngest brother.

He hadn't been home, but Sawyer had let himself in with his key and settled Lucy, hoping his brother would be home when he picked his dog up later.

"Hey," he said to Deni as she got to the table. He stood up and helped her with her coat, draping it on top of his own on one of the two empty chairs at the table.

"Hi," she said as she sat down next to him. Smart girl, she knew he'd want to be across from Ryan.

"Um…I'm not really sure why you asked me to join you…but…." She didn't finish her thought, just looked at him.

No, he wouldn't let her off with just that. "But what?"

She blinked her eyes at him. Yep. Brown. And yep, a flash of something in them. Of course, that could just be the exasperation she was trying to hide.

"But…" She looked down at her hands, running her finger along the pink nails of her other hand, as if she was surprised they were there. Then she clasped her hands together and looked straight at him. "But I guess I'm glad you did. This is good for me. It's not often I get to sit in with a client at this stage. I'm hoping I learn a lot."

"Prospective client," Sawyer clarified, and she nodded. "And if I remember Pete Ryan very well, you might learn a whole lot. Just exactly how many curse words do you currently have in your vocabulary?"

A tiny bark of laughter erupted out of her.

There were certain sounds Sawyer did not miss living the life he did. Crowds. Cars. Machines.

But the sound of her laughter—short, unexpected, and just a little husky—that was a sound Sawyer knew he'd miss if he were to hear it on a regular basis.

But he wouldn't.

He'd nail this down with Ryan. Maybe have to come back for a meeting or two, but basically hand it over to Andy to handle and head back up to the Harbor.

"You know," she said, "it was very disappointing to learn you weren't really the Brockway Mountain Hermit."

"Really? You're familiar with that legend?"

"Oh, yes. It's one of my favorites."

"I guess I had it in my head you weren't from around here. I vaguely remember seeing new-hire information from Andy, and I thought we hadn't hired any locals since Mac."

"I'm not. I'm from Farmington Hills."

"And you know the hermit legend?"

"Yes, I—" She was about to say more, but was eclipsed by the shadow of Petey Ryan.

"Hey, Sawyer Beck! How the hell are ya?"

Sawyer rose and shook the large man's hand. Sawyer was almost as tall as Ryan, but the NHL player was broader by about a foot.

"It's been a while, Pete. I've been good, how about you?" He was about to sit when he realized the tiny woman standing next to Ryan was actually with him. And it was someone Sawyer knew.

"Alison? Hi. I…" Sawyer stumbled on his words, shocked to see Alison Jukuri standing with Ryan.

"I know. We've just gone public recently, and everyone's shocked we're together. They can't believe she'd ever go out with me."

"Petey," said tiny Alison Jukuri, elbowing Petey in the gut. "Hi, Sawyer. Petey said we were meeting someone from your firm for dinner, I just didn't realize it would be you. I wasn't aware you—"

"I made it a point to come down for this," Sawyer said.

"Local hero and all that," he said as he took his and Deni's coats from the chair he thought would remain empty and put them on the wide window ledge behind him.

"Fuck off, Sawyer," Petey said as he and Alison got settled. "Hi, Petey Ryan."

"Denise Casparich," Sawyer heard her say as he situated the two more coats Petey handed him. He turned around to see Petey shake her hand and then point to Alison. "Alison Jukuri."

A moment passed, and Alison stuck out her hand toward Deni. He watched as Deni hesitated, then took Alison's hand and shook it. As she leaned back in the chair she said, "Actually, Alison and I know each other. She's my therapist."

Sawyer sat back down, looking from Deni to Alison and back.

Well, shit.

Five
———$\sim\!\!\sim$———

WELL, NUTS.

She looked at Sawyer for his reaction. Would he be repelled? Laugh? Mentally cross off her working on any large project due to emotional instability?

He looked back and forth between Alison and her and then quietly said, "I'm sorry if this puts either of you in an awkward position."

"Well, I don't feel awkward about that, but Petey didn't fully explain that this was a business meeting, so I'm happy to excuse myself," Alison said, starting to rise from her seat.

Petey clamped a huge hand around her tiny wrist and held her hand to the table. "It's not a *strictly* business meeting. Sawyer and I were just going to chew the shit about this thing over some beers and pizza." They shared a look that Deni couldn't decipher, and then he let go of Alison's hand. "But if you want to bail, I'll have Sawyer drop me off at The Ridges when we're done, and I'll meet you at your folks' place."

Alison gave a short nod and Deni realized she was leaving to get Deni out of a possibly uncomfortable position.

"This isn't strictly business, Alison," Deni said. "It really is a meet-and-greet and broad discussion, so please stick around."

Alison studied her for a moment, then nodded and sat back down. "Good, 'cause I've been thinking about Tostada pizza all day since Petey texted me."

The waitress came, and they all ordered beers—except Deni, who stuck with water.

"Not a drinker?" Sawyer asked her.

"Not on a Wednesday, no," she answered.

"Well, we'll have to come back on a Friday," Petey said as he studied the menu, oblivious to the other three looking at each other and knowing there was no way there would be a repeat of this dinner, on a Friday or any other day.

When Deni had started seeing Alison the previous October, Alison had told her that she left it up to all her clients as to how they wanted to deal with the possibility of seeing each other in public.

"It's a small town. Sooner or later, you see everyone somewhere. I'll leave it up to you as to how you'd like that to play out. If you want to pretend you don't know me, that's fine. If you'd like to speak, but act like we know each other from something other than therapy, that's okay, too. I don't think there's any reason to be ashamed that you're in therapy, but I do realize it's a private matter, and I'll just follow your lead," Alison had said at the time.

Funny that it took several months before they'd run into each other. Or maybe not so funny when you figured that Deni had started going home right after work at about that time.

She and Charlie had usually gone out for beers on Friday after work. And she'd been hiking on the weekends with her friend Claire whom she'd met at the gym. But she'd started taking rain checks on those activities around October, and Claire had stopped calling. Even Charlie didn't bug her anymore to go out for a cold one.

"You know what?" she said to the waitress as she brought Alison and Petey's beers to the table and set down Deni's water. "I will have a beer after all. Bud Light, please."

The waitress let out a sigh, but returned to the bar area.

"So, Sawyer. Shit, man, it's really good to see you. How many years has it been? Seven? Eight?"

"Ten," Sawyer said with dead certainty.

"Really? That long?" Petey said, and took a drink of his beer.

The waitress returned with Deni's beer, and she took a drink. Alcohol wasn't a problem. She and Alison had discussed the possibility of anti-depressants, but Deni had wanted to hold off on that step until she'd tried the light therapy. Her SAD was mild, relatively speaking, and she wanted to see if she could get through this season without medication, though she knew it may be the next option available to her.

"I would have sworn it was only—"

"Ten. It's been ten years," Sawyer said firmly. He took a long drink from his beer, draining it. He held it up in the air, motioning the waitress for a refill.

"Oh, shit. Right. Of course. Sorry, man," Petey said, looking sheepishly at Sawyer, then at Alison as if needing help.

She put her hand on Petey's arm and squeezed. To Sawyer she said, "Petey only has finesse on the ice."

Sawyer smiled at Alison and at the waitress, who handed him a fresh beer. The waitress sighed again, but in an entirely different way.

Deni didn't blame her. Good lord, the man was handsome when he smiled. Too bad he didn't seem to do it often.

His smile was so blinding that it took Deni a moment to realize that there was some undercurrent going on between the other three that she was unaware of.

"Dude, I'm really—"

Sawyer held up a hand. "It's fine. Don't sweat it."

One of those "guy" looks passed between them, and just like that it was dropped.

They took a moment to look at the menu, then put their order in. Petey ordered another beer for himself. Deni and Alison worked on their first.

"So, Deni, is it?" Petey asked her.

"Yes. Short for Denise."

"Becks here ever tell you he's the only guy in the Copper Country who ever knocked me on my ass on the ice?"

"Ummm. I just met him today—so, no."

"Well, he is. Only guy ever to do it. Shit, there are guys in the NHL who can't knock me on my ass, and Sawyer here did it a few times."

Sawyer snorted. "About a thousand years ago. And you were a freshman to my senior."

"No other senior did it," Petey said, then raised his beer and tipped it in Sawyer's direction, a salute of sorts.

"You played hockey, too?" Deni asked Sawyer. He didn't have the build that Petey Ryan did, but he was still a big man. Not having grown up in the U.P., Deni wasn't as familiar with hockey as the natives were, but she had season tickets to the Tech games.

Though she hadn't used them much this year.

"In high school," Sawyer answered her. "For Calumet. Petey went to Houghton. Alison went to Hancock. All Copper Country, but..."

"You're all rivals."

The three of them looked at each other and broke into smiles. "You betcha," all three said at the same time, causing Deni to laugh.

"How's your brother doing?" Petey asked Sawyer.

"Which one?"

"I meant Huck. I saw Twain not too long ago. He was at Katie's wedding last fall."

"I'm not really sure. I haven't seen him in quite a while. I left my dog there tonight, and I'm hoping he'll be home when I pick her up."

"Wait a minute," Deni said, holding up a hand. "You have brothers named Twain and Huck? And you're Sawyer?"

He nodded. "Yep. Mom was a bit of a Mark Twain freak."

"So why not Mark? Or Tom? Or Samuel? Or even Clem for Clemens?"

"Mom was also a bit of a nut job."

Deni laughed, and Sawyer smiled at her. The sheer voltage of his...his...manliness when he did that had her reaching for her beer.

"Baby, help me out here. Name some other Mark Twain novels," Petey said to Alison.

"*A Connecticut Yankee in King Arthur's Court.*"

"Arty," Petey proposed to Sawyer.

"*The Tragedy of Pudd'nhead Wilson.*"

"Willy," Petey threw out. They all laughed. Petey turned to Alison and said, "Damn, if it doesn't turn me on when you get all brainy."

"Be good," Alison said, warning in her voice. She looked embarrassed, which made Deni feel better about sitting at a table having beers with her therapist.

Petey leaned over to Alison, but Deni could still hear him when he whispered to Alison, "But baby, you don't like it when I'm good."

The look of intimacy that passed between them was so strong, so raw, that Deni had to look away.

And met Sawyer Beck's gaze as he watched her.

He had the most expressive green eyes. Green, not brown as she'd thought back at the office. Everything else on his chiseled face was stoic, implacable. But his eyes... His eyes held a story. One that Deni couldn't read.

"Katie has friends in the golf world who are sisters named Franny and Zooey after the Salinger novel," Alison said, pulling Deni's attention away from Sawyer and his eyes. Then, for Deni's sake, Alison added, "Katie's one of my best friends, and she married Darío Luna last fall. Darío and Petey are the ones who came up with this idea of an indoor driving range."

"Yes, Andy told us a little bit about how the idea came to be," Deni said.

"Basically, Darío needs a place to practice in the winter, and I need something to do with my time now that I'm retired."

"Yeah, I heard about that. An injury? The knee, was it?" Sawyer asked.

"Yeah. But I'd actually decided this year was my last anyway.

It just sped the process up a little."

"I'm sorry about that," Sawyer said.

Petey looked at Alison as he answered. "I'm not."

Alison blushed, and Deni again felt like an intruder.

"So Alison, you and Petey? Are you sure it wasn't you who was injured? Like a concussion or something?"

"Fuck off, Becks," Petey said, then looked at Deni, "'Scuse my language."

"Well, Deni, you got Petey to do one thing no one else in this town has been able to do—apologize for his language," Alison said.

"I have two brothers—bad language doesn't bother me."

"That's good. 'Cause if we're going to work together, that's pretty much a prerequisite," Petey said, flashing a grin.

Wow. With a charm-filled grin like that, no wonder her mild-mannered therapist had fallen for this potty-mouthed brute of a man.

"Speaking of which," Sawyer said, a bit of edge in his voice, "let's talk a little business."

Their food arrived, and as they ate, Petey brought them up to speed on what he was envisioning.

"The challenge is keeping costs down. First in building it and then in maintaining it. Because it's never going to be a big revenue generator. And that's not even the purpose."

"What exactly is the purpose? Your main goal in this undertaking?" Deni asked. She wiped her hands on her napkin and pulled a tablet out of her bag.

"Well, I was only half kidding when I said it was for Darío to practice and me to have something to do. That's a big part of it." Deni jotted a few things down, then looked back to Petey for him to continue. "This area is golf crazy, second only to hockey crazy. And the golf season is so damn short, it just seems like it could be something people would use."

"So, even if we used materials that let in most of the light during the day, we'd need enough lighting to clearly light it up in the evenings for night golf," Deni said, writing again.

"Yeah, exactly. It'd have to be open late into the evening, so people could go after work, after dinner. You might even get a crowd of guys who go after they put their kids to bed, or would go do this instead of going out for a beer with their buddies. We're even toying with the idea of trying to get a liquor license and having a few tables where guys could have a beer after they hit a bucket."

"Weekends, of course, would be big," Deni said, not even looking at the others anymore, now quickly writing notes. "So you'd be looking at energy costs almost twenty-four/seven."

"Yeah, and that's the bitch of it all. I don't know if that makes this thing even feasible."

"That's for us to figure out," Sawyer said. There was a sense of authority, of confidence, in his voice that made Deni look up from her notes. He leaned forward, his forearms on the edge of the table. "Let us take this on, Petey. If there's a way to do this, we'll figure it out."

Petey looked across the table at Sawyer, then he took a quick glance at Alison. Deni thought she saw Alison give a small nod, but it may have been her imagination.

"When you say 'us,' who exactly do you mean? Are you going to be working on this yourself?" Petey asked Sawyer.

Deni sat back in her chair, waiting for Sawyer to explain the process, and groups of people, that Petey would work with at Summers and Beck. The survey team, then the costing process, and then finally—hopefully—the choosing of the contractor and the actual building. All of which would be overseen by a project coordinator, most likely Jim or Bob, or possibly Andy himself. Although Snide Randy had been made lead on more projects lately, making Deni feel that Andy might be grooming Randy for a partnership.

"Yes. I will be seeing this through every phase," Sawyer said, shocking Deni.

Today, Andy had made it seem like Sawyer was here merely

for the meet-and-greet schmooze dinner. That he'd make the pitch for Petey to use Summers and Beck and then head back up to the mountain and his hut.

Okay, so not a hut. And maybe not even on Brockway Mountain. But still. She hadn't expected him to lie outright to a client. Unless he wasn't lying and was indeed going to take lead on this one.

Deni wasn't sure which scenario was less likely.

"Of course, others will be involved. First thing, we'll get our survey crew up to your land and get some specs. And then our costing guys will start working on a budget and ongoing cost-versus-revenue analysis."

Oh, okay. He was easing Petey into the idea that others would take over for him when he headed back up to the mountain.

"But I will be the lead on this and will oversee every step of it myself," Sawyer said, looking straight at Petey.

The man was not lying. He was going to come out of hibernation for this job.

Which was an important, high-profile job, but not one that would make the company much money. There were a lot of other projects—some of the new buildings at Tech they were trying to land—that could have used the attention of a partner more.

But you didn't hide away on a mountain if you didn't have at least a touch of eccentricity—and possibly a little of downright crazy.

"Deni's going to be my second on this. Like I said, others will be involved, but you'll be working with the two of us."

Petey was nodding, chewing on a piece of pizza. He finished, wiped his mouth with a napkin, and said, "Let's do this. You guys start. I won't go anywhere else with this thing until we take a look at what you come up with. If the numbers can work, you have the business."

He wasn't even going to bid it out? Deni kept her mouth shut. Either this Petey Ryan was the world's worst businessman or...

She watched as something, some look, passed between Petey and Sawyer. A measurement of some kind. A judgment. Something Deni didn't fully understand. But Alison did. Deni could tell by her therapist's body language that Alison approved of whatever was passing between her man and Sawyer.

Deni had been in the Copper Country long enough to know that things were sometimes done quite differently than in the real world, but this exceeded anything she'd seen before.

Still, she kept her mouth shut, not even bringing up the fact that surely tomorrow her role in this project would be turned over to somebody with more experience in this type of structure.

"How about Darío?" Sawyer asked. "How involved will he be?"

"Not very. He's here for the next month while the tour is on the west coast, and until the baby gets a little older."

"Right. Andy mentioned something about somebody having a baby." He sat back, his arms falling from the table. He took his beer bottle and noticed it was empty. He motioned to the waitress, then looked around at the level in the others' bottles and held up three fingers. Deni eyed her nearly full bottle.

"Yeah, Darío and Katie had a baby girl about, what"—he looked at Alison—"three weeks ago?"

"Four," Alison said.

"Right. Four. Two of which were the longest two weeks of my life," he said, still gazing at Alison. She put her hand on his arm. Deni thought she heard Alison whisper, "Mine, too."

"Anyway…." Sawyer said, trying to guide Petey back. "Darío's involvement?"

"Right. So, he'll be around for another few weeks until the tour hits the Florida swing, then he and Katie and Peaches will hit the road for a while."

"They're going to take a two-month-old baby out on tour?" Deni asked. By the shrugs coming from both Alison and Petey it seemed they'd asked the same question.

"She says she wants to try it. I think she's going to be

home with Peaches in about two weeks, but Katie seems pretty determined to spend this spring and summer on the road with Darío," Alison said.

"So, anything we can have ready to show Darío, the sooner the better. Obviously we can email him anything and conference call and all that. But for the most part you're going to be dealing with me on the day-to-day stuff."

Sawyer nodded and ate some pizza.

"First thing, we're going to want to get our survey guys up on your land and see what's what."

Petey nodded and motioned to Alison, who reached down, pulled a large envelope out of her bag, and handed it to Sawyer.

"This is all the stuff on the land, measurements, specs, all that crap," Petey said as Sawyer took the envelope from Alison and put it on the ledge behind them with their coats.

"We should probably talk about budgets a little more in depth," Sawyer said.

Petey waved a hand. "Just give me a bottom line. I wrote in there"—he motioned to the envelope—"our rough estimates on revenue, hours open, that stuff. I'm working on a more detailed business plan now."

"You are?" Alison and Deni said at the same time.

"Yes. I am," Petey said with attitude. Deni didn't blame him. Both she and Alison had sounded doubtful. Deni had only met the man an hour ago, but he did not seem like the type to spend time developing a thorough business plan. And Alison apparently agreed, and she obviously knew Petey much better. And much more intimately.

"What? No comment from you?" Petey said to Sawyer.

"Nope. No comment. Except good for you, man. I hope it works out and we can help you."

Petey seemed taken aback by this, but quickly recovered.

"Thanks, man."

"If you need any help writing the plan, let me know. It's been a while, but I've written a few of them over the years."

"Thanks. Lizzie Hampton's helping me with it. She's helped a few of her clients with them. Dumb jocks who need to put their money somewhere."

"Hey, don't call yourself a dumb jock," Alison said in a soothing voice, then smiled and quickly added, "That's my job."

"Ain't that the truth," Petey said, but his smile at Alison said she could call him anything she wanted.

The three of them started talking about the Lizzie person Petey had mentioned, and then others they all knew. Deni only half listened as she ate her pizza.

"Sorry to go on and on about people you don't know... Deni," Alison said after a while. She only knew Deni as Denise, and the nickname didn't seem to roll off her tongue easily.

"No, that's fine. It's nice that you're getting a chance to catch up."

Soon after, the dinner came to a close, and Sawyer said he'd be in touch with Petey soon about the surveying and moving forward.

"Great. We're sorry to cut this short, but we need to stop by The Ridges and see Al's parents tonight."

"Your parents are in The Ridges?" Sawyer asked Alison.

Deni knew The Ridges was an assisted-living facility in the area. It'd been designed by Summers and Beck. She wasn't a huge fan of Snide Randy's, but he'd done a beautiful job with that complex.

"Yeah, for a few weeks now. We try to get over each night. Petey goes to see my dad most afternoons."

"He told you about that? I didn't know if he remembers or not."

They'd risen from their seats and were putting their coats on. Alison stopped mid-sleeve and leaned over to hug Petey. "Thank you for doing that, by the way." She continued putting her coat on. Deni just watched her with part fascination at seeing her therapist as such a...human. And, yeah, okay, part envy at the easy, sweet, and yet obviously passionate relationship the two of them had together.

They all said their goodbyes, and the couple left, leaving Deni and Sawyer alone together. Sawyer's eyes were still on the doorway where Petey and Alison had exited, as he slowly shook his head.

"Petey Ryan and Alison Jukuri? Wow. I would not have seen that coming." He looked at Deni. "Still. They seemed pretty happy, eh?"

"Yes, they did. And oddly compatible."

"Yeah, exactly." He shook his head again. "Go figure." Then he took his wallet out and put some bills down with the tab. Sawyer reached for Deni's coat and held it up for her. She rose from the table and let him drape her coat around her, her hands bumping his arms as she reached for the armholes. She pulled her hat and mittens out of the coat pockets as Sawyer put on his own coat.

As they walked out of the Commodore, Sawyer said, "So, Petey Ryan is in a committed relationship and seems happy."

Deni turned around, ready to agree with him, but she stopped short when he added, "Guess I didn't need to bring you."

Six

DENI WALKED OUT OF THE RESTAURANT, SAWYER'S words becoming clear as they reached the sidewalk. The frigid air wasn't nearly as shocking as his meaning.

"I was…what? A token girl to dangle in front of the town horndog? You were going to pimp me out to a client?"

"No. Of course not. I mean, nothing that nefarious." He had the grace to look chagrined.

The numbness Deni had been feeling for weeks switched gears into the irritability Alison had warned her may be coming. She put her mitten-clad hand in the center of Sawyer Beck's chest and pushed. "How *dare* you." He backed up a step, but she followed and put her hand on his chest again. "I'm a very good architectural engineer, I'll have you know."

"I don't doubt that," he said, taking another step back.

That, for some unknown reason, infuriated her even more. "I may be the only female engineer at Summers and *Beck*"—she nearly spat the name at him—"but I'm nobody's…bait!"

"I know that. That's not—"

"And another thing," she said, pushing his chest again, sending him backing into the brick facade of the Commodore. "I'm not the right person for this job. There are any—"

The words were cut off as he grabbed her upper arms and whirled her around, placing her back against the building.

"Why didn't you say any of your ideas today?" he asked.

Growled.

"What?" she asked, confused. This was her rant. What was he blathering about?

"Today. In the meeting. You had it all down in your notes. Why didn't you speak up?"

"You were looking at my laptop?"

He shook her arms, stepped closer to her. The envelope under his arm rustled, but held. His breath came out in frozen clouds. She could see hers as well. Why was she breathing so hard?

"I even gave you the opening about the methane, but you let the others bring it up. Why?"

She tried to think back to the meeting, but her mind shut down. She couldn't think, she could only feel. Feel his strong hands on her arms, even through the thick wool of her coat. Feel his breath against her face. Feel the weight of his gaze as his eyes searched hers.

"I don't know...I... What do you mean?" she asked, her voice not sounding like her own.

His eyes dropped from hers to her mouth, and she bit her lip. In anticipation.

"Aw, hell," he whispered, then leaned forward and kissed her.

SHE TASTED LIKE PIZZA. And beer. Which were two of Sawyer's favorite things. But both paled in comparison to the taste of... just...her.

He'd watched her all night at dinner. She'd been good with Petey and Alison, had fit in. She knew when to pipe up and when to let the client talk.

But all Sawyer could think about was the way her mouth wrapped around that beer bottle.

It was wrong. On *so* many levels, not the least of which was she worked for his company.

But, good God, she tasted great.

And, good God, she was kissing him back.

He opened his mouth over hers, and she followed suit. He

darted his tongue inside, and hers greeted him. He moved his hands down her arms to her waist and pulled her closer, the envelope falling to the ground. She wrapped her arms around his neck. He felt the wool of her mitten on his nape when she slid her hand under his hair.

But that mouth.

Her lips were silky warm—even in the cold—and moved against his in a rhythm they found in seconds. Natural. It felt so natural to be kissing her.

But it wasn't—it wasn't natural at all.

Shit.

He pulled away. Stepped away. The warmth from her mittens left, leaving his neck suddenly cold.

"I'm really sorry," he said, not quite meeting her eyes, his gaze on her lips, now a deeper shade of red and so wet. He bent down and retrieved the envelope. "I shouldn't have done that."

He expected that cute red wool mitten to poke his chest again, but her hands remained at her sides. Awkwardly, as if they didn't know what to do now that they weren't wrapped around his neck.

He almost stepped back to her, just to give her arms something to do, but then she whispered, "Why did you, then?"

Because I could not look at that mouth one second longer without knowing how it tasted.

Because seeing those out-of-place-on-you pink nails wrapped around a beer bottle gave me ideas of something else they could be wrapped around.

Because…because…

"Because I couldn't…not."

She looked up at him then. Her brown eyes grew wider, then narrowed slightly in suspicion. She didn't believe him.

"It's the truth. But I'm still sorry I did it."

"Because you're my boss?"

That reason was pretty damn low on his list. "I'm not your boss."

"Maybe not directly, but it's your company. You could have me fired."

He took another step back, yanked his chook out of his coat pocket, and pulled the knit cap over his head, making sure to cover the tips of his ears, which were growing colder in the frigid air.

"If I walked into those offices tomorrow and told Andy I wanted you fired"—she started to open her mouth, but he held up a hand—"or that I wanted you off this project or even expressed some doubts about your abilities, he'd laugh me out of his office."

"Why? He seems to trust your judgment. Why else get you down here?"

"He got me down here because I knew Petey—not well, and not for a lot of years, as you could tell from our conversation. But he thought Petey might feel more comfortable, more at ease, with me."

She looked down, probably thinking about where he was going, then looked back up at him and gave him a forgiving shrug. She was quick and didn't need him to go on, but *he* needed to.

"Which was one of the reasons I wanted you here, too. I wasn't pimping you out. I knew Petey Ryan likes pretty girls—women. I knew he likes to flirt and posture, and I figured he wouldn't do that with me." He smiled, thinking about the man he remembered. "But he'd particularly love to do it in *front* of me." Then he thought of the man he'd just had dinner with. "But it seems it was all for naught, because he is blissfully unaware of all other females than Alison Jukuri."

"Okay, so you weren't pimping me out."

"Nope. And…." He didn't finish his thought.

"What?"

"Nothing."

"Come on. What?" she said with a bit of resignation in her voice. Like he was going to tell her it wasn't like she'd be Pete Ryan's type anyway. Which was about a thousand miles away from what he was actually thinking.

Which was: "Besides, by the end of the night, if he'd made one move toward you, I would have put him on his ass…again."

"Because Alison is your friend, too? I don't think he'd—"

"Not because of that. Even if Alison hadn't been there. By the end of the dinner—hell, even by the time I'd walked out of the office—I did not want Petey Ryan flirting with you. And I really didn't want you flirting back."

"Why?" No resignation in her voice now. She knew. She knew how attracted he'd become to her in such a short time. Seemed surprised by it, but she wasn't being all coy about it.

Which was part of the attraction.

"Why?" she asked again, challenge in her voice this time.

He liked it. It felt so different from how he'd been feeling for so long now. And more than being attracted to her—which was odd in itself—he *liked* her.

When he realized that, he knew he had to step back—and not in the physical sense.

"Why?" she asked once more, this time on a whisper, her breath trailing into the space between them.

"Because of your pink nail polish," he said, shocked at what came out of his mouth. He wanted to be straight with her, but Jesus, he didn't want to make her think he had a fetish or anything.

"My nail polish?" There was a sly smile on her face that he couldn't quite read.

"Not that, exactly." He took another step back and waved a hand that encompassed her from her cute, striped hat to her furry boots. "You kind of have this tree-hugger vibe going"—she groaned, and Sawyer guessed that maybe she got that a lot—"but then those hot pink nails. I don't know, they just seemed so… unexpected, I guess."

She was looking at him like he was crazy.

He shrugged. "Now you know why I don't go out much."

She laughed at that, even though he wasn't truly joking. He liked the sound of her laugh—not a giggle, but not deep and throaty, either. Just a normal, amused laugh.

He liked normal. Appreciated normal.

Craved normal.

And the pink nails were just the tiny twist that made it all so interesting to him.

"The pink stood out to me," he said. "And then *you* stood out to me." He shrugged. "Plus, my dog liked you, and she usually won't go to strangers."

She started to speak, but he didn't want to know what she was going to say. "But, I shouldn't have kissed you. Not because you work for me—which again, by the way, you don't. But because I have no business starting up anything with you." He took another step away from her, almost to the curb.

"I have no business starting anything with anybody." He looked at her one more time—so adorable, all bundled up—and then turned around and walked to his car.

WHAT THE HELL JUST HAPPENED? Deni watched Sawyer get in an old, beat-up Bronco and drive away.

Her pink nails? *That* was why he'd kissed her?

The irony of that washed over her as she made her way to her Subaru. She got inside and turned up the defroster and the seat warmer to the highest setting.

Most people would have just gotten in their cars and gone. Definitely most Yoopers. But Deni waited until every last vapor of frost disappeared from her front and back windshields before driving to the house she rented in Hancock's East End. It was a gorgeous Victorian that she was able to afford only because the owners didn't want to sell, but were living in a place they'd built on the lakefront.

They were basically looking for a paying caretaker for the place, and Deni fit the bill perfectly, even restoring the original woodwork herself.

It was tall and picturesque and had an awesome view of the lift bridge. And steps. It had a lot of steps leading from the garage, detached and at street level, down to the house, built into the hill.

Deni had finally surrendered last winter and hired a kid to come and shovel them at six every morning. Most days, when she came home after work, they were covered again. But today they hadn't had much snowfall, and the steps weren't hard to navigate.

She made her way inside, divested herself of her layers, turned the heat up, and went to her bedroom to change out of her work clothes.

As she hung her cardigan up in the closet, Sawyer Beck's words "tree-hugger vibe" came back to her.

It wasn't the first time she'd been called that. And it was a label she was okay with, though it usually signaled someone much more militant than she was. She barely even recycled.

She just liked natural fibers, not a lot of bright colors, and really comfy clothes. Which was a good thing, because this past winter her normally baggy clothes were tightening up just a smidge on her.

She looked down at the shoe rack. And, okay, she liked Birkenstocks. Lots of Birkenstocks.

It was a fine line between tree-hugger and Yooper dress, with their flannel and Sorel boots.

She changed into sweats and pulled a different cardigan around her turtleneck. Slipping her feet into her fuzzy slippers, she eyed her bed. It beckoned to her, as it did most evenings when she came home from work.

"It's warm in here. Relax. You've worked hard. Just curl up in here for a while," the rich chocolate comforter called out to her. Most nights that was all it took, and Deni would crawl in, sometimes not taking the time to change out of her work clothes, and wrap herself in that delicious comforter like a burrito. Some nights she wouldn't get out until morning, not even to make some dinner for herself.

Tonight she bypassed the bed, giving it a wide berth lest she succumb.

She went downstairs, her hand caressing the oak bannister that she'd lovingly restored two years ago. After unpacking her laptop from her bag, she set it on the kitchen table at the far end from the light box and booted it up.

She'd cut out her regular cup of strong tea after dinner and instead put the kettle on and plucked a decaf tea bag out of a ceramic pig where she kept all her teabags.

Once the kettle was ready and her mug was full, she settled in at the table. She started to open her personal email software, but instead opened her browser and got on the company's webmail site, checking her work email. Nothing since she'd left the office two hours ago.

Only two hours, and yet it seemed like it had been days since she'd been in her own cubicle, quietly doing her job, thinking about how best to restore a small section of a project that Charlie was working on.

Now that project—one she'd been delighted to work on— seemed far away and insignificant. A monstrosity in the shape of a billowing, oversized bed sheet now took up her thoughts.

Well, not all of them. Some corner of her mind—and just a corner, not an inch more!—was thinking about Sawyer Beck. And an even smaller portion—too small to even signify, really—was replaying that kiss.

She took a sip from her tea, the hot liquid not nearly as scorching as his mouth on hers had been.

She didn't know what had gotten into her when she'd pushed him. The irritability that she'd been feeling as part of the SAD had been something that she'd hidden well from friends and coworkers. Certainly she'd felt the urge to snap responses, and terse comments whistled through her mind. But she'd held them in check, knowing it was the mood talking, and she had to keep a lid on it for sheer common decency's sake.

Well, the lid had blown tonight. And, really, over nothing. She instinctively knew that Sawyer Beck wasn't really going to offer her sexual favors to Petey Ryan for the job. And putting clients with employees whom you think the client will like working with was a part of the job—really just good business.

Buried under the numbness, her mood had been looking for something to explode over for weeks. And Sawyer had given her the opening she needed.

Too bad it was with her boss. And that she'd poked him in the chest several times while yelling at him.

She went to the company's website. She'd been on it years ago when she'd interviewed, and then again when she'd been added as a project engineer, but she hadn't poked around too deeply.

She went to Andy's bio, and there was a mention of Andy and Sawyer Beck founding the company eighteen years ago when they'd both graduated from Tech. But there was no bio page for Sawyer. No photo, no nothing.

But that kiss hadn't been nothing.

Finally, she got to her personal email and answered the ones from her mother. There was one from Claire asking Deni if she wanted to go cross-country skiing this weekend. A year ago, Deni would not have thought twice and would have quickly responded with a yes. But this year, this winter, thoughts of leaving the house on a weekend when she didn't have to be anywhere seemed larger than she could handle. The dark blanket started to wrap around her shoulders, and she began to type a response that said she was going to have to work this weekend and asked if she could take Claire up on it some other time.

She knew she'd refused Claire—and Charlie, and all her other friends—too often. In fact, she was surprised Claire even made this offer, as frequently as Deni had said no lately.

She rolled her shoulders, as if trying to dislodge the phantom weight, and deleted her response. Instead, she typed that she might have to work this weekend, and asked if she could get back to Claire on Friday.

It wasn't true. That was one of the things Andy was pretty strict on—family life. If at all possible, his staff kept normal working hours, able to be home on weekends and most nights for dinner. It wasn't always possible, especially when active construction was going on, but it was something Andy felt strongly about.

Deni sent the reply off to Claire before she could delete it once again. It was a small step not to say no right away. Even if she'd most likely pass on Friday, she felt like she'd taken a positive step.

She logged out of the laptop, rinsed out her teacup, and patted the light box as she exited the kitchen.

Seven

"DID I EVER TELL YOU ABOUT MY FATHER BRINGING US here—to the Copper Country—when I was about eight years old?" Deni said to Alison on Friday.

Alison was just getting seated, having brought Deni and herself a cup of tea. She seemed taken aback by Deni's jumping right in before Alison could prod with questions, as was their normal pattern.

"No, I don't think you did," Alison said, nodding for Deni to go on. They both knew that Alison would have remembered if Deni had told a story about her father. She'd barely mentioned him her whole time in therapy. And Alison forgot nothing.

Deni launched in with the story of standing on top of Brockway Mountain for what seemed like hours trying to find the hermit's hut, her father patiently waiting for her to do so.

Her shoulders felt lighter than they had in weeks as she went into minute details of that long-ago day. How she'd tried to see Isle Royale, but couldn't. How clean the air had been, but she'd been too young to realize how special that was. Even the smell of the grass.

"And how did you feel that day? Can you remember that?" Alison asked her, then took a sip from her teacup. She set it down on the end table next to her chair and quietly waited for Deni to answer.

"I felt…I don't know."

"You seem to remember that day pretty clearly. You can't recall how you were feeling?"

She was just about to give a pat answer of "happy" or something like that when she stopped. She looked at Alison and said, "Treasured."

"In what way?"

"Well, there we were on top of that mountain for, what seemed at the time, most of the day. Although now that I think about it, it probably wasn't really that long. But it felt like it." She stopped and took a sip of the tea. It had cooled off some since Alison had handed it to her, and Deni realized she'd spent most of her hour telling the story without taking a break of any kind.

"My brothers were doing God knows what on the other side. Although my dad probably was checking up on them while I was looking through the telescope thingy. And my mother probably had an eye on them the whole time she waited in the car."

"And yet, your father waited with you while you tried to find the hut."

"Yes."

"And that made you feel treasured?"

"Yes. But you know what? I felt that way all the time then. I couldn't have put a name to it, of course, but I knew my world was safe. I knew that I was loved, and that if I desperately wanted or needed something, my father would be there for me."

Alison waited patiently, but Deni just sat on the comfortable couch, willing whatever heat was left from the mug of tea to seep into her hand, her arms, her entire body.

After a moment, Alison said, "And when was it that your father died?"

"Six months later," Deni said without hesitation. She took a gulp of the lukewarm tea and looked at her watch. "I guess it's time to go."

Alison didn't look at the clock that sat on the table and faced away from the patient's couch.

"We have a little bit of time if you'd like to—"

"I really need to get back to work. I do this on my lunchtime so I don't like to take advantage."

Alison nodded and started to ask her the wrap-up assessment questions she asked her most sessions. Sometimes they varied but were basically the same. When they got to the one where she asked about the small thing Deni was going to work on for the following week, Alison said, "I noticed the pink nail polish the other night at dinner. It's really striking. Did you enjoy that? Shopping for something different? Doing or wearing something different than you normally would?"

That had been her "assignment" from last week. To spend time shopping for something—and it could be small—that was not something she would typically buy and then to incorporate it into her life.

She'd thought about sexy lingerie or something like that, but she'd walked out of ShopKo with a bottle of hot pink nail polish instead.

"It was interesting," she now said to Alison. "It wasn't what I thought I'd buy."

"I find it interesting that you chose something that *you* would see as much as somebody else would see."

"What do you mean?"

"Well, you see your hands all the time—eating, getting ready, working, especially if you work with computers as much as I'm guessing you do."

"Yes?"

"You could have chosen something that you wear outwardly that other people see more than you do, like a necklace or something. Or, you could have chosen something that *only* you see, but not very often, like different undergarments."

Deni should have been embarrassed, but she'd passed that line with Alison a long time ago.

"But you chose something that *you* would see as much—or even more—than others would."

"What does that mean?" Deni asked. Surely they were over

her session time by now, but Deni didn't dare look at her watch again. She didn't want to stop Alison's train of thought.

"I'm not sure it means anything. I just find it interesting. And"—she started to rise from her chair, causing Deni to do the same—"it's a very bold choice. I like it."

"Sawyer Beck said the reason he kissed me was because of my nail polish."

Alison sat back in her chair, a look of shock on her usually composed face. "Sawyer Beck kissed you?"

"Yes. That night we met you and Petey."

Alison waved Deni to sit back down, which she did. "Do you want to talk about that?"

"Aren't we out of time?"

"I don't have another appointment for an hour."

"Oh, okay. Um…what should we talk about? I mean about him kissing me?"

A devilish smile crossed Alison's face. One Deni had never seen during therapy but which seemed to go with the woman who'd been Petey Ryan's date the other night. "Well, what I'd really like to know is what kind of kisser Sawyer Beck is, but I guess that would be unprofessional to ask."

Deni laughed, out of shock as well as amusement. "Um… that was *so* not what I thought you were going to say."

"I am a therapist. But I'm also a woman. And Sawyer Beck… Well, let me just say, he was the older bad boy from Calumet, and we Hancock girls thought he was…." She trailed off, but Deni knew what Alison was thinking. She'd thought it herself.

"Dangerous," Deni whispered.

Alison chuckled. "Yes. Exactly. Of course, we all got to know each other as adults, and of course we all changed. But Sawyer Beck was always kind of this elusive figure."

"Like some kind of white whale?"

"A sexy-as-hell white whale."

"I *guess* so," Deni added, and they both laughed.

"So, he kissed you the other night. Was that all there was?"

It was Deni's turn to flash the devilish smile. "Are you asking as my therapist or because you want to finally know what kind of kisser Sawyer Beck is?"

"Both," Alison answered with a smile.

"Then will you tell me what kind of kisser Petey Ryan is?" Deni teased Alison. They were probably on the fringes of professionalism, but it felt good to joke with someone. Even if that someone knew all her issues.

But apparently Alison was willing to let the boundary shift a little as she smiled and said in a near whisper, "Dangerous."

"You seem like such an unusual match," Deni said, hoping she wasn't offending Alison.

"I know. We are. We fought it for a long time because of that." She glanced away for a second, then looked back to Deni and shrugged. "I got tired of fighting something that made me feel so good."

"Is it that easy?" Deni asked. They both knew she wasn't asking about Alison and Petey any longer.

"No. It isn't easy at all. It's a struggle. It may be a struggle for a long time. Or it might get better once spring is here."

Deni nodded.

"So, last week you spent time out, shopping for something that you don't typically wear."

Deni nodded, one finger tracing across the pink nail of another.

"This week I'd like you to try going to a place in the area that you haven't been to before. And take some time planning it. No spur of the moment trip to, like, the hardware store if you've never been there."

"I go to the hardware store all the time. McGee's was one of the first places I stopped in when I moved here."

Alison chuckled. "I forgot who I was talking to for a moment. So, maybe a restaurant that you haven't tried. Maybe in Baraga or L'Anse, some place that you have to plan for, think about, and take some time getting to."

A sense of dread started to crawl up Deni's back. "I don't know if I can. I'm going to be putting in a lot of hours trying to do some research on this indoor driving range thing." She didn't know that to be true. Sawyer had said something to Petey the other night about keeping her on the project, though that might have changed since that kiss.

And the truth was an indoor driving range wasn't even something she was very interested in.

Or hadn't been before….

"Are you becoming nervous just thinking about doing it?" Alison asked, and Deni realized she'd hit the nail on the head.

"Yes, I guess so."

"All the more reason to do it."

Deni nodded, knowing Alison was right, yet getting the creeps just thinking about it. She tried to see herself finding a neat little hole-in-the-wall restaurant that was new to her and enjoying a meal there. Maybe she'd even invite Claire or Charlie. But the vision of her bed and its warm covers supplanted her happy vision.

"You can do this, Denise," Alison said. Deni nodded again, though she didn't feel quite as confident. "I was surprised at dinner the other night when you introduced yourself as Deni. Is that the name you prefer?"

"Yes," Deni said, with a bit of sheepishness. "I don't know why I didn't tell you that. I think I thought therapy was supposed to be, I don't know, more formal or something."

"Therapy works best when you're comfortable."

"Then, after a while, it seemed weird to tell you I go by Deni, you know?"

Alison was nodding. "Of course. No worries, we'll go with Deni moving forward." She made to rise from her chair, and Deni followed suit.

As Deni was putting on her coat and boots, Alison said, "I'm not sure how often I'll be with Petey when he might be working with you all on this project. My guess is not very often, but are you okay with situations like the other night?"

Deni thought about it, wanting to be totally honest with Alison. "I am. I was kind of nervous about what Sawyer would think knowing I was in therapy, but I didn't want to pretend I knew you from somewhere else or start lying, you know?"

"I don't think Sawyer would have any issue with you being in therapy. He may have the hermit reputation, but he's hardly a caveman. He had the skills and savvy to build up that company before he…took some time off."

"Time off?" Deni thought there was a big difference between taking time off and living a life that made people think you were the Brockway Mountain Hermit.

"After his wife died."

The words seemed to hang in the air between them. "I… didn't know. I guess I assumed hermits didn't marry."

"I'm only telling you what anyone in town would tell you— he was always kind of a loner, but he didn't really check out until after Molly died."

"Molly." The name conjured up the vision of a vivacious blond with a ponytail and teasing laughter. Someone vibrant and full of life. "How'd she die?"

"Car accident," Alison said, but there was just a tiny hesitation in her voice that made Deni want to ask more. But then, she didn't want it to seem like she was interested in the life of Sawyer Beck—even if he had kissed her.

"That's really sad," she said as she did the final buttons on her coat.

"It was. It is," Alison said. Deni moved to the door, and as she turned to say goodbye, Alison reached out and put a hand on her arm.

"You know, I think the light box may be having a good effect," she said to Deni.

"You do? Why?"

"You may not have realized it, but not once today did you mention your mother."

Deni left Alison's offices feeling more confused than ever. But she thought that might be a good thing.

Eight

—m—

"DOING OKAY?" SAWYER ASKED DENI AS HE DROVE them both back to Houghton from Green Bay. She'd been quite talkative during their meeting with the owners of a now-defunct indoor driving range. She'd asked good questions—even a couple that Sawyer hadn't thought to ask.

It'd been a good meeting, other than feeling even more so that this thing might be a pipe dream.

He'd set up this Saturday meeting yesterday morning. He couldn't even explain to himself why he'd then emailed Deni and asked her to join him. She'd responded that she was available and had been interested in this particular range because of the fire that had put it out of business a year ago. After seeing her laptop Wednesday at the meeting, he wasn't surprised that she'd already found this place and done the homework on it. He'd responded that he'd drive and would pick her up at the office at 8am to get to Green Bay by noon. The owners were only giving them two hours to ask questions and take a look around the site.

Other than an initial assessment of their meeting when they'd first left Green Bay, she hadn't said a peep since he'd begun the drive home.

"Deni? You okay?" he asked again.

Her head nodded, but she didn't say anything.

"Hey," he said, taking a good look at her now. "Seriously. Are you okay?"

"Could you please keep your eyes on the road?" she answered.

But it wasn't a bitchy tone in her voice. It was…fear.

Sawyer assessed the road conditions and the blowing snow. It wasn't great out, but he'd driven in much worse. Besides, he'd taken his F-150 today instead of the Bronco. New tires, four-wheel drive, big-ass truck. They were fine.

"The roads aren't that bad," he said calmly, trying not to sound like a stereotypically boastful male driver. Just his luck that right then a particularly strong gust created a white-out, not allowing them to see more than ten feet in front of them.

Out of the corner of his eye, he saw her hands clenched in her lap. Totally white-knuckling it.

"Hey, Deni, it's okay. Really. I'm not stupid. I wouldn't drive in weather I thought was truly dangerous."

Another short nod, but her hands clenched harder, if that was even possible.

"Would you like me to stop for a while? Pull over?"

She looked over at him with a look of relief. "Would you? Just for a little bit? Maybe until the wind calms down and visibility gets better?"

Sawyer didn't mention that the visibility wasn't likely to get much better as the day went on. It was late afternoon now and would only be getting darker. But he was becoming concerned. About her, not the roads. He'd driven in crappy weather like this, and a lot worse, his whole life.

"Sure," he said, getting his bearings. "We're coming into Iron Mountain. We can go to a coffee shop or something and wait till it gets a little better."

Only when he saw the tension in her shoulders ease did he realize just how nervous she really was.

"You went to Tech, right?" She nodded. "And you've been with the firm since then?" Another nod, her hands still clenched. "Are you just really nervous because someone else is driving, or are you like this on iffy roads all the time?" Before she could answer, he added, "And if so, how are you able to function up here?" As soon as he said it, he wished he could take it back. Maybe she had issues about fear or anxiety that were heightened by winter driving. Maybe that was why she was seeing Alison.

The day after their dinner, he'd briefly wondered about that—the reason Deni was in therapy. But then his mind went back to the time he himself had seen Alison on a professional basis, and his mind had shut down, not wanting to relive that awful time in his life. Instead, he'd strapped on some snowshoes and taken a walk along the Lake Superior shore, letting the vast white frozen landscape cleanse his mind.

But it hadn't. Even though he'd stopped pondering Deni in therapy, he couldn't stop thinking about her pink nails. Or the little dimple that appeared in her left cheek when she'd laughed at Petey's jokes. Or if her body was as lean and strong as it appeared to be under her baggy clothing.

And he kept coming back to that kiss.

It wasn't even as if it'd been the first kiss since Molly had died.

A woman he'd known at Tech had reached out to him when Molly died to express her sympathy. She'd known them both, though Molly more than Sawyer. At the time, she'd been married. But about a year later she'd divorced and again had gotten in touch with Sawyer. He'd made the drive to Superior, Wisconsin, every other month or so for a couple of years, neither wanting more than the comfort of the other's body.

She'd started dating someone a couple of years ago, and Sawyer had to admit he was relieved when she'd put a halt to their get-togethers. And was genuinely happy for her when she told him she was remarrying.

There'd been a few hook-ups with other women since then. All out of town and none more than a couple of nights, if that.

But not one kiss in any of those encounters had affected him like kissing Deni in front of the Commodore.

He'd realized walking along the shore, Lucy sinking into the snow beside him, that what he'd felt kissing Deni had scared the hell out of him.

And he liked that.

She hadn't answered him about how she coped in the Copper Country with the winter driving.

Her hands were still clenched in her lap, and he thought that her breathing sounded heavier than it had a moment ago.

He looked around for someplace to pull off the road. He wasn't sure she'd make it the next couple of miles to Iron Mountain.

There was a large commuter lot just before the turnoff from Highway 141 to Highway 2, and Sawyer pulled in. The lot was nearly deserted, being a Saturday. The three cars that were parked had heavy burdens of snow on their hoods and roofs, clearly having been left for longer than just ridesharing to Green Bay for the day.

The lot had been plowed recently, but there were already drifts being formed from the blowing snow. Sawyer stopped near the entrance of the lot and put the truck in park, but kept it on for the heater.

If they were here a while, he'd have to cut the heater or at least get out and make sure snow hadn't blown a drift onto the tailpipe.

Back in drivers' ed, they'd told the story of couples parking in the Copper Country and backing into snow banks that covered the cars' tailpipes enough that the young lovers died of carbon monoxide poisoning. Sawyer had never known if the story— legend? myth?—was a deterrent to kids making out or a safety lesson, but it'd stayed with him.

Not enough to stop high school make-out sessions, but he always checked the tailpipe beforehand.

But there'd be no lengthy make-out session here. Not as silent as Deni had been with him today. Besides, he just wanted to make sure she was all right, then he'd get them to Iron Mountain and some hot coffee and food.

That always helped him.

But where to start? "Deni?" he cautiously said. "Are you—"

"My father was killed in a car accident," she said. Her

shoulders eased a little, making Sawyer realize how tense they'd been.

"Oh. I—"

"In a snowstorm," she added. Her shoulders fell a little more. She rolled her neck, and he watched her chestnut hair sway across the back of her wool coat. Her hands unclenched and lay limply on her lap. She looked down at them like they were foreign objects. He watched her. And waited.

"He was on a business trip north of Detroit. A trip he took at least a couple of times a month. No big deal, right? But this time… Apparently the visibility was really bad." Her hands smoothed her coat against her thighs, the flash of her nails mesmerizing to him as he waited for her to continue. He knew exactly how hard this was for her to talk about.

"I was eight, and we were really close. And…and…."

"You still miss him," he finished.

She nodded, but didn't look at him. Then she took a deep breath, her shoulders coming down to what he now realized was their normal posture.

"I do miss him. And winter driving has freaked me out at times, when there's really bad visibility."

He didn't say that he'd seen much worse. She'd been in the Copper Country long enough to know this was maybe a five on a scale of one to ten.

"And I know this isn't that bad," she added, and he smothered a smile by bringing his hand to his mouth. She finally turned to him, and he could see those big brown eyes. It wasn't fear so much as resignation that shone through. "And most times it doesn't even faze me. I've gotten used to it. I just seem to be having a hard time with it lately. The roads are bad, or it's a heavy snow, or poor visibility, and I start thinking about my dad. And then I get on kind of an obsessive loop about it, and it grows into a much bigger fear than normal." Her eyes broke away from his, but not before he saw a flash of something that resembled embarrassment.

"Hey," he softly said as he reached a hand out to lay over

hers. The heater had been running steadily since they had left Green Bay, and the cab was warm to the point of hot. But her hands felt like ice.

This must have been what she was seeing Alison for. Residual feelings about her father's death seemed to be causing her problems.

Well, shit. He knew all about that.

"Hey," he said again. "It's okay to still miss him. And to get freaked out about driving in crappy weather. It's perfectly natural."

"But it's more—"

"My wife died in a car accident, too," he said, shocking himself.

It wasn't that he kept Molly's death a secret or anything. It was common knowledge in the Copper Country, but it wasn't something that he just casually mentioned.

Apparently he did with Deni.

"I'm sorry. And here I'm going on about—"

He pulled his hand from hers and pressed a finger against her mouth—against those magnificent lips. "That's not what I meant or was going for. I only brought it up to say that it's been ten years, and there are times when I go crazy thinking about it." So true. "And then…" He paused, not sure he was ready to put into words the thoughts that he'd been having lately.

"There are times when it seems so long ago, like it happened to another person and has no bearing on my life today." Her head moved in the tiniest of nods, as if she didn't want to dislodge his fingers from her mouth any more than he did. "And then I feel like a total shit for those feelings…for forgetting her." He dropped his hand. Her mouth, her skin, felt so good, but to feel so good as he explained his feelings about his dead wife? It didn't seem right.

"You're not a total shit. And it's not about forgetting. It's about moving on," she said.

They sat like that for a moment, not precisely looking at each other, but not looking elsewhere either.

"Umm…" she said, just as he was about to suggest they drive

on to Iron Mountain.

"Yes?"

"I need to talk about the other night."

"Yes?" He was hoping it'd be about something Petey said about the project. But he knew it wasn't. He was about to get called on the carpet, and he deserved it.

"I need to talk about that kiss."

Yep, just as he'd thought.

Well, shit.

Nine

—⚋⚋—

WELL, NUTS.

Deni watched as Sawyer dodged her stare. It was obvious that he regretted the kiss and didn't even want to acknowledge it.

And it was all she'd thought about for the entire day as she sat next to him first in the warm, cozy truck, then at the meeting with the driving range owners, and now in this deserted parking lot.

Oh, okay. It was all she'd thought about since Wednesday night. Talk about obsessive loops!

She'd been able to put the replay aside for bursts of time to work, go to therapy, and basically lead a normal life, or as normal as her life had been since this funk had overcome her last October.

But today, being so close to him—smelling his scent, feeling his physicality beside her—it'd been almost hypnotizing until she'd looked outside and seen nothing but white. It was like a switch had flipped inside her, and a bubble of anxiety rose up, almost suffocating her until he'd pulled into the lot in which they now sat.

"The kiss," she said again, as if to get herself back on track. The track she'd thought of the whole drive down and most of the way back.

"Listen, I'm really sorry. I was totally out of line. You're a professional, I'm a professional...."

Did he truly regret it? That would mess everything up. She

looked at him, and his sentence died as his gaze dropped to her mouth. Self-consciously, she licked her lips. The flare of hunger she saw in his eyes gave her the courage to go on.

"I'm not," she said.

"Not what? A professional? I think that meeting we just had proved you wrong."

"No. I'm not sorry about the kiss."

"No?" he asked, tilting his head, as if measuring her or waiting for the other shoe to drop. "You got pretty riled up at me."

"I did, you're right," she admitted.

That. That was exactly why she needed to do this. "And, honestly, getting riled up at you was the most emotion I've felt in a long time. And I…" She looked away. It was all well and good to think she could be so aboveboard with a man, to lay it all on the table. But in reality, she'd never been the aggressor with the guys she'd dated.

Not that this was a date. Or that she was asking Sawyer to be her boyfriend or anything. Her mind started to whiz out on tangents, fragmenting her focus. She willed herself to pull it together. This was what she needed right now. All she had to do was ask for it. She stared at him, unable to speak.

"What are you saying, Deni?" he asked. There was confusion in his voice, but also…hope?

"I'm saying, that…um…if you'd maybe want to kiss me again, that…."

"Yes?" He was closer to her now, nearly in the middle of bench seat. His hand moved, and suddenly her seatbelt was unbuckled, sliding over her body to the door.

"I wouldn't mind—"

He was on her.

She wasn't sure which delicious sensation she felt first—his hands nestling into her hair or his lips on hers. But the playing in her hair quickly floated out of her mind as her lips opened under his, and she felt the warm glide of his tongue. She tangled hers with his and heard his breath hitch. Her brain turned off, but not in the dull haze of late. It was a haze that fogged her up but in no way was it dull.

Lust. A haze of lust. It was the last coherent thought she had before turning everything over to her body and how Sawyer's kiss was making it come alive.

She wound her arms around his neck, scooching over across the seat, wanting to touch him, to let the haze spread.

Seeming to know what she wanted—or wanting it himself— his hand slid from her hair, over her coat, lifting it up enough to curve a hand around her butt and nudge her body closer.

She'd made out with boys in cars before, but it'd been a while, and Sawyer's truck was nothing like the cars the boys back in Farmington Hills drove.

And Sawyer Beck was in no way a boy.

As he continued to lift her to him, she touched the side of his face. He'd been clean-shaven when they'd met this morning, but now there was a tantalizing amount of stubble that she stroked.

"Jesus," he mumbled, then kissed her more deeply as he pulled her ontop of him while he edged his body to her side so that she'd be able to straddle him.

Breathing heavily, she broke away from the kiss, needing to see his face. The wind howled outside, and the whiteness of the snow seemed to give a glow to the truck's cab.

His chest was heaving, and she put her hands on him there, pushing aside the lapels of his wool pea coat. It wasn't enough, so she pushed the coat off him. He leaned forward enough so that she could drag it out from behind him and toss it on the seat next to them. Better. She smoothed her hands down his strong chest, then glanced at his face to find his green eyes on her. She inched closer to him on his lap, her full skirt rising along her thighs. Her tights and his khakis were the only things between them. His breathing had slowed now, but the rise and fall of his firm chest became deeper. The chambray of his shirt felt almost repulsive to her when his skin was just underneath. She started plucking at the buttons, almost in a fury to see his chest.

His movements were slower, more deliberate, as they eased her coat from her, tugging her hands away from his shirt momentarily, before he tossed her coat on top of his.

He began to unwind the scarf that she'd so laboriously configured this morning, using a picture from Pinterest as her guide.

"What the…?" He was tangled in the intricate design, yanking at the gossamer material.

"It doesn't matter. Leave it," she whispered, having his shirt finally undone. She yanked it free from his waistband and opened it wide. His chest was strong, developed, and covered lightly with hair that her fingers itched to touch. As she reached for his skin, her arms were pulled away by his peeling of her cardigan off her body, leaving her in only her camisole and bra. She wasn't even sure where her sweater wound up. She certainly didn't care.

Her hands ran over his chest, and she was delighted when he involuntarily flexed at her slightly colder touch. The muscle was strong and firm, and she leaned forward to nuzzle him. Breathing in the clean, fresh scent of him, she ran her cheek along his chest, up to his throat, then burrowed deeper. Her body was responding, coming out of its funk, and she reveled in the feelings that had been dormant for so long: desire, attraction, and, okay, horniness.

"Holy wah," he said as she nipped his neck, then put her tongue on him. She smiled at the Yooperism that she hadn't quite been able to add to her vocabulary, then returned to tasting his skin. She nibbled her way up, his hands pulling her body even closer, then clenching her butt as her mouth finally made its way to his.

Their kiss was hungrier now, with tongues tangling. The pressure was exquisite. She felt him slide her camisole and bra straps down her shoulders and was torn between leaving his mouth and wanting that mouth elsewhere. She moved away from him, giving him the room he would need. The slide of her body along his erection had them both gasping.

"God, I feel like I'm in high school. I haven't dry humped

like this since then," he said.

She smiled. "Do you want to stop?" She moved against him again and delighted in the flare she saw in his eyes.

"Hell no." Her straps now dangled at her elbows, but her bra and camisole stayed in place, covering her. His hands skimmed up her arms and curved around her shoulders. "Deni," he whispered, his eyes staring into hers.

She felt beautiful, desired. The fact that she felt anything so deeply after months of the fog would have been enough, but the penetration of his gaze helped. She moved her hands to his head, guiding him to her chest.

"Sawyer," she said, also whispering, "I want—"

Three short raps on the window made her jump out of Sawyer's embrace while frantically pulling up her bra straps. Trying to be gallant and shield her, Sawyer pushed her to the side, which made her nearly topple off the seat.

The snow had stopped blowing, and although the windows were pretty fogged up (no surprise!), she could see the blue jacket of a state policeman clearly enough.

"Jesus, I really am back in high school," Sawyer mumbled as he too recognized the occupation of the man once again tapping on the truck window.

"License and registration," the officer said, and Deni scooted out of the way as Sawyer reached across her and opened the glove box. His arm grazed her boobs, and she lamented the fact that in only a few moments she would have had his hand and mouth on her. He must have been thinking the same thing, if she could read his frustrated groan. And the slamming of the glove box door after he'd pulled out an envelope. And his heavy sigh as he looked over at her—or her now-covered chest—after handing the envelope and his license over to the policeman.

She smiled, shrugged, and finished buttoning up her cardigan, which only made him sigh again.

"We were just trying to wait out the storm," he said to the cop.

"Good way to do it," the man answered.

"It *was*...."

It was hard to tell, but Deni swore she saw a small grin quickly squashed by the officer.

"Beck? From Calumet?" the cop asked Sawyer, holding up the license.

"Yep."

"Any relation to Huck Beck?"

Deni watched as Sawyer's shoulders tensed. "Yeeees...?" He seemed to prepare himself, like he wasn't going to like what came next.

And what came next looked like the officer reaching for his gun. Deni almost dove to the footwell. But when his hand reappeared, the officer was holding open his own wallet and flipping through it, all while trying to balance Sawyer's information. He pulled out two twenty-dollar bills and handed them to Sawyer.

"Give this to him the next time you see him, and tell him it's from Bonehead."

Deni leaned closer and peered at the officer's nameplate over his badge. It did not say Officer Bonehead (nor did she expect it to).

"Um...yeah...okay," Sawyer responded, taking the money from the other man's hand. "I don't see him much, though. You might be better off mailing it to him or something."

"Nah. It's already waited a few years. It can keep until you see him."

"I have to pick up my dog from his place tonight. I'm not really expecting him to be there, so I'll just leave it on his kitchen table with a note or something."

"Great. Thanks." He put his wallet away and then handed Sawyer back his information. He pulled back as Sawyer reached for his license. "If I run this through the system, am I going to find anything?"

"Nope. I'm clean as a whistle."

The officer handed over the license, then chuckled. "And

you're sure you're related to Huck Beck?"

"That's what my mom tells me," Sawyer answered as he put his license back in his wallet and then shoved it in his back pocket.

Nuts. She'd been moments away from having her hands all over those back pockets—and the divine butt they covered.

"We're hearing the storm has blown to the east of us, missing the route you're taking. And the plows are out right now in Iron Mountain, so you're safe to get moving." He gave Sawyer a pointed look to which Sawyer nodded his understanding. After the officer got back to his car, Sawyer waited a moment and then sighed and put the truck in gear.

"I guess he's going to wait until we're out of here."

"Oh," she said, the disappointment in her voice a bit too obvious.

"Exactly. 'Oh.'"

As they pulled out of the parking lot and onto the main road (freshly plowed, just as the cop had said, though they'd been too occupied to notice), Deni asked, "So, he was really going to trust you that you had no unpaid parking tickets or outstanding warrants or anything?"

He shrugged as he made the turn and started the last leg of their journey. "Yeah. I guess. I mean, he'll probably run my name now, but…"

"You wouldn't see that happen in Farmington Hills."

"Nope. You gotta love da Yoop." His Yooper accent was exaggerated and thick, and Deni smiled.

Realizing she couldn't remember the last time a genuine smile crossed her face for something so tiny, she made up her mind that pursuing something physical with Sawyer Beck was exactly what she needed right now. It would be a distraction from her SAD and give her something else to think about so she wouldn't get into the obsessive loops of late over insignificant things.

He made a turn, and she watched as his shoulder filled out his chambray shirt, the muscles on his forearm clenching where he'd rolled up his sleeve.

Okay, she might be trading in one obsessive loop for another—namely how hot Sawyer Beck was. But those kinds were ones she knew how to deal with. She had since she was thirteen and started noticing Jimmy Gaston's chest in gym class.

And God, it felt good just thinking about how quickly she could get home and get Sawyer Beck in her bed rather than how quickly she could get home and just go to bed.

He looked over at her as they stopped at a light in downtown Iron Mountain. He gave his head a tiny shake. He gazed at her mouth, and when she licked her lips he gave a soft chuckle.

She wanted to say something, but his eyes returned to the road and he started off again.

There were a lot of reasons not to start something. For starters, he was older than she was. Not crazy older, but older than she'd ever dated before. He was the owner of her company, if not her actual boss. And to top it all off, he was dealing with understandable residual grief from his wife's death. Seemed like three big strikes.

But this wasn't about dating Sawyer Beck. This was about feeling a flash of emotion—namely lust—for the first time in a long time, and it felt good. It felt right. Even if Sawyer was the wrong choice for this lust, she was going to act on it.

She spent the next two hours trying to remember what state her house was in and if her sheets were relatively clean. She knew the bed wasn't made but was hoping desire-induced neediness would make that point moot.

She didn't even think an invitation would be necessary—not if the bulge that she'd felt beneath her was any indication. No. He'd be following her home for sure to finish what they'd started.

Still, just so there'd be no awkward "should I or shouldn't I" on his part, as they pulled into the Summers and Beck parking lot and he parked next to her snow-covered car she said, "Will you follow me to my house?"

He grinned and said, "Absolutely. Give me your keys, and I'll get your car warm for you."

She dug the keys out of her bag and handed them to him. He left the warmth of the truck cab to start up her Subaru.

She watched as he turned on the car and then reemerged with her heavy-duty snow brush to clean off the inches of heavy white stuff that had fallen throughout the day.

She'd had gentlemanly boyfriends before. They'd held doors for her, held her coat for her, things like that.

But it was amazing the lump that rose to her throat as she watched Sawyer clean off her car as the heater warmed up the inside.

When he got to the front passenger side, he stilled as he cleared it off. For a moment, Deni wondered if he'd wrenched a muscle or something. And then selfishly wondered if it would hamper his performance. Ha! It felt so good to have her body sparking again, to be thinking thoughts about performance and orgasms and Sawyer's hot, sweaty body heaving over her.

She hadn't had sex in a long time, and even the desire to… take things into her own hand…had completely disappeared since the blanket of numbness had wrapped itself around her.

She squirmed on the seat. Oh yes, the sparks were there and were ready to be ignited.

Sawyer rose from leaning over the windshield, and he seemed to be okay, although he was walking slowly back to the truck. There wasn't quite the same spring in his step as when he'd left it.

"Are you okay?" she asked as he got into his seat and shut the door.

"No. Well, yeah. I'm fine." He was staring straight ahead at the building. Then he turned to look at her and said, "I'm not going to follow you home."

"Oh," she said. She wanted to come up with some alternate plan about her following him, leaving her car here, or, hell, just peeling their clothes off in the warm truck and finishing what they'd started in a different parking lot.

But logistics weren't the problem. It was most likely being back at the office. He must have seen the building with his name on it as he brushed off her car and realized what a bad move this was, business-wise.

Which was exactly what she'd told him the first time, when he'd brushed it off as easily as if it were snow on a windshield.

But that wasn't something she was going to throw in his face now. And she certainly wasn't going to try to convince him otherwise. If he thought it'd be a problem because he owned the company, she was going to respect that.

Even if the spark that had been humming through her body had just extinguished, and the heaviness seemed to envelope her once again. Like a lead blanket was being pulled around her, her arms were almost too heavy to even open the door. She wondered if she'd even be able to drive herself home.

"I'll follow you home, but just to make sure you get in okay. I think it's better if—"

She raised her hand (*hey, her arms did work!*) to stop him. "Not necessary. This is Hancock. I'm fine." He made to argue, but she quickly said, "I'll just see you at work on Monday?" Then added, "If you're going to be in on Monday? If I'm still on the project?"

He looked confused. "Of course you're still on the project." Then he seemed to get it. "Oh. Unless you don't want to be?"

This was her chance to gracefully exit this project. One that really held no appeal to her whatsoever as an engineer. "No. I still want to work on it" were the words that came out of her mouth, surprising herself and apparently Sawyer, if his expression was any indication.

He quickly recovered. "Good. Good. I'm really glad." He started to reach out to her but dropped his hand on the seat between them. "Monday, then. Why don't we plan on meeting at the site around ten?"

"Sounds good."

"Dress warmly. The wind can be a bitch on the hill."

"Will do." She sat for a moment more. She was waiting, but not really sure what she was waiting for. She looked at him once more and saw a look of regret that should have taken some of the sting out of going home alone. But it didn't.

"Bye," she said as she climbed out of his truck. She thought she heard him answer her as she shut the door.

Her Subaru was toasty when she entered it; he'd turned the heat up full blast. Thoughtful.

She drove away from him toward her house where she knew she'd crawl into bed as soon as she could.

Nuts.

Ten

━━ꝏ━━

DAMN IT. SAWYER WATCHED AS THE LITTLE SUBARU made its way out of the parking lot and toward the bridge. He sat for a while longer. From where he was parked, he could see her car cross the bridge. At Bob's Mobil, she turned toward the houses of East End.

He was tempted to throw the truck in gear, try to catch up to her, and then troll the three or four streets of East End looking for her car. But he didn't. Instead, he slowly left the parking lot and headed toward Tech, to the part of town where Huck lived, to pick up Lucy.

He'd fully intended on going home with Deni. His imagination had run wild for the two hours after they'd left the lot in Iron Mountain. He'd almost reached for her several times but thought that touching her might not be the best move with her being nervous about the roads. Because once he touched her, he'd want to keep on touching her, and they'd end up in a ditch for sure.

And she'd invited him to follow her home, which was all the encouragement he'd needed, until… Damn, he never should have brushed off her car. He hadn't noticed the mittens sitting on her passenger seat when he'd hopped in, started it, and turned the heater up. But as he cleared the snow from her windshield, he'd seen them sitting on the seat. Bright, multi-colored wool mittens that sent him spiraling back to Molly's death. She'd had on a pair just like them when she'd been in the car accident that claimed her life.

Guilt and grief bubbled up inside him, pushing out the past two hours and all his thoughts of Deni naked.

God, Molly would have been right about the age Deni was now when she'd died. Which just slammed home how young Deni was. Whatever thoughts he still had of sleeping with her tonight blew away like the snow from her windshield.

When he got to Huck's house, he parked in front, noting the drive had been plowed and the sidewalk shoveled. Maybe he'd be able to give Huck his money from that cop in person.

But no, unsurprisingly, Huck was nowhere to be found, though Lucy's water bowl seemed to have been refilled. He let Lucy out into Huck's fenced backyard and wrote his brother a note explaining the forty dollars and thanking him for keeping an eye on his dog.

At least he thought it was his brother who'd refilled the water bowl. With Huck, though, you never really knew.

After Lucy had done her business, he loaded her up in the truck and made the drive home.

DENI TURNED AROUND as she heard barking to see Sawyer's dog dashing through the snow toward her. She bent down to receive the yellow lab's affection, grateful to have a moment before Sawyer was upon her. She'd come with Charlie and Mac and was taking in the site as they set up surveying equipment. They'd only get preliminary specs due to all the snow, but they'd be able to cross-check them against the set Petey Ryan had provided. Besides, if they could make this project work—and after what the men in Green Bay had told them, she wasn't sure they could—they wouldn't be breaking ground until the snow melted anyway. And in the Copper Country, that could be as late as mid-May.

She thought about her day yesterday, spent in her pajamas going from her bed to her couch just so she felt like she'd moved. She wasn't sure if the light box would be enough if spring made such a late showing this year.

She'd done a lot of thinking, though. About Sawyer not coming home with her. And more about what would have happened if he had.

And even more about what would have happened after that.

"Hey, girl," she said, bending down and pulling off her leather glove to give the beauty a good scratch. Which prompted the dog to assume a submissive position and give Deni her belly, an expectant look on her face.

"Lucy, don't be so easy. Play a *little* hard to get," Sawyer said as he met them. "Hey, guys," he said loudly in greeting to Charlie and Mac, who looked up from their clipboards and instruments and gave him a wave before returning to their task.

Deni finished scratching Lucy's belly, gave her a couple of sturdy pats, and then stood back up and faced Sawyer. "She's a gorgeous dog."

He nodded, looking down at Lucy, a soft smile crossing his hard face as he watched his pet. "She's been a good friend."

Maybe she should get a dog. But then she thought about having to get out of bed to let the dog out or not being able to go to bed at eight because the dog would need to go out after that. The whole thought suddenly felt very daunting to her. Her arms became weighted down, and the heaviness seemed to seep up her limbs.

Okay, not a dog. Don't worry. Shake it off. Stop the cycle of thought. It was what she told herself when just thinking about certain tasks made the fog creep up. Sometimes it worked, sometimes it didn't.

She met Sawyer's gaze and saw something that looked like puzzlement in his eyes. Nuts. Had she said the whole "clear your mind" thing out loud?

But no, it wasn't puzzlement. The quick glance at her mouth that he snuck looked very much like the look he gave her right before he kissed her.

But then let her go home alone.

As if he remembered it at the same time, he cleared his throat and looked around the terrain.

"Well, he can cut his prep costs down. No trees or anything to get rid of. In those terms, it's a good location. Halfway between Hancock and Calumet, so you could pull both areas in."

"Do you know why he bought this property? It's commercially zoned and close to the airport, but there's nothing much else that's great about it."

The land was a blanket of snow now, a huge parcel not far from the county's airport. Slightly higher elevation would have given a fantastic view of the Portage canal. At this level, though, all you could see was the airport and a tree line at the edge of Petey's property.

"No, I'm not sure what he was thinking. I don't know if he knew at the time. I remember that a few years after he went pro he bought up some vacant property around here. I was paying attention to that type of thing then."

What was left unsaid was that Sawyer Beck didn't pay attention to that sort of thing now. A flash of Sawyer with a long beard dancing in front of a ramshackle shack floated through her mind. Lucy would be there, prancing around beside him, hopping up on him.

"What?" he said, bursting her hermit vision.

"Huh?"

"What were you thinking? Just now?" His head tilted as if trying to read her mind.

She was grateful for the blistering wind, which had surely already turned her cheeks pink, hiding the blush she felt creeping up her face.

Ducking her head, she said, "I was thinking that the wind up here may make this thing more expensive. The material for the dome is going to have to be heavier than it would elsewhere."

"*That's* what you were thinking?"

"Yes," she said, meeting his skeptical eyes.

"Okay. If you say so." There was a teasing in his voice, and she couldn't help but smile at him, which he returned.

"Hey, Deni," Charlie said, startling her. She hadn't even realized he and Mac had approached them. Her buddy's eyes shifted from her to Sawyer and back again. "I think we've got everything." He turned to Sawyer. "It's a good site for what Ryan and Luna want to do. It's going to be a bitch to heat, though."

She heard the sigh come from Sawyer as he put his hands on his hips and looked over the vast expanse of white again. "Yep. I don't know that it's going to be a viable idea for them, as little revenue as it will bring in. Too bad. It'd be nice for the golfers in the area."

"Yeah. I'd be up here once a week all winter for sure," Mac said, a bit of regret in his voice. "Wouldn't be able to swing a club wearing a parka, though."

They all nodded and looked around again, as if trying to find some solution.

"The guys we met in Green Bay didn't give us much hope either," Sawyer said. "They lost their place to a fire, and the city doesn't want them to rebuild due to the huge amounts of power the place used up."

"They were barely making a go of the place, anyway," Deni added. "And their average snowfall is a lot less than ours. Not to mention the average winter temperatures, which aren't as low as ours."

"You went to Green Bay together?" Charlie asked.

Sawyer had turned away from them, slowly moving in a circle, hands still on his hips. Lucy nudged his side. "Yeah. Saturday. It was good to talk to them. They didn't really tell us anything we hadn't already been thinking, but it did drive home the potential risks and costs of this type of thing."

Deni could feel Charlie watching her. She hadn't told him or Mac that she'd gone with Sawyer to Green Bay. And now it felt like a thing. She took a peek at Charlie, but couldn't make out his expression. Her closest work friend, and probably her best friend in the whole area, was looking at her with puzzlement. And was that disappointment?

"Well, we don't have to figure out whether or not the business can make it. All we can do is give them a bid and build the thing. The rest is for Ryan and Luna to figure out." Sawyer had made his slow circle and was now facing them again. "But if we can figure out a way to keep building costs down, and a way to help out with ongoing costs to heat it…"

"And build it so snowfall doesn't collapse it every year," Mac added.

"Well, there are heavier, sturdier materials," Deni said, though she knew they all knew this.

"Cost," Mac said, and they all nodded.

"And structural reinforcements. Putting double the beaming in," Charlie added, another point that they all probably knew.

"Cost," they all chimed in.

"But if there was a way to work both those in…." Deni added.

They stood in a circle, all thinking, all visually surveying the land. Though it had been windy all day, a huge gust blew up at that moment, nearly knocking Deni from her feet. She took a step back and Charlie, being the closest one to her, reached out a hand and grabbed onto her arm, as if to keep her from taking flight. She smiled at her friend, and he chuckled and dropped his hand.

Glancing at Sawyer, she froze at the look in his eyes. She didn't fool herself that it was jealousy, but it was intense and burned into her. He then looked at her coat, where Charlie had grabbed her. Then his eyes went upward, to the sky. She could see his gaze follow snow that had been kicked up from the—

"Wind," she and Sawyer said at the same time. His glance came back to hers and locked on. It was if they were reading each other's minds. The feeling was so strong, so deep, that it penetrated the fog and numbness, making her brain snap to attention.

It was almost more stirring than grinding against him in his truck.

Almost.

Suddenly, Deni wanted this project to come to fruition. She told herself that it was good for the Copper Country to have a new business and that the golfers would love it. But deep down she knew that working on this project—the type that did not interest her in the least—might be the most interesting project of her life.

"Yeah, sure is," Mac said, thinking he was agreeing with their simple statement.

Sawyer grinned at her. *Dear Lord, when that man smiles....* Their simultaneous brainstorm was a shared secret between them. He nodded at her, wanting her to speak up.

"Wind power," she said, and his grin turned to a genuine, wide smile.

"What?" Mac said. Charlie looked between her and Sawyer again and seemed to get the connection between them.

Connection. Yes, that was exactly what it was. And on a more elemental level than the physical. It was the harmony of a great idea shared. Of knowing someone thinks like you do, even if you're the only two that do.

"Wind turbine. Or turbines, more likely. Power the damn thing with wind. Hell, there's enough of it up here."

Mac was looking around again, as if seeing the property in a new light. Charlie was watching her, she could feel it. And yet she could not take her eyes from Sawyer's.

"Holy wah," Mac said, "That just might work." She smiled at her coworker's Yooper accent slipping through, but her eyes never left Sawyer's.

"Mac," he finally said, breaking the spell. "Can you start researching it?" Mac was nodding, still turned from them, his mind already working it through. "And Charlie"—Sawyer turned to him—"can you check out any restrictions there might be on turbines? We might have some compliance issues because we are so close to the airport. Height restrictions, zoning stipulations, that sort of thing? Sue probably has most of that stuff."

"Yeah, I'll get on that," Charlie said. Whatever hesitation he might have had evaporated, and he too looked at the area again, mentally calculating, taking in the height of the tree line. He was no doubt measuring the distance to the airport in his head with pinpoint accuracy.

After a moment, they all faced each other in the circle again, smiles of anticipation on their faces.

Engineers were such geeks.

"Let's get going," Mac said, excitement in his voice.

They started moving toward the cars. Sawyer put a hand on her arm, stopping her. "You guys go ahead. We'll meet you at the office in a bit," he called. Mac just waved over his shoulder, but Charlie turned around and glanced at Deni.

"See you in a bit," she said, then made her way to Sawyer's car instead of Mac's. She could feel Charlie's eyes on her as she got into Sawyer's old Bronco—thankfully not the truck they'd taken to Green Bay. She pushed the seat up so Lucy could hop into the back onto what was obviously her blanket.

Once they were in the car, Sawyer cranked the heat and followed Mac's car to the highway. Mac turned left, heading back to Hancock. Sawyer turned right, heading to Calumet.

"There's something I'd like to show you," he said.

She burrowed into her coat, letting the hot air warm her. But his words, and being alone again with him, had her hot well before the heater did.

Eleven

—⁓—

HE PULLED ONTO SIXTH STREET IN CALUMET. NOTHING
but silence in the car since they'd left the site. When he pulled over
and parked, he saw Deni's shoulders drop. She was biting her lip,
which he now knew meant she was debating saying something.

He didn't want to think about how well he knew her in such
a short time or how much he'd rather be biting on said lip.

"Um," she said, and he waited. "Thank you for thinking of
this, but I've already seen the theater." He started to open his
mouth, but she rambled on. "I mean, it's beautiful, of course, and
I'd love to see it again. It's just…I thought I should mention that
I've been in it before. Several times, in fact." She looked at him
almost apologetically.

He eyed the famed Calumet Theater, then looked at her and
smiled. "That's not where we're going," he said. He got out of the
car, folding his seat forward to let Lucy out on his side.

He rounded to her side, but she was already out by the time
he got there.

"So where are we going?"

He pointed to the run-down building next to the historic
theater. "There."

"A bar?"

"Not just any bar. Tootie's."

"Looks like a neighborhood bar. Not that there's anything
wrong with that. But why bring me here on a Monday"—she

took a quick look at her watch—"afternoon?"

"Just wait." He led the way and held the door open for her. He had a moment of wondering if the bar would even be open on a Monday just after noon, but yep, it was.

He recognized the woman behind the bar as a Kilpela girl and knew one of her sisters had been in his class at Calumet. Damn if he could remember his classmate's name, though, let alone that of her younger sister.

He nodded to the old-timer at the end of the bar, already through half a glass of beer. Leading Deni to a stool at the bar, he took in the room, trying to see it from her perspective. The establishment was long and narrow, with Formica tables on one side and the bar running the entire length of the other. At the end of the room, three steps took you up to a smaller area that housed two pool tables and the restrooms.

"This is what you wanted me to see?" Deni asked him as she settled onto the stool. She surveyed the room as he just had, confusion on her face. Typical dive bar, nothing worth seeing here.

He reached to her stool as he sat down on his and turned her so she was facing forward, toward the bar.

"*This* is what I wanted you to see." He waited while her eyes scanned the woodwork of the bar—nice and well kept, but nothing special—the obligatory rows of bottles of booze, and the mirror above it. She almost turned back to him when she—

"Holy cow," she said.

"Honey, 'round here it's 'holy wah,'" the bartender said to Deni as she made her way to them.

"I can't quite seem to master 'holy wah,'" Deni said, her eyes still on what Sawyer had brought her here to see. "I don't have enough Yooper cred to pull that one off yet," she added.

He watched her eyes scan and examine, her head turning this way and that. Finally she looked at him. "Is that Tiffany glass?"

He smiled. "Yep. Well, the experts think so. No one knows for sure."

She turned from him and studied the stained-glass hood that

ran the length of the bar and was mounted above the mirror on the wall opposite where they sat.

"It's amazing," she said in a soft voice.

Something clenched in Sawyer's gut. Somehow he had known she'd get it. See how special it was.

"The village owns it. Not the bar owners, who have changed hands over the years. It can't be removed. It has to be kept as part of any deal. The canopy, bar, and bar back area."

The bartender was looking at it now. "Is that right?" she said. "What can I get you two?"

"Just a Coke," Sawyer said. Deni nodded her agreement.

Before the Cokes were brought to them, Deni left her stool and walked to the end of the bar. "Would it be okay if I came back and took a closer look?"

"Um… We're really not supposed to." Sawyer gave the bartender a "come on, please?" look, one he hadn't pulled out since he'd been married and in the dog house for one thing or another. Apparently he still had it, because the woman nodded for Deni to go ahead.

"You're Sawyer Beck, aren't you?"

He nodded. "Yes. And you're a Kilpela, but I'm sorry—I can't remember your first name."

She seemed proud that he'd gotten that much right. "I'm Linda. I was in Twain's class."

"Right. And how's…your sister?"

Although there were at least five Kilpela girls that he could remember, Linda knew which one he meant. "Sarah. She's good. She just had a baby."

"How many does that make for her?"

"Six."

Not entirely unusual in the U.P., but still. Sawyer couldn't imagine having six kids. Then the familiar pang hit him as he remembered Molly teasing him that she wanted three boys, just like his mother had and him bantering back that he wanted only girls.

"Good for Sarah," he said automatically, not really aware anymore. "Tell her I said hi." He turned away from Linda, took a drink of Coke, and willed himself not to fall down the rabbit hole of regret right now.

Instead, he looked at Deni, who was by now examining the glass on the canopy, standing on a stool that must have been under the bar. Linda had backed away to the other end of the bar, as if distancing herself from the proceedings.

She needn't have worried. Deni revered the glass with the same delicate touch that Sarah probably had with every one of those six babies. Tapping the glass ever so slightly, she put a finger on each side of a corner piece as if judging its density. Then she stuck her head up under the canopy so that all he could see was her lithe body—once again dressed in gray and black work clothes that hung on her.

Her head came back into view, and his breath caught as he saw the look of pure passion on her face.

"This is amazing," she said, looking at him. "I'm not an expert in stained glass or anything. But...but...." She didn't finish, instead sticking her head back under the canopy and rotating slowly on the step stool.

He had the urge to go over and stand next to her, beneath her, lest she lost her balance, but he didn't. Her tiny movements were surefooted, and although he really would have liked to put his hands on her hips and steady her, Deni was a woman who didn't need steadying.

And, God, that appealed to him.

And, God, he was dying to see what lay beneath those sweaters and skirts.

Finally, she left her perch and came back to join him at the bar, thanking Linda.

"It's so clever how the plasterwork along the archway mimics the arch of the stage at the theater, right down to the light bulbs and scrollwork."

She was facing him as she said this, her back to the archway that she spoke of.

He hadn't even realized she'd noticed it when they'd come in. And he sure as hell hadn't expected her to pick up on the tie-in to the architectural design of the Calumet Theater, though he'd planned on pointing it out to her.

"When was the last time you were at the theater?" he asked, as he took a sip.

"Hmmm. Probably three summers ago. Charlie and I saw some old-timer who came in for a concert. We'd never heard of him before, but he was pretty good. The place was packed."

Sawyer didn't want to ask who the artist was. No doubt it'd be someone he'd heard of. And then something she said struck him. "Charlie from the firm, Charlie? From just now at the site, Charlie?"

"Mmm-hmm," she answered. She'd swiveled in the stool and was now facing the archway, her back to him.

Damn, he wanted to see her face as he asked, "Are you and he...a...thing?"

Body language counted for a lot, and hers had noticeably stiffened, but he wasn't sure why.

She spun back around quickly, stopping herself by catching the rung of his stool, her foot placed between his.

"That kiss you planted on me in front of the Commodore would have ended with a slap to the face instead of me...."

"Participating?" he offered up.

She waved his spot-on description away. She was becoming animated now, a tiny bit riled, and he had to admit he liked that in her. Oh, he liked the clear-headed, logical engineer in her too, but when she was like this, with a flush coming to her face and a heat in her eyes....

"Whatever. And I *certainly* wouldn't have...umm...initiated anything in your truck on Saturday if I were with Charlie. Or *anyone*, for that matter."

"I know that," he said softly. It was true. He didn't know her that well, but he inherently knew she wouldn't be making out with him if she were seeing someone. She just wasn't the cheating type.

She was about to go on, and though he liked her fire, he reached out and took her hand in his, laying them both on her thigh. "I know that. I do. I don't even know why I said it."

She calmed at that, her head dropping just a little as she stared at their joined hands. She didn't pull hers away.

"Well," he said, "I guess I do know why I asked. I saw the way he looked at you today."

"How did he look at me?" she asked, but not in a real way. She knew. On some level, she knew.

"He's got a thing for *you*." As the words came out of his mouth, he realized he could have easily switched the opening pronoun to "I" and the statement would still be true.

Thank God, Deni didn't realize it.

"I know," she said quietly, then lifted her head to look at him. "He's never said anything. Or made any kind of move. And he's my best work friend." She ran her hand through her hair, tossing the mass over her shoulder. The wind on the hill had ruined her neat ponytail, and she'd taken it out of its holder on the way to Calumet.

He liked her cute ponytails, but dear lord, her hair was beautiful loose and flowing like now.

"He's actually kind of my best friend, period," she said, pulling his thoughts back.

"But he'd like to be more."

She nodded, tentative. "I don't know that for sure. And I'd never do anything to hurt him. I just don't…you know…feel *that* way about him."

She quickly glanced at him, then away. He leaned toward her, his thighs bracketing her legs. Letting go of her hand, he placed his on her thigh and squeezed. "What way? What way don't you feel about Charlie?"

He was baiting her, but not in a cruel way. And even though he'd been the one to call a stop to their night on Saturday—a move he'd kicked himself for all day Sunday—he needed to hear her say it.

"The way I'm starting to feel about you," she said softly, but firmly, looking him straight in the eyes.

God, so brave. So much braver than he was. He wouldn't leave her hanging, not for being so honest.

He brought his other hand to her leg and slid both hands down and around to the back of her knees, as if holding her in place. "Me too," he told her.

"Really?"

"Really."

"Then why'd you bail on Saturday?"

He didn't think he could adequately explain what seeing her mittens had done to him, but he wanted to try.

And that feeling—wanting to try with a woman, to communicate with her, to make her understand him—had been so long dormant that it took a moment for him to recognize it.

"While I was brushing off your car, I got...blindsided by memories. It really shook me, and I knew I couldn't go home with you." He moved his hands up a little on the back of her thighs, the wool of her skirt catching ever so slightly on his rough palms. "Much as I wanted to," he added.

She studied him, much like she'd just studied the stained-glass canopy. Her head turned from one angle to another, as if checking him for cracks and imperfections.

Both of which he had in abundance, but they probably didn't show much on the outside.

"I did some thinking yesterday," she said.

His thumb, which had been stroking the top of her thigh, stilled. Had he blown this whole thing before it had even started? And though that idea would have been fine just three or four days ago, it now sent a chill through him much like the wind on Quincy Hill had.

"And?"

"I know I said I wanted you to kiss me. In the truck...."

He reluctantly nodded for her to go on. It sounded like regret in her voice. Shit.

"And I was telling myself all the way home from Iron Mountain how it would be so nice to just have a little...*snack*."

"Snack?" He grinned at her euphemism. Oh, he'd definitely planned on snacking on her. Until he'd seen Molly's mittens.

"Yes, snack." She gently swatted his arm, but then kept her hand on his forearm. "Not that way. In the sense of...not a full meal. Nothing heavy. Just a little something to squash the hunger pangs."

"Okay." He wasn't sure where she was going with this, but he didn't think he was going to like it.

"But then on Sunday I started thinking."

"That does not sound good."

She smiled, and that tiny dimple appeared on her left side. Adorable. "I'm not really a snacking kind of person. I like regular meals. And as tempting as in-between-meal snacks can be...." She took a deep breath, raised her hand, and gently touched his cheek. "I thought it would be good for me. But now I think that it would probably just ruin my appetite."

Panic. Sheer panic coursed through him. But he couldn't tell which emotion was stronger—the urge to flee at the idea of a woman wanting more from him than he had to offer, or the thought of Deni walking out the door and never kissing her mouth again.

He reached up and took her hand from his face, turning it and placing a soft kiss on the middle of her palm. He was just about to agree with her, to tell her he admired her honesty and her ability to see so clearly what he would have gladly ignored.

Instead, he said, "I can try to be more than a snack. I can't promise appetizer through dessert, but I want more than just a snack, too."

He wasn't sure who was more surprised by his statement. Judging by her look, she probably was.

"I mean it," he said quietly, and realized that he truly did. "I won't make promises because quite honestly I don't know what I even have to offer a woman these days. It could end up being a sloppy Joe with chips, but I don't just want a snack with you, either."

Deni curled her hand, holding on to his, and then set them both down on his thigh. They were already close, but she leaned just that much closer so that her lips were almost—*almost*—on his.

"I happen to like sloppy Joes," she whispered, then briefly touched her lips to his before pulling back.

He leaned after her, but she was already scooting off the stool. "But first we have to figure out how to harness the wind."

He watched as she gathered up her things, tossing him a knowing smile. Sawyer felt the ice that had been around his heart for ten long years start to melt.

Twelve

—⌇⌇⌇—

"THAT WAS ON MONDAY?" ALISON ASKED DENI AT HER regular session Friday morning.

"Yes."

"And how has the rest of the week gone?" Alison kept her calm, cool professional tone, but Deni noticed just a hint of a smile as she asked the question.

"We've been working nonstop on the project. First with Mac and Charlie on development, then with Larry and Gerry on costing. So, we've been together every day, but not…you know… *together*."

"It's okay to take things slow."

"I know. And it's been great working with him. God, I love how his mind works. Sometimes it just amazes me."

"His body ain't so bad either," Alison mumbled softly to herself, but Deni still heard her.

"Umm…are you complaining about the body you're going home to?" Deni said, and then instantly regretted it. Alison hadn't meant for Deni to hear her. Had Deni crossed a line?

"A-men, sister," Alison said, smiling at her, though looking a little embarrassed. At Deni's snort of laughter, and then her struggle to cover it up, Alison said, "Listen Deni, I don't want you to be uncomfortable during therapy. And the fact is we may be seeing more of each other out of this room if Petey is working with your firm. I'd like to continue on and I can keep a professional attitude. But…I'm…sometimes very different when I'm not in this chair. Just so you know."

"Different how?" Before last week, Deni had never really thought of her shrink outside of the office, but assumed she'd be the same capable, nurturing, sensible person who sat across from her now.

"Well, I think it's safe to say that my friends would call me a complete smartass."

"Really?"

"Yep. And it's no secret around town that I've never had great luck with men." She looked away from Deni then, out the huge window. A small smile crept across her face, and Deni knew what she was thinking.

"Until now," Deni supplied for her.

Alison nodded, turning back. "My point is therapists are people too. And you may see a side of me that you didn't see before. And that side of me—the personal side—wasted a lot of time with the man she loved because she wasn't able to articulate what she wanted and what she needed from said guy.

"That's why I'm so impressed with you for laying it on the line the way you did with Sawyer. Letting him know you wanted more and setting your expectations. I wish I could have been that direct many times."

"Really?"

"Oh, yeah. I'm really impressed."

Deni inwardly preened. "I really like him—I mean as a person. And I wanted to be honest with him. I've never really been good at the whole yin and yang of flirting and dating. It just always seemed more logical to say something."

"That's the engineer side of you." As Deni was about to object, Alison added, "It's a great side. Trust that side."

The rest of their session went about like normal and wrapped up with the assessment questions Alison always asked. And then she reminded Deni about last week's "assignment."

"It was business, so I'm not sure if it counted, but going to

Green Bay for the day with Sawyer and making out in his truck should qualify for going somewhere new and different."

"Making out in a truck wouldn't be considered too different for most Yooper girls."

Alison *was* a smartass. How fun.

"But it qualifies for you."

"It sure felt out of my comfort zone."

"Uncomfortable?"

Deni thought about that. "Yes. But in a good way, you know?"

Alison nodded. "This week I'd like you to try wearing something different."

"You don't like how I dress?" As soon as she'd said it, Deni knew she'd sounded like a middle-school girl thinking she didn't pass judgment.

"I like how you dress very much. You have a nice, understated style. And I wish I could do the cool things with scarves that you do."

"Pinterest."

"Really?"

"Yes."

"Good to know. So no, don't change your style. This is all about stepping out of your comfort zone again." Deni must have been showing the discomfort she felt, because Alison held up a hand and said, "I'm not talking about sexing it up or anything. More like an orange tee-shirt, or those socks that have toes in them." She waved her hand again. "Whatever. It may be something in your closet already. I'm not saying you have to go on a shopping spree or anything."

"Good," Deni said, relieved.

"Does the idea of going shopping seem daunting to you?"

Deni nodded. "Yes. It just feels exhausting, you know?"

"That's the SAD. It'll pass, or at least ease, and you'll find that everyday tasks just feel normal again, not daunting."

"I have noticed it's not as hard getting out of bed in the

mornings."

"That's good," Alison said, though she was probably thinking the same thing Deni was—that Sawyer Beck being back in the office had a little something to do with that.

SHE GRABBED SOME LUNCH and ate in her cubicle, answering emails until late afternoon when Petey Ryan came in the office with Sawyer and Andy. They'd planned on taking him to lunch to walk through the team's ideas and then coming back here to present the proposal and show him the mock-ups that they'd been working on all week.

And it had felt like all week. They'd been at the office night and day, trying to pull this together quickly so, if accepted, they could be in place to start construction as soon as the snow melted.

Which could be as soon as four weeks, but would probably be more like seven.

She'd told Alison how much she'd liked working with Sawyer. She could have gone on and on about his creative—yet practical—thinking on this project, about his take-charge attitude, and about how damn fine his shoulders and ass looked as he wrote on the whiteboard.

All equal turn-ons to her.

There'd been a few stolen kisses throughout the week when they were absolutely sure no one was around. But those times were few and the kisses short and unsatisfying. They shared many more stolen glances than kisses. Deni would often look up from her laptop and see Sawyer staring at her, which made her uncomfortable at first, but then only made her feel warm and full of anticipation.

They'd ordered most meals in, eating in the conference room that Sawyer had commandeered for the week. But Mac, Charlie, and Andy were usually there, too.

Sawyer must have been staying somewhere in town since they worked so late, and he'd be back by eight each morning, freshly shaved and with Lucy in tow.

After this meeting with Petey, Deni wasn't really sure what would be happening with them, but the too-long touches that Sawyer gave her when passing her a file told her that he was feeling the same things she was.

As the three men made their way to the conference room, Sawyer's gaze sought her out. When their eyes met, she saw a subtle softening of his features, and he motioned for her to join them, which was normal for something like this since she was the second on the project.

She got up from her cube, grabbed her laptop, tablet, and pen, and made her way to the conference room, Lucy at her heels. Whenever Sawyer wasn't around—and even sometimes when he was—his dog stuck to Deni like glue.

Sawyer's welcoming smile as she entered the room helped put any butterflies about the presentation at ease. As did Petey's comment of, "Finally, the brains behind the whole operation. Now I can get some questions answered."

Everyone chuckled and settled in. Petey sat where he'd be able to see the screen. Deni opened up the PowerPoint deck they'd added to all week and she'd polished up late last night. She motioned to Andy that she was ready.

"Well, we hit the broad strokes over lunch, Petey. Now we want to show you the specifics," Andy said, then nodded at Deni to move on to the next slide.

"Actually, you know what?" Sawyer interrupted. "Deni, why don't you take the lead on this one? You don't mind, do you, Andy?"

"Umm." Andy stalled, looking at Sawyer and then Deni. She'd presented to clients before but never on a project this large, and never when a senior project manager was in the room—let alone the two partners.

Ignoring Andy's look of confusion, Sawyer said to Petey, "She knows this inside and out. She'll be the best one to explain it all."

Deni flashed Sawyer a look. *He* knew it much better than she did. He nodded to her laptop. She looked at Andy, who only shrugged.

"Yeah, this is good," Petey said. "I like having things explained to me by women much smarter than me. It'll feel like being at home."

They all laughed and the moment of unease passed. Petey Ryan was no dummy, either.

"Well," Deni began, "this is how we can make the brutal winds on Quincy Hill keep your costs down and make your business viable."

TWO HOURS LATER, they were still going over the renderings. They'd placed one of the 3D models up on the screen, rotating it this way and that. Petey and Sawyer were standing, moving back and forth from the screen to the papers now littering the table.

"Okay," Petey said, stretching his enormous back. "I think I've got it. It's actually fucking brilliant. Darío and I never would have thought of wind power."

Deni stole a glance at Sawyer, who was watching her. She couldn't help herself and broke into a large grin, which he returned.

"So, next steps," Petey continued, though it seemed to Deni that he had caught the look that'd passed between her and Sawyer. "I'll take this all to Darío. If he likes it, and I think he will, we'll go to the bank and sign the papers, set up the funds."

"You aren't going to get another bid? Another plan?" Sawyer asked what she was thinking.

Petey walked closer to Sawyer and stood right in front of him.

"Is anybody else going to have a better idea than wind?" he asked.

"No," Sawyer said without hesitation.

"Is this a fair, honest bid? No extra padding?"

"It's a good bid. We aren't going to take a loss—"

"I'm not asking you to."

"—but there's no padding."

Petey looked at Sawyer for only a second before nodding.

"Okay. That's good enough for me. We won't be bidding it out elsewhere."

"Probably not a good way to do business, Petey," Sawyer said quietly.

Petey shrugged a massive shoulder and said, "Aw, hell. You know I'm going to be a shitty businessman, Sawyer. Thank God, Al's got a good job." Then a grin spread across his face that had Deni guessing Petey was a lot sharper than most gave him credit for.

"Let me get your final packet, and Darío's, too," Andy said, leaving the conference room. They'd left clean copies in Andy's office so they'd feel free to pull apart and mark up the copies in the conference room—which they definitely had.

Deni started gathering up the various papers, sketches, and other things that had been strewn around the room. Sawyer paid some attention to Lucy, who'd been so good during their meeting, quietly lying under the table with her head on Sawyer's feet.

Petey joined Deni at her end of the large table. "This is a nice room," he said. Deni looked around and nodded her agreement.

"I don't know what I expected. Lots of mechanical pencils and protractors and shit lying around, I guess."

"You really haven't been in the professional world much, have you?" she asked him good-naturedly.

"Nope. I have a degree from Tech in business, if you can imagine that, and I've handled my money and endorsements and stuff like that. But the day-to-day, show-up-at-the-office stuff? Never."

"Think you'll like it?" she asked. She'd finished straightening up and leaned a hip against one of the chairs, watching Petey as he thought about her question.

He looked at her and let out a long sigh. "I honestly don't know. All I ever knew was hockey. And yet...today...right now? I'm kind of the happiest I've ever been."

"Alison?" Deni asked. It wasn't really a question. And she didn't need an answer. The goofy look on his face gave him away.

"Yeah. Hey, I'm sorry about the other night, bringing her to dinner. I guess that shit happens to her a lot, small town and all, but I don't want to put you in an awkward position."

"You didn't. It was fine. We actually talked about it and know that there is the potential to cross paths a lot more if Summers and Beck is doing your driving range. It's fine."

"Okay, good. I just don't want you freaking out because the woman sitting next to you at the Commodore knows all your dirty little secrets."

Before Deni could answer, he leaned in and said in a conspiratorial whisper, "Because she knows all of mine, and it sure freaks me out."

A bark of laughter escaped her. "No freak-outs, I promise. Besides, in my sessions I mostly just bitch about my mom."

"Ha! And then she comes home and I bitch about my dad."

"At least she gets paid to listen to my bitch sessions."

He gave her a wink. "Oh, she gets paid to listen to me. It's just in a different currency."

As Deni was laughing again, an arm slid around her shoulders.

"Wanna knock off early and get something to eat?" Sawyer said in her ear. His hand stayed around her shoulder.

"Sure, where—" Petey started.

"You're not invited," Sawyer said.

Petey laughed. "Yeah, I know. I was just busting your balls, Beck. Not that I haven't invited myself before."

"But not this time," Sawyer said, pulling her a little closer to his body.

She was stunned. They'd been very careful to not show any PDA in the office. And he was the boss. And there were glass windows all around. Yep. Sure enough, Andy was standing at the door, handle in hand, frozen at the sight of them. She craned around Sawyer. Double yep. Charlie and Mac were standing by Charlie's cube staring. There was surprise on Mac's face and what looked like resignation on that of her dear friend.

"I can't even suggest a double date. Al's doing the girlfriend thing tonight with Lizzie."

"Another time," Sawyer said.

"Sure. Absolutely. Well, thanks again. We'll get back to you as soon as we have an answer."

Andy had recovered and was now fully in the room, handing Petey the folder they'd prepared for him and Darío. "And if you have any questions in the meantime, anything at all."

"I've got your number," Petey agreed, shaking Andy's hand. Nodding at Deni and Sawyer, he left the conference room and then the office.

"SERIOUSLY?" ANDY SAID to them both. Sawyer knew that tone. He was about to get a sermon. "In front of a client?"

"Petey Ryan," Sawyer said, as if that explained everything.

"Still a client. And only a potential client at that."

Sawyer took his arm from around Deni's shoulder, already missing the feel of her body against his. He couldn't explain why he'd felt the need to be so demonstrative with Deni—other than he'd been dying to all week. It was seeing her laughing with lady-killer Ryan that made him do it. And damn, but he wasn't sorry. Even with Andy giving him the stink-eye and poor Charlie burning a hole in the back of Sawyer's head with his undoubtedly hangdog eyes. Unless….

"Are you okay?" he asked Deni quietly.

"No, she's not okay," Andy said, getting heated now. "You treated her like arm candy when she's a respected part of this team. She'd just given a stellar presentation—great job, by the way"—he directed this to Deni, who tried to answer, but was cut off by Andy continuing—"and you reward that by treating her like your girlfriend. It totally—"

"She is my girlfriend," Sawyer said.

"What?" That made Andy stop in his verbal tracks.

"It's early days, but yeah, we're…um…shit, can you be forty and have a girlfriend?" he asked Deni.

She gave a small smile. "Yes. My mother is fifty-eight, and

she has a boyfriend."

"I'm not even going to do the math to know if I'm closer to your age or your mom's."

"Smart man," she told him, the smile still on her face. Then she seemed to remember the glowering Andy and sobered up. "But Andy's right. This is the office. Petey is a client, and—"

"Did you mind?" he asked her as he stepped closer to her. "Honestly?"

"I should have. I'm one of two females in this office. You're a partner. Professionalism is—"

"Did you mind?" he asked again, meeting her eyes and holding them with his gaze.

"No," she said softly. "But don't do it again," she said, probably for Andy's benefit.

Good enough for him. "Mea culpa," he said to Andy, his hands up in surrender. "It's been too many years since I've been in a professional setting."

"Oh, bull. Don't play the hermit card. You know perfectly well not to paw the employees."

"Well then, we're going to get out of here so we can paw each other properly."

Deni stifled a giggle. She was so damn cute.

"Oh no. Not just the two of you. You're taking the team out for drinks to celebrate all the hard work they put in this week to turn it around so quickly."

"I'll give 'em my credit card. I'm happy to pay." He stepped aside and motioned for Deni to lead the way, which she did. Quicker, he silently tried to relay to her, so Andy wouldn't—

"Good news, everybody," Andy said from behind them once they were out of the conference room. "Sawyer's treating everyone to drinks and dinner to thank you for all the hard work. Let's skip out of here early and enjoy the evening"—Sawyer could feel Andy's eyes on his back—"at the Indian River Steak House."

Of course he'd pick the most expensive place in town.

Well, if he didn't get to paw Deni over dinner, at least he'd get a damn good T-bone.

Thirteen

CHARLIE WASN'T SPEAKING TO HER. OR AT LEAST IT FELT that way.

Oh, he and Mac cornered her right away when she arrived at the restaurant, to pump her about the presentation.

Sawyer arrived a short time later, after dropping Lucy off at his brother's house. And from that moment on, Charlie moved to the other end of the bar area, ostensibly to talk to Snide Randy.

Yeah, right. Charlie liked Randy's company about as much as she did.

Sawyer had stood behind her while they commandeered the bar area waiting for a table for them all. Sue had declined, wanting to attend her grandson's high school hockey game, as did Bob, who had other plans, but the rest had made it on short notice.

When Randy made his way over to Andy, no doubt to suck up in some way, Deni excused herself and made her way down to Charlie, taking Randy's empty stool.

Alison had applauded her today for being so open and honest with Sawyer about what she wanted, but in truth Deni was just not good at playing social games. Not with potential boyfriends or platonic friends. That was why she liked being around engineers so much; most of them were the same way—literal, logical, and to the point.

"Hey," she said to Charlie as she sat beside him.

"Hey," he answered, not looking up from the beer in front

of him.

She took a sip from her own beer bottle, then set it down on the polished oak bar.

"So, out with it," she said.

He just shrugged his shoulders, started peeling the label off his bottle and said, "Out with what?"

"Come on, Charlie. This is me." She jostled his stool with her foot.

He turned to her but took forever to look her in the eye. When he did, she could see the hurt. "I know. That's the problem."

She could pretend she didn't know. That was kind of what she'd been doing for the past couple of years, on some level. She'd not thought about it because she loved spending time with Charlie and didn't want that dynamic to end.

But it looked like it was going to.

She put a hand on his arm and said quietly, "I'm sorry it couldn't have been you." She meant it. Life would have been great if she'd fallen for Charlie. But she hadn't.

"And it's *him*?" he asked, with not a whole lot of surprise in his voice.

She shrugged. "I don't know. Maybe not." She looked at Sawyer talking with Andy, engaged and yet…not. "He'll probably end up breaking my heart."

"Yeah, that's what I was thinking," Charlie said, with no emotion. "I mean, the guy totally checked out since his wife died. He's older, not to mention your boss."

She could argue with each of his points, but he was right. She'd told herself the same things. And yet she'd turned to Sawyer on that stool in Tootie's and told him she wanted more from him than just a fling.

And he'd said he wanted it, too.

"I know. But there's…something there, Charlie. Something I haven't felt before."

"Do you think maybe it's just the SAD? That feeling any emotion is such a good thing right now that you're making it out to be more than it is?"

Charlie and her mother were the only two people she'd told about being diagnosed with SAD. She had a mild form of it, and there was no reason to believe that it wouldn't lessen and disappear when spring came around. So it wasn't something she shared with people like her brothers or friends back in Farmington Hills or her other coworkers.

"I don't think so," she answered. "Who knows? We're taking it very slowly."

Except for kissing in front of the Commodore on the day she met him. And grinding on him in his truck four days later.

"We haven't actually had a real date, yet."

She couldn't even imagine Sawyer on a date—dinner and a movie, or something as normal as that. And she wanted normal.

She looked over at Sawyer again. He was being talked to by Snide Randy now, who had wisely stayed down at that end of the bar. But he wasn't looking at Randy. His eyes were glued to her.

He wasn't quite as tall nor nearly as broad as Petey Ryan, or as classically handsome as Andy. He was nowhere near as sweet and friendly as Charlie, and he sure had a lot more baggage than the guys her age. But....

He mouthed "You okay?" to her with a look of concern.

She nodded to him, then turned back to Charlie.

"But I need to see where it's going." Her voice became so quiet she barely heard herself as she added, "I have to know."

There was a moment when neither of them said anything. Then Charlie said, "Well, don't think you can come crying on my shoulder when he leaves you to go be a hermit again." There was more teasing than venom in his voice.

She smiled at her buddy. "I won't." She started to get off her stool. "We're good?" she asked. She knew they'd probably never get back to the hanging-out pals they'd been. That had shifted, but she still wanted Charlie in her life.

"We're good." As she started to walk away, he reached for her hand and held it. "You can, you know. You *can* come crying to me if it doesn't work out. I'll be there if you need me."

Oh, how she wished she could be in love with sweet, wonderful Charlie. "I know," she said. She took her beer bottle, squeezed Charlie's arm as she passed him, and returned to Sawyer.

THE DINNER SEEMED to go on forever. Sawyer watched as Deni, sitting across the long table from him, tried to hide a yawn. Yeah, they had worked a ton of hours this week. Burning the candle at both ends was nothing new for him—though doing it in an office setting was. He'd been hoping to have a quiet dinner with her and then to *finally* finish what they'd started in that Iron Mountain parking lot. It'd only been a week ago, but it seemed like forever since she'd been straddling him and moaning as he—

"Sawyer? Did you hear me?" Andy pulled him out of his truck memory. Stupid Andy.

"What was that? Sorry, lost in thought." He gave Deni a look that hopefully told her exactly what thought had him lost. By the flush that rose in her face and the way she dropped her eyes, he guessed she got it.

"I said, thanks for dinner, and more importantly, for taking on this project."

"We don't have it, yet," he reminded the ever-optimistic Andy.

Who waved the negative thought away. "I know, I know. But it's a great plan, and we wrote a great quote. If they do it at all, they'll do it with us and follow the plan you came up with."

"The plan we *all* came up with," he quickly pointed out. He'd expected a level of resentment from the group—him swooping in and leading a large, high-profile project when he hadn't shown his face in ten years. But no, everybody had been great to work with. Except maybe Charlie when he'd caught Sawyer staring at Deni various times during the week.

Poor kid. He had it bad for Deni, and she only thought of him as a friend. They seemed to have made some kind of peace earlier, though. He'd ask Deni about it later when they were alone.

She yawned again, and he realized that this night was going to end just like all the others in the past week—with them both going home alone, exhausted. She would get some much-needed shut-eye. He would battle sleeplessness, and think about getting Deni naked while he jerked off.

His sigh of frustration coincided with the waitress putting down the check in front of him. Everyone laughed, thinking that was the cause, but Deni knew. She had a look that said the night hadn't gone how she'd wanted, either.

He had a moment of thinking they'd rally and salvage it, but she yawned once more. He shrugged his shoulders and reached for the check.

Somehow, they managed to be the last of their group in the parking lot. He walked over to her car, where she stood as if waiting for him.

"Hey," he said softly. "Long day."

She nodded. "Long week."

"Very." He put a hand to her cheek, which was already cold from the frigid night air. "But a good one."

She smiled. "It was."

He leaned in to kiss her, but the lights of a car pulling into the lot shone in his face, stopping him. He hadn't thought it through, but blurted out, "I'd like to take you somewhere tomorrow. Are you free?"

"Yes."

"It's a bit of a hike. It'd be better to spend the night, but I don't want to rush or presume—"

"I'd like that," she quickly said.

"Great. I'll pick you up at nine. I know you live in East End, but what's your address?"

She told him and he memorized the number. There were only five or six streets in that cluster of older homes, and he knew hers well.

"Dress warmly. We'll be outside for a while. Very, *very*, casual. Like long johns or ski pants. Warm and casual."

"How romantic," she teased.

"That's what I'm going for," he said, and they both smiled. "And pack light. Like a backpack, if you have one."

Another car entered the lot, shining on them. She moved to get in her car. Sawyer opened the door for her and held it. "Okay," she said. The same reluctance to leave that he felt came through in her voice. "See you tomorrow morning."

He kept his hand on the door longer than needed but then finally shut it. She looked at him through the window, then turned forward and started up her car. He walked to his as she pulled away and turned out of the lot.

He got in his truck and pulled onto the highway that led back into Houghton. Deni's car was within sight. He kept his eyes on it, the ache that he'd felt each night when he left the office— and her—returning once again.

When he got to Agate Street, where he should have turned to go get Lucy from Huck's, he kept going. Through Houghton and across the bridge, taking a right at Bob's Mobil and heading up the hill into East End.

Ahead of him, Deni made the last turn onto her street and disappeared.

Keep going, don't turn, don't turn, don't turn. Go back to Houghton.

The sheer strength of the urge he felt to follow her shocked him. He hadn't felt anything this strong, this desperate, in…God, years and years. He turned.

She lived in one of the older homes that were built into the hill. You parked in back and then walked down steep steps to get to the house. She'd already exited her street-level garage and had made her way down the stairs when he pulled up to her house.

"Deni, wait," he shouted as he got out of his truck. She whirled from putting her key in the door, startled.

"Sawyer? What's wrong?" She must have sensed his urgency, which wasn't hard since he was racing down the steps, losing his footing on the snow-covered incline. He righted himself and nearly sprinted to her.

"What is it? Is it Lucy?"

He shook his head. He couldn't explain it to her. Hell, he couldn't explain it to himself. "Just...this," he whispered to her, then held her head in his hands as he kissed her.

Hard, and yet softly. He wanted to devour her and also gently taste. He needed to own her but to share what he was feeling for her.

Except he couldn't explain it—let alone share it. So he kept his mouth fused to hers, tangling with her tongue, tasting the coffee and sweet Amaretto of the tiramisu she'd had for dessert.

Her arms wrapped around him and a soft sigh escaped her mouth, floating against his cheek, warming him. His hands moved from her face to her nape, holding her in place as he tilted his head, wanting more. The leather of her gloves felt foreign on his neck...but he liked it. Liked everything about how well their bodies fit together, even through the many layers of warm clothing and coats.

"Come inside," she whispered between kisses, and then swept her tongue back to his mouth, searching for his. She started to step back, toward her door, pulling him with her.

And, dear God, he wanted to go inside with her. But he stopped. Stopped this kiss. Stilled his hands and just laid his forehead against her.

"Wait," he said, catching his breath. He didn't look at her, just kept his eyes closed and forged on. "I'm going to explain this badly, so please bear with me. Sometimes I get these...visions in my head."

She pulled away, and he opened his eyes to see her studying him. "Like...psychic visions?"

"No, not like that. Like visions of what could be. Like at a building site. I can see the final thing in my head...like seeing the rendering."

"Oh, okay. Yeah, I get those, too."

He nodded. He guessed most engineers and architects did.

Hell, maybe everybody did.

"And...I have this very clear...vision of where we'll be the first time...we're together."

"So you want to wait?" If there had been incredulity or petulance or anything like that in her voice, he would have brushed his stupid ideas of their first time aside and grabbed the keys from her hand and had that door unlocked and them inside in no time.

But there wasn't. There was understanding and what sounded like anticipation. But it was the understanding that clinched it for him. "Yes. I want to say good night and pick you up tomorrow morning at nine like we planned."

She didn't say "Then why the hell did you follow me home?" which was kind of what he was thinking.

"I just...wanted to kiss you good night," he said to the unspoken question.

She smiled and the little dimple appeared. "I'm glad you did," she said softly. Then she turned around, let herself into her house, and shut the door behind her.

Fourteen

—⚮—

SAWYER ENDED UP CRASHING IN HUCK'S GUEST ROOM. And even though there was a fresh pot of coffee made, water in Lucy's dish, and Sawyer was sure he hadn't slept more than a couple of hours, there was no Huck when he woke up in the morning.

He knew that after ten years of basically checking out on his family he had no right to start playing concerned big brother now. But should he be concerned about Huck?

He left his brother a thank-you note, filled two travel cups with coffee, and started out with Lucy. He went to Jim's Foodmart and stocked up on easily transportable food and a good bottle of wine. Then it was time to pick up Deni.

She must have been waiting for him, because he had no sooner pulled his truck over than she was out the door, a backpack slung over her shoulder.

He got out and opened the passenger door for her. "Morning," she said as she breezed past him and stepped up into the truck.

"Morning," he answered, taking her backpack and putting it on the floor of the backseat, giving Lucy something new to sniff.

"Hey, girl," she said to his dog as he shut the door and walked back to his side. By the time he was seated, Deni was halfway over the backseat giving Lucy a belly rub. Much as he would love to look at Deni's ass for the entire trip, he put the truck in gear, which caused her to turn around and buckle up. He motioned to the two coffee cups. She picked one up and took a long drag of what was now probably lukewarm coffee.

"So, where are you taking me?" she asked, setting the cup back in the holder.

"In general terms, Copper Harbor," he answered. He drove them out of East End, up White Street, and then turned right, heading to Calumet and ultimately the Harbor.

"And in specific terms?"

"A very remote piece of property that I own."

"We're not camping, are we? At this time of year?"

"Plenty of people winter camp."

"Yes, but I'm not one of them."

"I didn't picture you as the high-maintenance type," he teased. He stole a glance her way and saw she was smiling.

"I'm not. But that doesn't mean I want to be in a tent and sleeping bag when it gets down to ten below zero."

"What if I said I'd keep you warm?"

She laughed at that. "I'd say that was very romantic, but I still want a mattress, heavy comforter, and furnace."

"How about a mattress, heavy comforter, and a roaring fire?"

"Walls? And a roof?"

"Yep."

"Sold," she said, and gave him a brilliant smile as she reached for her coffee.

He stepped on the gas.

THEY RODE IN SILENCE, Lucy's occasional sighs the only sound. That was fine with Deni; she'd never been one who needed to have silence filled. Besides, their silence was a comfortable one, neither feeling the need to talk for talking's sake. And it wasn't awkward at all, even if a sense of…*anticipation* hung in the air.

When they got to the point where you could turn off to go the longer route, or stay on the shorter one, Sawyer put his blinker on and made the turn.

"You did say Copper Harbor, right? Not Eagle Harbor?"

"Yeah, Copper Harbor. Beyond Copper Harbor, actually."

"And you're taking this route instead of Covered Drive?"

"I didn't know you knew your way around up here so well. Do you get up to the harbors much?"

"Not a lot, no. Not as much as I'd like. It's beautiful up here." Lucy let out a soft snort, as if agreeing with her. "I usually get up once or twice during the summer. And I try to get up during color season. When I do, though, I tend to take Covered Drive up and then go through Eagle Harbor on the way back."

"That's a good route. I just thought this way would be prettier for you. Covered Drive isn't as great this time of year with no leaves. Without that, it's just a twisty road—not always the best for winter driving."

Something about the way he said the last part put Deni on alert. If this were to be just the beginning of something lovely, but short—a snack, as she'd said—she would have just let it go and sit back to enjoy the ride.

But instead she asked, "Is that where your wife's accident happened? On Covered Drive?"

For a moment he didn't answer her, and she thought maybe it was too soon for those types of talks. Then slowly, he nodded his head, his hands tightening on the wheel.

"Yes. And it's not like I've *never* been on it since. It's just I prefer to go this way if I have the time."

She was glad he'd answered her, but she could tell he didn't want to talk about it, so she didn't push.

"And we have the time today," she said. "And Eagle Harbor is so pretty. I don't think I've ever been up here this deep into winter. I'll bet it's gorgeous in a different way."

He smiled at her, with gratitude for the changed subject, it seemed.

"It has its own kind of beauty. The snow and ice, the stillness of it all. It might be my favorite time of year up here."

"That's because there's no one up here now. No tourists, no

seasonal workers. Perfect for a hermit."

"Geez. Enough with the hermit thing, please," he said, but in a good-natured way.

"I think it's kind of cool. I've never dated a hermit before."

"The non-hermits you've dated before? Anyone special?"

Part of the conversation seemed so normal—a new couple doing the "get to know you," "tell me a little about your past" conversation. And yet, she was teasing him about being a hermit, and he was going out of their way not to drive by the site of his wife's death.

So, *not* normal new couple stuff.

"Not anyone really special, no. I had a boyfriend my last two years at Tech. And we tried the long-distance thing for a while after graduation. It was hard, though, and we didn't feel that what we had was worth...fighting for, I guess."

"Where'd he live?"

"He got on with GM."

"And you had no desire to move back to your hometown area?"

They were making the turn into Eagle Harbor now. The beach was deserted, and the harbor itself was frozen over up to the point where it joined Lake Superior.

"No, I really wanted to stay up here."

"Not the greatest career move," he said, but he got it.

"Nope, but I'm okay with that. I get to work on some really interesting projects. They're all different, and many of them involve restoration of original structures. I like that. And I love the Copper Country."

He just nodded.

"Besides, you're not really one to talk about making great career moves, Mr. Hermit."

He laughed. "You've got me there."

"How has it been for you the past week and a half coming out of your cave?"

"Cave?"

"Shack? Fortress of Solitude?"

He snorted at that, then after a moment answered. "It's been okay. Better than I thought, actually."

He looked over at her and flashed a grin, his green eyes glinting with amusement. "Besides, there's been a nice perk."

Dear lord, she wanted him to pull off the road so she could straddle his lap like she'd done in Iron Mountain. Only this time without all these pesky clothes in the way. She just smiled and said, "How much farther?"

He laughed and said, "Too damn far."

They passed through Copper Harbor and then drove on, past Fort Wilkins. Deni shared the story of Caleb climbing on the cannon when she was eight.

"Did you come up every summer when you were a kid?"

"No, that was the last one until the summer after my junior year in high school. I came up for the Women in Engineering summer program to see if I'd like it."

"And obviously you did."

"Yes. I thought maybe it would just be nostalgia, or some kind of legacy thing because my father went to Tech. I figured that once I got back up here, I'd realize it was too far away or too remote and would cross it off my college list."

"But you didn't cross it off."

"No, it moved to the top of my list. Much to my mother's chagrin."

"She didn't want you that far away?"

"No. I'm the baby, and Caleb and Josh were gone by then. She wasn't really keen about the looming empty nest, and it wouldn't be like I could just pop home for a weekend being ten hours away."

"I heard you say something to Petey about bitching about your mom to Alison…."

She waved that away. "Yeah, she's been a little…much… lately. She's…concerned about me, and that tends to come across as smothering. It was really bad for the first few years after my father died, but then she eased up. But lately…." She didn't continue. There were two reasons Deni felt her mother had become a tad overbearing lately—she knew about Deni's SAD and was understandably worried, and the last of Deni's single hometown friends was getting married this summer and Deni was still single with no prospects.

Which didn't bother Deni in the least, but she still kept both those factors to herself. She didn't want Sawyer to think she was husband hunting. Just because she wanted more than a few hook-ups, didn't mean she was trolling jewelry stores and checking out rings.

"She started dating again," she said. "My mom. And I think it's great, but she's a little freaked about it all. So the calls and emails have ratcheted up in the past year." All true, if not the whole truth.

"Moms dating. It's a different kind of hell," he said.

"Yours too? Is your father living?"

He nodded. "Living, yes. But he hasn't been in the picture since we were in high school. He was a Tech student who loved the area, married a local girl, and stayed. But it got too much for him, and he wanted to move south. Mom didn't want to leave, and the marriage was pretty shaky by then anyway, so he moved and we stayed."

"Did you see him much?"

"A little at first. Longer holiday breaks and a few weeks over the summer. I only had a year left of high school, so I didn't go down for the summers like Twain and Huck did. I lived on campus at Tech, so it didn't feel that much different for me. It affected Huck most of all, being the youngest."

"And now?"

He shrugged. "Oddly enough, my mom ended up moving after all. She fell for a guy who was up here on a fishing trip with buddies, and moved out east with him. That was about eleven or twelve years ago.

"It's nice that she's happy and everything, but when they

started dating it was just...so weird, you know?"

"Yeah, I know," she said, taking her eyes from him and looking out the window.

They were farther north than Deni had ever been before. "I didn't know this road even went this far up."

"Oh yeah, all the way to the tip. But we're not going that far." As if to prove his point, he turned left onto a snow-covered road, which, gauging by the tread marks and new snow in between, hadn't been driven on in a few weeks.

"Will your truck make this road?"

"Not all the way in, no. But we only need to make it"—he took a wide curve and a pole barn came into view—"this far." He reached up to the visor and pushed a button on a remote, and the garage door, which took up half of one side of the large building, opened.

"This place has a mattress, a comforter, and a roaring fire?" she asked as he pulled the truck inside.

"Nope, not this place. This place holds the transportation to the next place." He pointed to the snowmobile parked to one side of the huge structure.

"We're going on that?"

"You've never been on one? And you've been up here how many years?"

"Ten, if you count my years at Tech."

"And you haven't been on a snowmobile?"

"I haven't had the pleasure, no."

"Well, there is another way." He pointed to several pairs of snowshoes lined up against the wall.

Normally she'd love to go snowshoeing, but she hadn't had much exercise this year—opting to stay home in bed in the evenings and on weekends. And the thought of falling in a snow bank, overcome with exhaustion, put a damper on the whole "getting naked and sexy with Sawyer" thing.

"I'll try the snowmobile."

"Atta girl. Besides, it's not very far. It's just terrain that can't be driven by truck. It's a beautiful hike in the summertime."

By her estimation, they were about two miles from the end of the Earth—so, yeah, it probably wouldn't be a long ride.

They left the truck, and Sawyer took some grocery bags and walked over to the snowmobile. Lucy bounded outside and quickly found a spot to make the snow yellow.

"I'm going to take Lucy up first and then come back for you," Sawyer said as he started transferring things from the grocery bags to a sturdy duffle that he took down from a shelf. "If I take you first, she'll try to follow us, and the snow's too deep for her. I could put her in the truck, I guess—"

"No, it's fine. Take her up first, but how…." Her voice trailed off as Sawyer pulled some sort of harness from another shelf and started strapping it on to the machine. Lucy knew what he was doing and started barking with excitement, butting her head against Sawyer's back as he knelt at the machine.

"Hang on, girl, give me a second." When he finished, he stood up and took a step back. Lucy jumped up on the leather seat in a position she was obviously used to.

Deni stepped forward and started to examine the harness and straps while Sawyer fastened them around his dog.

"Did you make this?"

"Yep."

"Did you *design* it?"

"Yep."

"Is it safe? Legal?"

"Very safe. I made sure of that," he said, patting Lucy as if to reinforce how precious the cargo was that the harness protected. "But crazy illegal," he added with a grin. He hadn't shaved this morning, and the stubble suited him much better than the clean-shaven look he'd had yesterday.

He handed her the keys to his truck. "Go back to the truck and put the heater on. I'll be back in about twenty minutes."

"What if something happens to you?" she asked, momentary panic rising up inside her.

"Nothing's going to happen. I do this all the time."

It didn't help, and she felt an irrational fear bubbling up.

He must have recognized it. He set the packed duffle down on the machine in front of Lucy. He took his cell phone out of his jeans pocket, handed it to Deni, and then put his hands on her shoulders.

"If I'm not back in an hour, drive back to Copper Harbor. That's the closest place to get a signal. Find my brother Twain in my contacts. Call him and tell him where I am."

"And where are we?"

He smiled. "Tell him I'm between my garage and the ice cube. He'll know what to do."

"Okay," she said, grasping his keys and phone.

"But there's nothing to worry about, really." He looked at her again, then turned and started taking the duffle bag off the snowmobile. "I'll take you up first and then come back for Lucy."

Damn the SAD. Deni knew it was making her more emotional than she would normally be. "No, don't. Keep her on and bring her up. I'm fine, really. I just wanted a backup plan."

He studied her, and must have believed she meant it. He came over and gave her a swift kiss that ended all too quickly.

"Well, you wouldn't be much of an engineer if you didn't think of a backup plan, would you?"

"That's right."

"Okay, I'll be right back. Make sure you go warm up in the truck." He grabbed a helmet from an old hat rack, strapped it to his head, and then swung a leg over the machine. He jostled the duffle bag and checked on Lucy, who promptly licked the glass shield of his helmet.

"Okay," she said, but her answer was swallowed up by the roaring of the motor as he started up. Good God, the thing was loud. Being on a concrete slab only amplified the noise, and she backed away, deeper into the garage.

He gave a wave, throttled the handlebar, and drove slowly out of the garage. He went past the truck and up onto a bank of snow that had well-worn snowmobile tracks trailing away. As soon as he'd cleared the area and was on the trail, he sped up.

In seconds, he was gone.

Fifteen
—∞—

In twenty minutes on the dot, Deni heard Sawyer's snowmobile. She hadn't gone to the truck to keep warm as he'd suggested, but instead had been mesmerized by the various gadgets that lined the shelves throughout the large building.

Tools, yes, but also small machinery and many things that Deni could not identify. Was the hermit a mad scientist as well?

"What is all this?" she asked him when he'd cut the engine and taken off his helmet. He'd left the machine outside, already facing the trail back to…wherever they were going.

"Junk, mostly." He set his helmet on the seat and took the now-empty duffle bag over to where the rest of his grocery bags were and started transferring things.

"How much do you think we're going to eat in two days?" she asked.

"Each time I try to bring as much non-perishable food as I can, since I have to use the snowmobile in the winter."

"Kind of like stockpiling?"

"That makes it sound like I'm getting ready for Armageddon or something."

"Well, it does feel like the end of the Earth up here. In a good way, of course," she said with a smile.

He laughed at that as he finished with the supplies, zipping up the duffle and swinging the heavy bag over his shoulder. As he passed her, he stopped, leaned over, and whispered, "Maybe I should have just said we're going to work up an appetite."

She turned, but he'd already passed, shooting her a grin over his shoulder as he made his way back to the end of the garage.

"Ready?" he asked, plucking another helmet from the hat rack.

Ready and raring. At least to get to their destination, if not for getting on the machine.

He put the helmet on her and showed her how to sit on the machine. He must have left Lucy's harness up at the…the whatever. Log cabin, she supposed. One that smelled great and had a huge stone fireplace.

He closed the garage door behind him, got on the machine, and showed her how to hang on to him. She didn't need much direction with that and was happy to oblige.

They took off with a jolt and then rose up the incline to get up onto the trail. After that, the path smoothed, and Deni found she enjoyed the ride.

They wound through a trail with huge pine trees on either side of them, truly in their own world.

It wasn't long before the tree line broke and Deni saw Lake Superior. With a wall of stone in front of it.

They were coming at the building straight on, so she couldn't see the sides at all, but this was surely no log cabin. The thirty-foot-wide front was made of some kind of funky stone mixture. The structure was a single story, but it was clear that it had a high ceiling. She could barely wait to get off the snowmobile and check it out.

There was a door in one corner and a chimney protruding from the top at the center of the building. She arched her head trying to see the peak of the roof, but couldn't see beyond the stone wall.

There was what appeared to be an outhouse (oh God, she hadn't thought about *that*) on the side of the building, a discreet distance away. Another small building that had the shape and size of a sauna house stood farther down, closer to the lake.

"Come on," Sawyer said, helping her off the snowmobile. "Bring the helmet inside," he added as he put the duffle over his shoulder and took her backpack from her, carrying that as well.

She took the helmet off and tucked it under her arm as she followed Sawyer to the door. He'd parked as close to the door as he could, and the path was pretty stamped down, making for easier walking.

He opened the door and stood to the side for her to enter. She didn't see anything at first besides the four steps up and Lucy's big body greeting her.

"Hey, girl," she said, as she made her way up the stairs. She petted the dog. "Did you have a good ride up here? Did you? Good girl."

As she got to the last step, Lucy backed away, content that they were all here to stay. Deni was finally able to view the whole cabin.

For a few brief seconds she thought she'd been duped and there was no building at all. It looked like there was just the big stone wall with stairs leading to…what seemed to be just the other side of the wall. She seemed like she was still outside.

But no, she wasn't outside. The cabin had glass walls. This wasn't just a wall with large windows. No. These were glass walls. She looked up, but didn't really need to, as the amount of natural light alone could have told her that there was also a glass ceiling.

"Oh my God," she said, walking farther into the room. And it was just one large room. A cube made completely of glass, except for the stone wall—which ran the entire length of the room and the hardwood floor.

She set the helmet on the floor in an area that had a throw rug and seemed to be the general hat, coat, and boot area. She quickly took her outerwear off, dying to explore.

She heard Sawyer behind her, but she didn't wait for him to take off his things or set down the duffle and backpack. She needed to see this…this…glass house.

The room was as wide as it was long. She reconfirmed her

estimate of around thirty feet. It was a perfect square. She made her way to the far wall, which overlooked the lake. Although it seemed like every wall was overlooking something. She felt as if she were in some sort of life-sized snow globe. Or snow cube, in this case.

She walked past the low platform bed, which sat in the middle of the room, in front of the fireplace, which took up the middle third of the stone wall. In one corner of the room sat a glass table that was used as a desk. It was turned at an angle so the person sitting there would be able to see through either "wall" to the lake and the forest. In the opposite corner was a large, well-worn leather chair and ottoman with a cream fleece throw draped over its back.

That was it—bed, desk, and chair, and chair and ottoman. And yet, that was truly all you needed with this spectacular view encompassing you.

"What do you think?" Sawyer said from behind her.

She whirled, ready to tell him how incredible it was, when she finally saw the stone wall from the inside.

A huge fireplace was in the center, roaring as promised. Or if not roaring now, it would soon be again, as Sawyer was adding wood from a built-in wood box to the side. He must have started the fire when he'd dropped off Lucy and the first round of supplies. Now that she thought of it, she should be freezing, but the room held a warm glow from the fire. That was the reason he'd wanted to bring Lucy up first—to get the fire going so it wouldn't be so cold inside.

She watched as he bent over to add another log, not sure if she was more impressed with his thoughtfulness or his awesome butt in those jeans.

The butt, definitely. It was nice to walk into a cozy, heated room. But it was going to be heaven spending the weekend with that lean, muscular body.

"Well?" he asked, standing up and putting his hands on his hips.

"Spectacular," she answered without hesitation. *And the house ain't bad either.*

She moved toward the stone wall, taking it all in. To the right of the fireplace—the side without the entrance door—there was a sink, countertop, cupboards, and a pantry, which Sawyer was now filling with items from the duffle.

To the left was more shelving—some open, some with doors.

"Go ahead, poke around," he said. "I know you're dying to."

She was. And not in a girlfriend sort of way—curiosity about her date—but from an engineering standpoint.

"You sure?"

"Have at it," he said, sweeping his arm to encompass the entire place.

She had at it.

After examining every bit of the stone wall and all the different cubbyholes and shelves, the practicality weighted with the creativity astounded her. The shelving and fireplace, as well as the sink, were the depth of the four-step entryway, giving the whole wall an even, flush feel, even though some of it was open and some not.

And then she had at it with the glass cube itself, admiring the sheer genius that came up with not only the idea, but also the know-how to be able to pull it off.

"You did all of this yourself?" she asked.

"The design and most of the construction, yes. There were things I couldn't do by myself, and my brothers would help when I'd get to those parts."

"How long did it take you to build it?"

"About three years. I'd work on it on and off. Couldn't get much done during the winters."

"Do you live here?"

"No. Although I spend more time up here in the summer." He chuckled a little. "I can rough it okay, but I need more than a biffy and a jump in the lake on a permanent basis."

He pointed through the wall—*through the wall!*—at the

outhouse, or "biffy," apparently.

"See, I'm truly not the Brockway Mountain Hermit."

"No. More like the Tip of Copper Harbor Semi-Hermit."

"Exactly," he said, and their eyes met. And held. And suddenly the intense daylight seemed very, very bright.

Sixteen

—ɷ—

NOW WHAT? SAWYER WONDERED AS DENI BROKE EYE contact first and turned around to face the lake.

He'd wanted to get her up here early, so he'd suggested the 9am start. Now it was noon, with the whole day and night ahead of them. And as much as he wanted to get her naked, he supposed he should let the girl get past lunchtime first.

He watched as she ran her hands along the seams of the clear braces he'd created to bracket the large, double-paned thermal glass. Her fingers glided up and down, and he imagined those fingers gliding up and down his chest.

Preferably down.

She stepped even closer to the glass and blew on it, ostensibly to see if it would fog up. It didn't. He'd made sure of that, given the extreme weather this property endured. He could think of something else she could breathe on to see if it would steam up.

Okay, enough. He wasn't some fourteen-year-old boy. His brain knew that, but his cock was having a hard time believing it.

God, her ass looked incredible in those snug jeans. He should talk to Andy about making them mandatory in the office.

"It's just amazing," she said.

His eyes still on her ass, he answered, "It is, isn't it."

She turned around, and he didn't even try to hide that he was checking her out. He grinned at her, and that pretty flush splashed across her cheeks.

Suddenly, the room seemed very small and very warm, even though the fire had just barely taken the chill out of the room, and he was tempted to pull their coats back out until the place warmed up a bit more.

But that went against every instinct he was feeling right now—to get more clothes off of them both, not more on.

He kept his eyes on her as he walked back to the fireplace and threw another log on for good measure.

"It should be bearable soon."

"It's fine now." Her voice was soft and quiet. She took a step toward him. "I have to tell you. I want to be here, and this place is so great. But I have to admit I'm…a little…nervous."

"Listen, if this is too soon, let's forget it. We'll have some lunch, maybe take the snowshoes down to the lake to look around, and then head back to town." He walked the small distance between them and took one of her hands in his. It should have been cold, but it wasn't. He could almost feel the blood coursing through her.

"It's not too soon," she said, and he almost dropped to his knees in gratitude. And then the thought of being on his knees in front of her made his cock jerk to attention. Not that he hadn't been semi-hard since she'd been sitting behind him on the snowmobile.

"In some ways it feels like"—he tried to focus on what she was saying and not on how he wanted to taste her all over—"not only isn't it not too soon, but it feels like not soon enough, you know?"

"Oh, I know," he said quickly, and she smiled.

"And it's been a while for me."

"Me too," he said.

"Since…not since…?"

"No, not since Molly died. But…a while. And the first time since Molly died that…." He stopped, not sure how to phrase it, not sure he really knew what he meant himself.

He moved even closer, sliding his feet to either side of hers, getting as close to her as possible. She was wearing a thermal Henley under her sweater, and he could see her pulse beat ever so slightly at the base of her neck. He ran his fingers along the back of her hand and felt the matching pulse point. Needing desperately to have his tongue on that spot on her neck, he leaned down, taking in the scent of her as he did.

"That what?" she said, then her breath hitched as his tongue flicked across her skin. At first it was almost a lick, but then he settled his mouth on her.

"Hmmm?" he said in answer, alternately kissing and sucking on the tender skin of her graceful neck.

"The first time since Molly that…what?" she said as she dropped her neck back to give him better access.

His head tried to clear, to return to what he'd been saying, what she wanted to clarify.

Oh. Oh, yeah. He left her neck and pulled his hand away from hers. He gently held her head with both hands and brought her face to his.

"It's the first time since Molly that it's mattered," he whispered.

And then he kissed her.

IT COULD HAVE BEEN A LINE. But why bother? She was already here and had just told him it wasn't too soon for her.

God, it had seemed like ages—this past week of being near him every day and not being able to touch him or kiss him.

Besides, Sawyer wasn't the type of guy to throw out lines.

It mattered to him. *She* mattered to him.

She wrapped her arms around his neck and returned his kiss, mating her tongue with his. He smelled so good, like pine trees and the outdoors.

She felt Lucy twining herself around their legs. Sawyer broke away from their kiss just long enough to say "Luce, go lie down." Which did the trick.

His mouth returned to Deni's with a different rhythm, a harder pressure, and it felt so right, so natural, to slide her feet forward so that her body was pressed tightly against his.

She could feel his hard-on and tilted her hips into it, eliciting a groan from him. His hands moved down her back and cupped her butt, pulling her even tighter into him.

Which still wasn't close enough. She twined her arms even tighter around him as his hands slid up from her ass to burrow under her sweater, pulling it up.

She broke away from him as he urged her arms up and the sweater off.

"Too many damn clothes," he growled.

"It's Michigan in the winter," she explained as she started unbuttoning his flannel shirt. "What do you expect?"

"I expect..." He started to work on her jeans as she finally got his shirt unbuttoned and peeled it off of him, leaving him in a green thermal shirt.

The green of his shirt made his green eyes pop even more as they bored into hers. "I expect," he continued, reaching once again for her fly, "to have you naked in about ten seconds."

"Sounds good to me," she said, brushing her hand against his erection before snapping open the button.

"Really?" he said with almost a hiss when she touched him. "You okay with not a lot of foreplay? 'Cause I'm dying to be inside you. Deep inside you."

The moisture between her legs intensified. "I think we've had a week of foreplay." She unzipped his fly. "I want you deep inside me, too. *Bad.*"

He had her jeans unzipped and was pushing them down over her hips when he stopped.

"Are you wearing long johns?" he said, amusement in his

voice. He stepped back, away from her. Her hand, which was just inches from his hard cock, fell away.

"You told me to," she said, maybe a bit too defensively. And it was a good thing she had, too, or she'd have been freezing on that snowmobile.

"I know, I know," he said as he moved back to her and quickly pulled her jeans down, helping her balance as she stepped out of them. "And I'm oh-so-glad that you did."

She moved to touch him again, but he stepped back out of her reach.

"My God," he said as he looked at her. "That may be the sexiest thing I've ever seen."

She looked down at herself. Red rag-wool socks, white long johns with pink roses, and a matching thermal shirt, also with roses.

"I did wear sexy underwear," she said, and reached to peel off her shirt. He held out his hand in a "stop" motion.

"No, don't you dare. I'm serious! You look so damn sexy right now."

"Seriously?"

"Oh, yeah," he said, taking another step away—*away!*—from her. His feet hit the wooden platform of the bed and he sank down onto it. The low height of the bed had his knees almost at eye level. He swung his elbows over them, his hands dangling between his legs.

"Lose the ponytail holder," he said. His voice was huskier than it had been a minute ago, and Deni felt her flush leave her face and move south to all her other parts. Her very achy other parts.

She reached behind her for her ponytail holder. Yeah, she didn't need to use two hands and probably didn't need to arch her back—pushing her boobs out—to do it, but she did it anyway.

And the glint of his green eyes told her he liked it.

"Shake your hair out," he whispered. She did, once again

using both hands and way more body swaying than was necessary.

The glint in his eyes was now matched by the grin on his face. "Back up a step. Put yourself right against the glass."

She expected it to be freezing against her butt and back, but it wasn't too bad. In fact, it felt refreshing on her quickly overheating body. She dropped her head back, but kept her eyes on Sawyer.

"Damn, but that's hot. Turn—wait. Slide your socks off."

She did, using each foot to pull the other sock off, still leaning against the glass wall.

"I've been wondering since the day I met you if…." She kicked the socks aside. He leaned forward, elbows still on his knees. "Yes, they match."

"What matches?"

"The hot pink fingernails. I wondered if your toes were done in the same color."

"Seriously? You wondered that?"

"Yep. And I'm not even a foot-fetish guy."

"But you're apparently a thermal-long-johns-fetish guy?"

"Apparently. Who knew?"

She placed her hands behind her, palms down against the glass, and ran them up and down the cool surface. The pink of her nails was shockingly bright in the sun.

She said a silent thank you to Alison for making her step out of her comfort zone.

"You look damn good anytime. But right here, dressed like that, with Lake Superior as your backdrop? Unbelievable."

She ached to touch him, to have him touch her. To taste and be tasted. She started to move toward the bed, and his knees straightened, legs dropping, opening wide for her. And then his head jerked, and he put a hand up for her to stop again.

"Wait. Did you say you had sexy underwear on underneath that?"

"Well, yeah. I knew what was going to happen tonight—

evidently *today*." She took back the step she'd just taken forward, placing her back once again against the wall. "I am a logical, sensible engineer and when you say 'dress warmly, like long johns warmly,' I'm going to dress long johns warmly."

"I love a woman who can take direction," he said with a grin.

"But," she continued, "besides being that practical engineer, I'm also a woman. A woman who wants…."

"To look sexy for her man?" he finished.

"Are you? Are you my man?" They both knew what she was asking. Was this to be a lovely "snack"? A fulfilling, passion-filled weekend that was a fitting conclusion to a week-long attraction?

Or was it the beginning?

"Take your shirt off," he said, the earlier humor gone from his voice. His tone made her nipples ache.

She reached for the hem of her thermal shirt but paused just as the skin above her long johns was bared.

"The shirt is going to come off either way. This *is* going to happen," she said. "But answer my question."

She didn't have to add "be honest." It was a given with Sawyer. She'd learned that even in the ten days she'd known him.

His eyes left her hand on her shirt, came to her face, her mouth, then held her eyes.

"I don't know how much of me is left. Ten days ago I would have said nothing was there…a void. That I couldn't be what you wanted, that a weekend, or two, would be the extent of it."

"And now? Ten days later?"

"I'm still not sure how much I have to give. And you need to know that up front. But, damn Deni, you make me want to try. You make me want to come out of my hermit cave and make love in the sunlight."

Her breath hitched, caught in her throat. Which was just as well, since she had no response to what he'd just said. She wanted to run the four paces to the bed and fling herself on top of him, but she stayed where she was.

"So, yes," he continued, "I *am* your man."

"Good," she whispered.

He nodded his agreement. "Now take off the fucking shirt."

Seventeen

—⟋⟍—

SHE SMILED, THAT LITTLE DIMPLE APPEARING ON HER left cheek.

"Take off *yours*," she said.

He loved the little flares of attitude that popped up from her. Not enough to be high-maintenance or irrational. But just enough to keep him on his toes...and make his already throbbing hard-on ache that much more.

His flannel shirt already on the floor beside Deni (next to those hot pink toes!), he reached behind him to the collar of his thermal Henley and yanked it over his head, throwing it to the side. It landed on top of his other flannel shirt with a soft noise, causing Lucy to look up from where she lay beneath his desk.

"Go to sleep, girl," he said. She eyed him warily and then looked at Deni before dropping her head to her paws. He would have put her outside, but it was too cold for her to be out there for as long as he intended to be naked with Deni.

He might emotionally scar his dog, but there was no way in hell he was going to stop now.

"Your turn," he said to Deni, nodding with his chin toward her top. Well, to her chest area specifically, which he was dying to see. Other than that brief moment in his truck when she was down to her camisole, this shirt was the clingiest thing he'd seen her in. He suspected that her loose sweaters were hiding a semi-spectacular rack.

She lifted the shirt and the pale expanse of her waist was slowly exposed. Then red—*red!*—satin bra cups, a milky-white chest, and that long, elegant neck. She tossed the shirt on the ever-growing pile of clothes on the floor beside her.

Nothing semi about it. "Spectacular."

A flush crept up her neck, but she didn't look away from him, didn't drop her head in embarrassment. Good thing, too, because there was no light to turn off, no blinds to close. Everything they were about to do was going to be in the cold light of day.

And he intended to do everything.

"Slide your long johns down just so they rest on your hips."

She furrowed her brows, confused at his request. Well, of course she didn't know how smoking hot she looked with the white cotton slung low on her hips and her red panties still mostly hidden.

What the hell were those kind of panties called? Boy shorts? Something like that? God, they made her look all woman— nothing boy about them.

"Unhook your bra but don't take it off." She reached behind her, making her tits rise, and unhooked the bra.

"Drop your arms." She did. The bra straps stayed on her shoulders, the cups in place, but there was something about seeing the back flapping loosely, like at any minute the whole thing could just slide off her body.

He'd been picturing Deni naked or in some sort of undress every night of the past week when he'd come home after a long day of working next to her.

Been jerking off to that vision most nights. Okay, every night.

So it seemed entirely natural when he slid his hand down his belly to his jeans. She'd already undone his button, so he eased the zipper down over his erection and then stroked his hand up his briefs, never taking his eyes from her.

Her breathing grew deeper and her tits lifted a little higher, nipples straining against the red satin.

"You like that?" he asked as he stroked himself again.

She nodded, and—good God—licked her lips, then bit the lower one. That mouth. That full, juicy, so kissable, made-for-sucking-cock mouth.

He stroked himself a little harder, but not faster. Just as he was about to tell her to get her adorable ass over to the bed, she rubbed her thighs together, trying to give herself some relief.

He levered himself to the edge of the low bed. Hell, it was easier to crawl over to her than to get up and walk. And something seemed very right about crawling on his hands and knees to the woman who had quite possibly pulled him from a ten-year semi-madness. There was almost as much gratitude in what he felt for her as desire.

Her hips twitched, and her thighs rubbed against each other again as he neared her.

Nope. Definitely more desire than gratitude.

He knelt before her and looked up. She reached down, putting her hands in his hair. The bra gave way with the movement, sliding down her arms. She took her hands from him for just long enough to free the bra and let it fall to the floor, where it landed on one of her feet. He brushed it away, the red sliding away to reveal those pink toenails. He placed his hand on the arch of her foot, hoping she wasn't too cold. He could hear the fire crackle behind him, as the room warmed up fast, but the place had still been absolutely freezing when he'd dropped off Lucy and started the fire.

But no, her feet weren't cold, and her hips rolled once again at his touch. He placed his other hand on her bare foot and took hold of the knit material at her ankles. He skimmed his hands up to her knees and then back down, pulling the material with him, slowly revealing the red panties and then the white of her thighs.

His hands skimmed up again, grabbing her long johns as he lowered them. He could smell her arousal and he became that much harder. Thank God he'd unzipped.

Her long johns finally pooled at her ankles, he lifted first one leg and then the other and slid the underwear off. She held on to his shoulders for balance and kept her hands on him, stroking and massaging his tight neck.

"God, that feels good," he murmured against her belly, tenderly kissing the warm skin. He straightened, while still kneeling. Her tits were just a little too high for his mouth, but his hand skimmed up the back of her legs and squeezed that great ass—causing a cute little half-moan, half-squeak from her. He moved to her waist and then around to hold those high, firm breasts.

Definitely all moan from her this time. Her head fell back, her shoulders and ass leaning into the glass, pushing her hips even closer to him—right where he wanted her.

"God, I can smell how turned on you are. How wet you must be."

"I...it...." She seemed embarrassed now, for the first time. She started to take her hands from him.

His heart leapt. No way did he want to embarrass her. "Shhh, no, it's okay," he said softly, kissing her right above the waistband of her panties. "I love it. It makes me even harder catching your scent. Seeing your wetness...right here." He rubbed a finger along her cleft, her moisture showing through the thin fabric.

"Sawyer..." she gasped, "I'm so...."

"Ready" was the word she was looking for. He knew it firsthand.

"I know, baby. It's not going be long and languid this first time. It's been building since that night at the Commodore."

"Yes," she said. She dropped her head even farther against the wall, arching her neck and pushing the breast he currently held deeper into his hand.

He rolled her nipple between his thumb and finger and then pinched it lightly, eliciting a throaty moan from Deni.

He wanted to give her beautiful breasts the attention they deserved, to suckle them and fondle and lift and squeeze, but they were slightly out of reach of his mouth. No doubt she'd bend down if he told her to, but when faced—literally—with her sweet arousal at mouth level....

He trailed his hand down from her breast—much to her dissatisfaction, if her soft grunt was any indication. "It's okay. You're going to like this better, and I need two hands." She stroked her hands down his back as far as they'd reach and then up again, squeezing his shoulders.

Sexy as they were, the panties had to go. He nuzzled her right above the waistband as his hands peeled the red fabric over her toned thighs and down her long, shapely legs. He lifted her foot again to take the panties off, but this time he widened her stance when placing the foot back on the hardwood. Running his hands up the backs of her legs, he circled around and his thumbs slid through her damp curls to open her even damper folds.

Deni's sex was a place to study and revere, to lose yourself in experiencing its wonder. Pink and soft, with a hood to hide its buried treasure and a passage to hidden pleasure—an engineering feat to surpass all others.

"Jesus," he sighed as he put his mouth on her. She jerked, and her hands left his shoulders, one grabbing his nape, the other lodging in his hair. She tasted so good. Musky and sweet at the same time.

But it was her noises that made him even more excited and touched him in a place he'd long thought dead. Soft sighs and then a small grunt as he put a finger inside her. And then a full-blown gasp as he circled the finger before adding another.

"Sawyer," she said on a moan. "That feels so good."

He wanted to answer her, but he wanted his tongue on her clit even more. Unveiling the hidden nub with his thumb and middle finger he swirled a finger around, joining his tongue, while his other hand started a slow movement deep inside her.

"Oh, God. Yes, that's...."

One last wiggle against her bud and she let go, her muscles clenching against his fingers, her hips bucking, tits jiggling. A sight to behold.

Dear God, he was glad he saw her come for him for the first

time in the glorious, blaring daylight. She was beautiful and he felt his heart thaw even more.

He sucked on her longer, trying to make it last as his fingers worked her. Finally, she slumped forward, sliding her hands down his back. Rising from his knees, he put a shoulder under her and lifted, getting to his feet with her draped over his shoulder, that sweet ass within biting distance of his mouth.

A soft nip had her lifting her head, as if coming back from the dead. Before she could object that she was being carried like a sack of potatoes, he laid her down on the bed and then joined her, settling himself on top of her.

Her legs immediately fell open, making room for him as he propped himself up on his forearms so he could see her face, see her pretty brown eyes as she finally opened them and looked at him.

Eighteen

—◊—

THOSE GREEN EYES STARING INTENTLY DOWN AT HER were almost enough to make her come again. God, how could one man be so sexy? She raised a hand to run her fingers across the stubble on his cheek.

"Hey," he whispered.

"Hey," she answered. Looking at him, and seeing how he watched her, the numbness of the past few months felt miles away. Though she was surrounded by ice and snow, she felt warmer than she had in a long time. She curled her fingers around the back of his neck and gently tugged his face down to hers to kiss him.

She could taste herself on him, and though just a moment ago she'd thought herself completely sated, she rolled her hips underneath his, wanting more.

"I know." He answered her unspoken request. "I need to be there, too."

He sat up, kneeling between her spread legs, and then stepped back off the bed, standing up. He peeled his jeans and briefs down and off. The sunlight was directly above them now and it seemed as if it were directing a big solar spotlight right down on all his naked glory.

There was that sexy chest, built from what she now knew was a *ton* of wood chopping and various other projects around this place. Hair was sprinkled across his chest in just the right amounts. Just enough to make her tingle when it touched her. It thinned out to a trail that led down his abs to his large erection, which he now took in hand and stroked a few times.

How hot was that?

His thighs were muscled too, but there seemed to be a leanness to him as well.

If not able to accurately describe his physique in her lust-muddled thoughts, she was certainly able to appreciate it.

"Holy wah," she whispered, the phrase finally rolling off her tongue with Yooper ease.

He grinned at her and then bent over and pulled his wallet out of the back pocket of his jeans.

Guessing what he was retrieving, she said, "It's okay. I'm on the pill."

"You are?" he asked, trying to hide his surprise. "I mean… I didn't… I guess I just…."

"It's okay. I've been on it since October to try to regulate my periods. They were all over the place."

"Oh."

"Not that you get to comment on why I may or may not be on birth control."

It was the only time she'd seen anything resembling embarrassment on Sawyer Beck's face. "Of course not. I didn't mean—"

She let him off the hook. "I know. I was just playing with you."

He narrowed his eyes at her. "So, you want to play, do you?" He lowered himself to the bed and crawled up it so that he was looming over her on all fours. "You sure about that? I play to win."

She drifted her hand over those gorgeous abs and wrapped her fingers around him, taking up the stroking motion. "I'm sure," she said, giving a squeeze.

"Jesus," he hissed. He dropped his head and kissed her hard, devouring her mouth with his. Then he lifted his head and said, "Remind me never to challenge a woman who has her hand wrapped around my dick."

"Good life lesson," she teased, and stroked up and around the tip.

"So, you're on the pill. What about the other? I'm clean, but if you want me to wear a rubber—"

"I'm clean, too. And no, I don't want you to wear one. I want to feel every inch of you." As if to demonstrate her point, she stroked the length of him again. Her other hand slid over his back to his butt.

"Well, then," he whispered, and lowered himself to the cradle her legs created. He kissed her again, tenderly this time. He started at her mouth, then moved to her jaw and then her neck. His mouth next to her ear, he whispered, "Put me inside you."

She guided him to her, gently easing him into her opening. She ran her hand up his side and wrapped it around his neck as he drove into her.

A soft gasp escaped her and she tensed for just a second, getting used to him. He felt so right inside her, stretching her. Everything about being with Sawyer felt right to her.

"Okay?" he whispered as he kissed down her neck.

She moved her hips, eliciting a gasp from him, and answered, "Yes. Very okay."

He slowly started to move. He raised himself up on his hands and looked down at her body. "God, you're perfect."

She'd put on ten pounds this winter, thanks to the SAD-induced carb cravings and lack of desire to exercise. Happily, a small portion of that ten went to her boobs, making her a bit fuller on top than she'd been before.

Pretty much the only benefit to the disorder.

They were just as sensitive as always, though, which she quickly found out as Sawyer paid them an extreme amount of attention with his hands. And mouth. And tongue. And his hands again.

Her breathing, not quite back to normal from her standing-buck-naked-in-front-of-a-glass-wall orgasm, ratcheted up again, causing a truly heaving bosom.

Which only garnered it more attention as he sucked on one breast and then the other, pushing them together and gently biting on her nipples.

She squirmed beneath him, her tension building. Moving her hands from around his neck, down to his butt, she grabbed on, trying to pull him deeper, urging him to go faster.

"You need it now?" he said, his voice rough and lower than normal. Looking into her eyes, his mouth poised above her breast, he added, "Harder?"

She nodded.

"Faster?"

She nodded again.

"Say it."

She placed her feet on the mattress with legs spread wide and canted her hips. Digging her fingernails—the hot pink fingernails he apparently liked—into his ass, she said, "Fuck me, Sawyer. Hard and fast." She clenched her muscles around his cock.

"Sweet Jesus, you feel so good," he said on a moan as he arched up and started moving faster. Deeper strokes and then a couple of short, hard pumps. Just enough to keep her off balance and unable to meet him halfway.

She thrashed her head from side to side, frustrated.

"Can't get there?" he asked in a teasing voice as he once again slowed down his pace after three hard pumps.

"Sawyer...God, just...."

"Get yourself off. Do it, Deni. Let me see you."

She moved her hand and found her clit. Still so achy from Sawyer's mouth, it only took a few circles with her finger to make her explode.

"Yes, that's it. Christ, you're squeezing me like a vise."

His words in her ear kept the convulsions going as her body shattered. Just when she started to come down, he rose to his knees and held her hips in his hands. He splayed his thighs, draping one of hers over each of his and put his hands under her ass, holding her in place as he began to wildly drive into her.

She didn't come down. No, she spiraled even higher.

"That's it," he urged. "Come again, Deni. Come while I spill inside you."

His words, in that gruff voice, made the spiral shatter again and she gripped the sheets beneath her, Sawyer's body out of reach.

"Ride it out, baby," he said, pumping even deeper than she thought possible. "God, yes. Fuck." He groaned on the last thrust, and she felt the heat of him inside her, his moisture joining hers.

After one last piston of his hips, he collapsed on her, catching himself at the last minute with his hands, which he buried in her hair.

"Holy wah," he whispered in her ear.

She smiled, though he couldn't see her. Sliding her legs back down to the mattress and twining her legs with his, she wrapped her arms around his shoulders and kissed his neck.

Eventually he moved off her—and out of her—and lay beside her.

"That was amazing," he said, his hand moving up and down her body.

"You got that right," she answered, not even having the strength to turn on her side to cuddle into him.

"You know what I would love to do right now?" he asked.

Visions of kinky sex games floated through her mind. Some appealing, some not so much. "What?" she hesitantly answered.

He chuckled. "What are you imagining?"

"That's just it. I can't imagine."

"Well, relax. I was just thinking how much I'd love to take a nap, to hold you in my arms while I slept the afternoon away."

"Oh, well, that sounds lovely."

"You sound disappointed. Did you want to go snowshoeing or something? A trek through the woods?"

Both of those options would have sounded great six months ago, but they felt too daunting to her now. "No, thanks. The nap sounds lovely, really. I'm just surprised by the way you said it. Like it seemed so 'something new' to you. Don't most men fall asleep after sex anyway? Especially sex that…."

"Fucking good?"

"Strenuous."

He placed a kiss on her nipple and then moved up to kiss her neck and then cheek. He gently put a hand on her face, turning her head to look at him. He propped himself up on one elbow, looking down at her.

"I have trouble sleeping sometimes."

She'd only known him for ten days, but at times like this she felt she'd known him forever. He was prevaricating for sure. "Sawyer…." she said in her best scold.

"Okay. Not sometimes. All the time. I have a lot of trouble sleeping. So, yeah, to say I'd love to take a nap right now? And to actually be able to do it? Pretty 'something new' for me."

She reached up and ran her fingers through his hair, which was sticking up at all angles. Probably from her grabbing handfuls of it when he had his mouth on her.

"Come here," she said softly, and urged him down so that his head rested on her chest. She pulled the comforter around them and then put her arms around him.

"Sleep, Sawyer," she said.

And he did.

Nineteen

He woke first, shocked to find that he'd slept almost three hours. A near-record for him of late, especially because it was in the middle of the day with the sun right overhead. He'd designed the glass roof in the right direction and with just enough pitch so that the strong winds coming off the lake would blow most of the snow off. He made sure to get up here at least twice a month to shovel the roof in case there was a buildup. Roof cave-ins happened all the time in the Copper Country. One from a glass roof would be particularly nasty.

He got up, threw a couple more logs on the fire, and then fed Lucy, praising her for being so mellow during the wrestling match going on in the same room. After gobbling down her dinner, Lucy whined to go out and Sawyer opened the door for her. "Don't go too far," he told her, and Lucy nodded her head as if giving him a beleaguered "yes, Dad."

Deni was stirring by now, and he climbed back into bed with her. As she rolled over toward him, the sheet caught, baring her upper body. She started to reach for the sheet to cover herself, but he put his hand on hers, stopping her. She opened her eyes then, and a small, almost shy smile crept up her face.

"Did you sleep at all?" she asked.

He pulled the sheet back even farther, studying her as he nodded. "I just woke up. I slept like a log."

"That's good," she said, and stretched, giving him an eyeful. He noticed stubble burn all over her creamy skin—particularly on her thighs and tits. He could just imagine it burned elsewhere on her, too.

"I could say I'm sorry and that I'll shave next time before I have my mouth all over your body…but I kind of like that my mark is on you."

The flush rose over her as he leaned down and tongued one of the places that he'd paid particular attention to earlier in the day.

"So…no shower, right?"

"Uh-uh. That's okay, I kind of like the smell of sex on you," he said. He reached out and cupped a breast, brushing his thumb over her nipple.

"Mmm. That feels good," she said, sighing. "And I like the smell of you on me, too. But I'd really love a shower right now."

"Sorry, no shower. Sauna, though."

"That'd be nice. But you can't jump in the lake this time of year."

"The hardcores roll in the snow in wintertime to cool off instead of jumping in the lake."

"Seriously?"

"Yep."

"Have you ever tried it?"

He tore himself away from her delectable body and swung his legs to the floor. He swatted Deni on the butt, threw his flannel shirt at her, and said, "Nope, but it seems to be a day for firsts. Let's give it a try."

SHE WATCHED FROM THE HOUSE—cottage? camp? ice cube?—as Sawyer made another trek on snowshoes to the sauna house to feed the fire, Lucy prancing behind him. Deni still wore just the shirt that he'd thrown at her over two hours ago. It hung down her thighs with the sleeves rolled up.

While waiting for the sauna to heat, in between his trips of fire feeding, he'd fed her a lunch of cheese, meats, and crackers and had opened a bottle of wine, which was nearly gone.

When he disappeared into the sauna house and she could no longer admire his broad back and long legs, even clad in a parka and denim as they were, she moved and once again turned her attention to the marvel that was his secret hiding place.

In the winter, with the snow on all three sides, all it needed were some icicles hanging from the ceiling and it really would be the Fortress of Solitude.

She admired his creativity. In the corner next to the stone wall, he'd built a glass alcove that was one panel wide and two high, which opened like a refrigerator, creating a cooler of sorts. She didn't know what served that purpose in the summertime, but for now, she put the leftover cheese and meat back in their packaging and placed them in the "icebox."

She'd seen a couple of coolers on a shelf back in the pole barn. She supposed that's what he used in the summertime when he stayed up here for any length of time.

In the pole barn, she'd also seen an ATV. The path they'd taken up here had been wide enough for a pickup, but the terrain was too treacherous for Sawyer's truck, even in the summer.

She wondered if the harness that he'd made for Lucy to ride on the snowmobile was the same one he used on the ATV. She'd be interested to see. Knowing Sawyer, he'd have made sure it was multi-purpose.

She tried not to get ahead of herself and wonder if he'd bring her here in the summer or if they'd even be together by then. No way did she want to get on an obsessive loop about that. He said he wanted to try for something real, something more than just hooking up.

They had a ton in common. She was already three quarters of the way in love with him (the engineer in her calculating down to fractions even in this), and he seemed to feel strongly enough about her to come out of his hibernation.

She started to feel her focus fracturing, her mind going fuzzy. She turned to face the lake again and breathed deeply, forcing her brain to slow down.

Just focus on a point on the horizon and stick to that. Let thoughts of a future with—or without—Sawyer float away as if they were on a boat headed for Canada.

Memories of looking for Canada on that long-ago day on top of Brockway with her father came flooding over her, filling her with both happiness and grief.

She placed her hands against the wall and leaned forward, letting the emotions flood over her, careful to keep them in check and not get sucked in too deeply. No way did she want the lead blanket covering her on this weekend getaway.

She heard Sawyer come in, but stayed where she was, trying to regain her focus.

"Sauna's ready. We—" She started to turn, but he quickly and forcefully said, "No. Don't move. Stay just like that."

Afraid there was something wrong—were there snakes in the wintertime?—she stayed still. She heard him take off his coat and boots. "Sawyer? Is everything okay? What's going on?"

"Shhh," he softly said. He was right behind her now. Killing the snake or whatever it was? "You just looked so…Christ, so hot…standing like that."

Oh, was that all? No snake? She started to drop her arms, but he put a hand on her backside, which was slightly tilted out.

"No. Keep your arms up there. Brace yourself. I can't not take you like this. You look amazing. All long legs, with your hair streaming down the back of my shirt."

The timbre of his voice, and more importantly the words he said, had her leaving her arms where they were. Not only that, but she leaned over a little farther and spread her legs wider.

"Yes," he hissed. She heard his zipper and the rustle of

denim, then cool air as he lifted his shirt from where it fell over her bottom and the back of her thighs.

"Such a sweet ass," he said as he caressed her.

She was damp immediately and arched her back to give him better access. His rough hands took hold of her hips, tilting her even more. One of his hands left her hip, but she soon felt it probing her folds, sliding along her clit.

"So wet already. You want it like this too, don't you?"

"Yes," she said, and braced her arms. Her head fell forward, but she could still see the gorgeous view of the lake.

He was inside her quickly and powerfully. She had a moment's thought that it was a good thing these clear brackets were designed by Sawyer Beck. Otherwise, they'd likely be going through the glass panels the way he pounded into her, one of his arms around her waist to steady her, another in the middle of her back, his flannel shirt pushed up with his hand.

It was fast and desperate and they both came quickly. Breathing heavily, locked together, his head dropped to her back. She could feel his hot breath against her neck, making her clench with an aftershock.

"Holy shit. You're going to be the death of me," he said into her ear. "I'm not some guy in his twenties, you know. I'm an old fart of forty."

She snorted. "Yeah, you're practically decrepit. About time to get you a walker or wheelchair or something." She tightened around him again.

He nipped her neck and then pulled out of her, spinning her around. His mouth was on hers before the gasp left her. She sought out his tongue and sucked on it, which made him back her into the wall, pinning her to it with his body.

"One difference. If I were twenty, I'd already be hard again and back inside you."

She laughed. Twice already today and it was barely five o'clock. "I think you're doing just fine, old man." She stepped away from him and across the room, toward her discarded clothes.

"Did you say the sauna's ready? Because suddenly I'm feeling very dirty."

Twenty

—⚊—

HE LOVED SEEING HER IN HIS SHIRT AND NOTHING else. So he just wrapped her in a blanket and carried her out to the sauna so she wouldn't have to put everything back on just to take it off again once they entered the small building.

"Um...I need to...you know," she said. Once they were in the changing room part of the sauna house, he took off his boots, slid them on her feet, and got her into his snowshoes. She made her way around the small building and reappeared a bit later.

"Get me into the sauna," she said, her thighs already turning pink.

"Hop in. I need to water a tree myself."

When he had taken care of business and removed his clothes, he threw more wood into the small sauna stove and then entered the tiny room.

Deni was a naked vision sitting on the top bench, her legs stretched out across the cedar planks.

"Well, if I wasn't sweating already, the sight of you would do it."

She laughed and threw water from the buckets of melted snow onto the rocks, creating a screaming hiss of steam, which rose and swirled around them. She made to move her legs as he stepped upon the bottom bench, but he held them, lifted them as he sat and then laid them across his lap. He ran his hands up and down the length of them, then settled them on her feet.

His thumb glided over her pink toenails.

"Ah, this feels wonderful. I can't believe how worn out I am from basically doing nothing," Deni said, stretching and raising her hands over her head to touching the ceiling. Her chest rose, breasts jutting out. The room was steamy and sweat glistened on her pale skin.

"God, I love your body" slipped out of him before he could stop himself. The look of delight on her face made him glad he'd been so unguarded, if only for a moment.

She lowered her arms, but not before she lifted the heavy mass of hair off her shoulders and pinned it against the wall behind her head. "Thanks. I think it's safe to say I'm a big fan of yours as well."

He smiled, slicking the moisture off his arms. He'd built a strong fire, and the sauna was one of the hotter ones he'd taken.

"But thank you for saying it," she added. "I've actually put on some weight this winter and was a little self-conscious about the thought of being naked. Stripping down in front of a glass wall got me over that pretty quickly."

"You certainly had room for the extra weight." She was long and lean, but had nicely curved hips and legs. And tits that perfectly overflowed in his hands.

"I'm usually pretty active. Hiking in the fall and spring. Water stuff in the summer. Skiing in the winter."

"But you aren't lately?"

She shrugged and then leaned over, grabbed the small dipper from the bucket, and threw another ladle of water onto the rocks.

She didn't answer him. Was Andy working them all too hard at the office so that they didn't have time for their private lives? They certainly had this past week, but he'd thought that was only because of the time frame of the driving range bid.

"But why don't…." The words died as she swung her legs from his lap and climbed down from the bench, giving him a steamy view of her shapely ass.

"Let's just see if you aren't more of a twenty-year-old than you think, eh?" she said as she stood in front of him. She knelt on the bottom bench, bringing her even with his now-hardening cock.

"See?" she said as she leaned into him. "Why, you're a veritable teenager."

Then she closed her mouth over his cock, and he dropped his head back against the cedar wall, not sure that he could stand the heat.

THEY DID ROLL IN THE SNOW to cool off, the crystalline texture of the white stuff prickling her sensitized skin. Deni couldn't tell if the sensation was more pain or pleasure, but she liked it.

Sawyer had put several buckets of snow in the sauna room when he'd started the fire so they had plenty of warm water to shower with when they were finally ready.

Deni sat on the bottom bench while Sawyer poured dippers of water over her hair and then shampooed and rinsed it. He then lathered up a loofa and scrubbed her back—and other places.

When it was his turn, she knelt next to him on the bottom bench instead of sitting above him, and gave him the same treatment. He wrapped an arm around her waist, caressing her butt as she shampooed him. She returned the distraction by *accidently* shoving her boobs in his face as she rinsed conditioner out of his hair.

Squeaky clean, she kept only her towel on, hanging on to his flannel shirt as he wrapped the blanket around her after he'd dressed and donned the snowshoes.

As he carried her back to the glass house, she wrapped her arms around him and burrowed her face into his neck, breathing him in deeply.

He smelled of pine trees and soap, as she supposed she did, but it was incredibly sexy on him and just utilitarian on her.

It was dark now, the daylight hours in such short supply this time of year. (And she knew to the minute how much daylight they gained each day—she'd Googled it during a particularly SAD day.)

He set her on the steps inside the door and then called for Lucy, who happily went outside with her master.

"There are candles and matches on the mantel. Once you light a few of them, you'll be able to see the other candles that are in one of the cabinets. Light a bunch of them."

"Got it," she said, and made her way to the mantel, led by the glow of the dying fire. She threw the blanket off, tossing it on the bed. Dressed only in the long bath towel, she slid her hands along the mantel until she felt a pillar candle with a box of matches next to it.

She lit each of the candles on the mantel and then found the others—all thick pillar candles on holders—and lit those as well. She placed two of them on Sawyer's glass desk and one on the glass side table that was next to the leather chair and ottoman.

The glow from the candles bounced off the glass walls, creating an atmosphere of shadows and reflections.

She took the towel off and found her pile of clothes. She started to put on the red bra and panties, but decided to go with just the long johns top and bottom.

Something glinted from the mantel as she put a log onto the fire and stirred up the coals. Putting the poker back into its holder, she took the candle closest to her and held it up to what was a large glass vase filled nearly to the brim with stones. Turning the candle, the stones shone different colors and sizes, though none were more than the size of a quarter. Some were the size of pebbles. Agates, what looked to be more than a few greenstones, and some just plain-old-pretty rocks.

"I pick those up on my walks on the beach," said Sawyer from behind her. Lucy bounded up the stairs and came to rub herself against Deni's leg.

Deni absently petted the dog while still shining the candle along the collection of stones. "They're beautiful."

"Some are. Some are real finds. Most are just junk from the

beaches around here."

"Are you a gemologist, too? If not certified, do you study them?"

"Not really, no. I bought a couple of books on it when I first started showing up with them in my pockets. More for identification than anything, but that's about the extent of my studying."

"'First started showing up with them'?"

He crossed the room and sat in the old leather chair, pulling the ottoman up and placing his feet on it. The glow from the candle on the table beside him was slightly below him and gave what she could see of his face a haunted glow.

"Come here," he said softly, patting his lap.

She placed the candle back on the mantel and walked to him. The chair was large and there was room for her butt to one side of him. She climbed in with him and started to lay her legs down next to his, but he scooped them up and spread them over his, turning her at a slight angle.

He put his arms across the back of the chair and dropped his head back, looking up. Deni snuggled into the crook of his shoulder and did the same.

"Wow," she whispered, seeing the vast black sky and glowing stars above her.

"Yeah," he said just as softly.

She wanted to nudge him about the weird turn of phrase he'd used about the stones, but sensed he was working up to something. Staying silent, she kept her eyes up. On one of the panes directly above them, there was a faint cast from the candle and she could see the white of her long johns and the clean long-sleeved tee-shirt Sawyer had put on after their sauna.

Sawyer took a deep breath and let it out. One hand left the back of the chair and settled in her still-wet hair, stroking through it, not unlike the absent petting she'd just given Lucy.

"I'd go on these long walks along the shore. Here, at Eagle Harbor, lots of places. Just thinking. And I'd get home and throw my jeans in the dirty clothes and they'd be so heavy. I'd look in the pockets, and they would be full of stones. Pretty ones. Always really nice ones."

"But *you* collected them?" She was kind of confused and had this quick flash of a little man who looked like her vision of Rumplestiltskin, surreptitiously putting pretty stones in Sawyer's pockets while he was walking.

"Yeah, of course. But I never had any recollection of doing it. I always just thought of it as a nice long walk to get some air. To clear the memories." He paused. "Or maybe *to* remember."

"How long did this go on?"

"Oh, a long time. Sometimes I would remember bending down and looking for stones. But there were lots of times that I got home and put my hands in my pockets and there they'd be."

"Well, it was hard to see by candlelight, but they look beautiful."

"They are, most of them. I mean, people take vacations to come up here and hunt for agates and greenstones. And here I was not even fully aware I was collecting them."

"That's a pretty big container, and it's nearly full."

"I don't do it too much anymore. And, of course, I can't during the winters. When I built this place, I thought they'd look nice on the mantel."

"So, Molly never saw this place?" She felt him tense for a second but then relaxed.

"No. I bought the property before Molly died, but she never even got to see it. I hadn't started building this place or anything. I didn't end up doing that for a few years after.

"But I knew exactly what I was going to build, so when this piece of property went on sale, I jumped on it. Things were good at the firm, a lot of business coming in. We were crazy busy."

"Was Molly an engineer, too?" She'd never had any feelings of jealousy about Sawyer's wife, but for some reason she knew it would hurt if Molly had shared with Sawyer the main thing that had brought Deni and Sawyer together.

"No," he said, and she felt herself relax further into him. "We met at Tech, but she was a business major. Her mother was originally from Baraga, and Molly's grandmother was still here. She just really liked the area, so she chose Tech."

Deni knew the feeling, although for her it was also about the top-rated engineering program.

"Her parents died in a house fire during our senior year. Molly was devastated."

"Of course she was."

"We knew we wanted to get married, and that we wanted to stay in the Copper Country, but we hadn't made any timeline or concrete plans. Her parents' death kind of sped that up. We got married after graduation. I worked at one of the construction companies in town as a draftsman, but by then Andy and I had hatched our plan of opening our own shop. Thank God Molly had that business degree—Andy and I were just a couple of engineering geeks who wanted to build cool things."

"Andy seems to be quite the businessman now."

She could feel him nodding, his chin grazing the top of her head. His hand moved from her hair to her neck, which he gently rubbed. "We always knew Andy had the personality to get the clients. Molly had the business end of it covered...."

"And you built the cool stuff."

She felt the small rumble of a chuckle in his chest. "Something like that. We got the startup money from Molly's inheritance and the insurance payout from her parents' death."

There was just a tiny bit of tone in his voice as he said this. She could imagine Sawyer balking at using that money for his own business. "I'm sure it meant a lot to Molly to be able to turn her parents' death into something good."

"That's exactly how she put it. Anyway, business was good. We had a little place in Houghton that we loved. Molly wanted to start a family, but I wanted to wait a couple more years until the business was really solid. I didn't want to be one of those guys who didn't have time for their kids."

And then she died in a car accident, and they ran out of time. He didn't say it, but Deni knew that would be the next sentence out of his mouth.

"And then she started to change."

Those were not the words she had been expecting. She leaned forward to look up at him, but he held her neck in place, as if he didn't want her watching him. So she didn't. She dug her head into his chest and wrapped an arm around his waist, as if to protect him from where he was going.

From where he was taking her.

"She stopped going to the office. Which was fine, because by then Sue had pretty much taken over for the day-to-day stuff. I'd come home and she'd still be in her pajamas. Stuff like that."

Depression. A wave of discomfort spread through Deni.

"It got pretty bad. We saw a couple of doctors, and they tried a couple of different meds, but they didn't seem to help." He let out a long sigh. "She always loved Lake Superior, so I thought if I built a place that had a great view, it would help or something." She felt his head shake. "I was pretty uneducated about it all. And so fucking…helpless."

"I'm sure you were very supportive," she said, meaning it.

"No, not really. I mean, I wanted to be, but I also wanted to fix her, you know? That's what I do—fix things. Build things. Create. And I couldn't fix her."

"You get that you couldn't, right? On some level you get that?"

"Sure, now. With hindsight and education. But when you're in it? When the person you love is in pain or totally checked out? No, I couldn't see beyond my own failure to help. Totally selfish."

"Totally human."

He didn't answer that. And then she got a sick feeling in her gut.

"Sawyer? The accident? Was it an accident?"

The room seemed to chill. He must have felt it too, because he pulled the throw from the corner and draped it around them both.

"I don't know. We'll never know for sure. I was up here—at the spot where the pole barn is now—waiting for her to meet me so I could show her the property. I wanted to get up here first and unload the snowmobile from the trailer." He shifted in his seat. "God, if I'd just waited and we'd gone up together…."

Ten years later and he was still beating himself up. Probably always would.

"Anyway, it got pretty late and still no Molly. I couldn't get cell service up here, so I finally started back to town. I was concerned but not freaked out or anything. She'd missed meeting me—or others—at places lots of times and then I'd go home and she'd be safe and sound, sleeping at two in the afternoon."

Deni had mild SAD, not severe depression like Molly apparently had. It made her tired and irritable with a few other nasty side effects, but she knew it was temporary, and it didn't really affect her day-to-day life. She couldn't imagine wearing the lead jacket she felt at times day after day, but twenty times heavier.

"I knew she always took the Covered Drive way when coming up here, so I started back."

"Oh, God, were you the one who found her?"

"No, somebody else had and had already called the cops. I could see the flashing of the lights through the bare trees well before I came around the curve. As soon as I saw the red lights, I knew. And I knew it wasn't an accident."

"Oh, Sawyer." She wrapped her arm tighter around him, wanting to take away his pain, to ease his burden. But just like he couldn't for Molly, Deni was unable to do that for him.

"But the roads that time of year can be so iffy. There are so many accidents. Why don't you think it was just that—an accident?"

He shrugged, and the hand that was on her neck dropped to her back. "We'll never know, but there was a light snowfall—"

"See, she could have easily just…what? Slid into a ditch?"

"A tree. She hit a tree head on. And there were no signs in the snow of her losing control, or trying to right the car or anything. It looked…." His voice cracked, and he cleared his throat.

She almost told him to stop, but somehow she knew it was important for him to tell her the story.

"They ruled it an accident. But I knew."

"I'm so sorry." She whispered the inadequate words.

"She was pronounced dead at the scene, already taken away when I got there. I just kind of wandered around until one of the cops called my brother Twain, who came and got me.

"You know, I still don't know things like how my car got back to our house, or remember them taking my statement at the scene, stuff like that. But her mitten in the snow…God, I'll never forget that."

"Her mitten?"

"They wouldn't let me too close to the car, but one of her mittens was thrown a few feet away. They had some spotlights on or I wouldn't have seen it. But there it was. This cute little multi-colored mitten that she'd gotten at some arts and crafts show in Marquette the year before.

"I picked it up to…I don't know what I was thinking… to take it to her, I guess. And then for a second I thought the yarn had come unwound and was still in the snow. But it was her blood."

She moved so that she could wrap her arm around his neck, trying to soothe the unsoothable.

"You have them, you know."

"Have what?" she asked.

"Those mittens. They weren't the ones you wore the night at the Commodore. And the day we went to Green Bay, you had on your leather gloves. But when I was brushing off your windshield, I saw them on your passenger seat. The exact same mittens."

She knew the ones he meant. Like Molly, Deni had purchased them at a craft fair. They were probably made by the same woman.

"That's what made the memories flood back? Why you didn't come home with me that night?"

"Yes. It wasn't because I didn't want to finish what we'd started in that parking lot. But it just…I don't know, threw me."

"Thank you for sharing that with me. I know it wasn't easy."

He cleared his throat again, and this time when he spoke his voice sounded more like himself. "I do want to give this a shot, Deni, whatever we turn out to be. I meant what I said at Tootie's. But you have a right to know what I'm bringing to the table."

She briefly thought about telling him of her SAD, but didn't. For one thing it wasn't anything permanent, or anywhere near the severity that Molly's depression apparently was. And for another, this moment was about Sawyer, not her.

"So, stone collecting as therapy?"

He gave a small snort of laughter. "I guess."

"And glass-house building as therapy."

"Definitely."

"Any depth to that? Glass house. Stones?"

"Hmmm. Sounds downright Freudian when you put it that way."

She smiled, even though he couldn't see her. "Well, whatever works, I say."

"Actually, the stones and glass house came a little later, after I got over the worst hump."

"And how did you do that? Just time?"

"No. Alison."

"Alison, my Alison?"

"Well, first she was my Alison."

"You saw her professionally? She never mentioned it."

"Well, it wouldn't be very professional of her to, would it?"

Of course not. She felt stupid for even thinking it.

"She did tell me that your wife had died in a car accident."

He waved that away. "That's common knowledge, she wasn't breaking any confidences with that. In fact, I'm kind of surprised you heard that first from her, and not at the office."

"Nobody at the office ever talks about you."

"I guess that's better than speculating that I'm the Brockway

Mountain Hermit."

"So, Alison, eh?" She shook her head, still not quite believing it.

"Yep. Saw her for over a year. Huck and Twain staged a semi-intervention and got me to go. And I'm glad I did. She really pulled me out of it."

"Becoming a hermit is being pulled out of it?"

He laughed. "Compared to the road I was probably headed down, oh yeah."

She wanted to ask what that road was, but he spoke first. "In fact, I have Lucy because of Alison."

"Alison gave you a puppy?"

"No, but she suggested I get one. I made the mistake of telling Twain about that and the next thing I know, he's showing up at my door with a seven-week-old Lucy."

"I'll bet she was adorable."

"She was a pain in the ass, is what she was. God, it took me forever to housebreak her."

"Alison was smart. So was Twain."

"Yes, she is. Twain, maybe on his good days. But what do you mean?"

"She knew that you could stop caring for yourself and let your life fall into ruin. You had Andy to take care of the business, so in a way you could check out of life. But if you had to take care of somebody else, like Lucy…."

"She took a gamble, 'cause it was close to that little puppy being put out into the snow to fend for herself."

"Nope. No way in a million years would you let that happen, Sawyer Beck, no matter how much pain you were in."

He didn't say anything to that. What could he say? She was totally right, and she knew it.

"Hmmm. Whatever."

"No. She saw it in you. So did Twain. You weren't so far gone that you couldn't care for something, or someone, else."

"But I didn't want to. Didn't want to care for anybody. Ever."

A moment passed. Deni was afraid to ask the question that hung in the room. "And now?" she finally said.

He pulled her out of his embrace so that he faced her. He put a finger under her chin and tilted her face up to his.

"And now I want to," he said, and leaned forward to gently kiss her. "And now I *do*," he added, and kissed her again before hugging her tight.

Twenty-One

HE LIFTED HER FROM HIS LAP AND ROSE FROM THE chair with her in his arms. She felt so good in his arms, so right. He carried her to the bed and lowered her down. Then he went to the door and let Lucy in.

"Did you hear us talking about you, girl? Did you?" She wagged her tail excitedly, snow flying from her fur as she did. "Go see Deni," he said. Lucy did just that, bounding onto the bed and butting her head against Deni, who immediately began petting Lucy and cooing to her as Sawyer put some food in her dish and poured some bottled water in another.

"Come eat, girl," he said, and Lucy left Deni and found her food and water in the candlelight.

"Hungry?" he asked Deni, ready to pull some hotdogs from the icebox to roast over the fire.

"You know what? I'm really not. But you go ahead."

"No, that's okay. I'm not really, either." He made his way around the room, blowing out the candles. Then he put two large logs on the fire and joined her on the bed. He'd have to feed the fire throughout the night, but that was fine. He never slept longer than a couple of hours here and there anyway.

"God, I'm beat," he said as he lay down next to her and pulled her onto his chest.

"I can't imagine why? Outdoor activity, mucho sex, a blistering sauna, and an emotional purging. Hmmm. Wonder what wore you out?"

He kissed her, and they smiled at each other. She rolled off him and situated them like they'd been before when they'd napped, his head upon her chest, his arm around her waist, and both of her arms around him. "Sleep, Sawyer," she softly said.

She was wearing her long johns, but he could feel she was without the bra this time. He started to knead her breast, but she put a hand on his and held it in place. "Sleep," she whispered.

Oh, sure. How was he supposed to sleep with his hand on her tit? It was the last thought he had before falling into a deep slumber.

THE MORNING SUN COMING through the glass ceiling woke Deni. Or maybe it was Sawyer's hand on her hip, pulling her back into his front. Sunlight or Sawyer's erection—both seemed to have an effect on her mood that surpassed any kind of serotonin rush.

She let out a long sigh as his hand crept under her thermal top and up to cup her breast just as the sun rose over the eastern tree line.

"Way better than any light box," she said quietly.

"Hmm? What light box?" he asked, nuzzling her neck.

"Nothing," she whispered. "God, it's freezing in here." She bundled deeper under the covers.

"Sorry," he said, and was gone from the bed before she could stop him. "I…I guess I let the fire go out." He was shaking his head in disbelief as he tore some newspaper up and put it on the grate, and then put some kindling on top of that. He let Lucy out while the dying embers caught. After a moment, he added a log and then crawled back into bed with her. "I can't believe I did that."

"What? You were going to wake up every three hours and feed the fire?" She turned over and curled into him, sliding one leg over his.

"Um…yeah, I kind of thought I was." He still seemed slightly puzzled that he hadn't.

"Forget about the fire," she said, her hand moving down to his briefs. "Keep me warm some other way."

The grin on his face told her he definitely would.

THEY TOOK ANOTHER SAUNA in the early afternoon and then packed up and headed back to the pole barn the way they'd come up—Sawyer taking Lucy first, then coming back for Deni.

When he came back into the house from dropping Lucy off, he found Deni not looking out at the spectacular view but instead staring at his stone jar.

Should he have even shared that story with her? She was young and didn't have the baggage he had. Would knowing how he'd struggled after Molly's death scare her off?

Was that why he'd told her?

He did a mental gut check and came to the conclusion that no, he hadn't wanted to push Deni away. He'd just wanted her to know what she was getting into with him.

And now, this afternoon, seeing her staring at the manifestation of his near-madness, he found himself saying a silent prayer that she would stay with him—monstrous baggage and all.

When they got into Copper Harbor, where he would typically go straight to keep going to Eagle Harbor, he put on his blinker and turned left instead.

"Oh, Sawyer, you don't have to do this," she said. He wasn't surprised that she'd picked up on it so quickly—that he was taking *the* Covered Drive back to Calumet. And what that meant.

"It's okay," he said. And he truly meant it.

She scooted a little closer to him in the truck and put her hand on his thigh. Not in a sexual way, just to let him know she knew. Even Lucy seemed to sense something monumental was happening, sticking her head over the seat and resting it between them.

He didn't mention when they came upon the spot where

Molly—his sweet, outgoing, beautiful Molly—had died, but he must have tensed up or something because Deni removed her hand from his thigh at that point, as if trying to give him some privacy or something. As if she didn't want to intrude on his "time" with Molly.

He'd been oddly attracted to Deni since that first day in the conference room, standing over her shoulder. "Oddly" because she wasn't in any way like Molly or any other girl he'd ever dated.

And he'd really enjoyed seeing Deni's mind work this past week as they put the driving range proposal together. That was a major turn-on to him.

Well, not as much of a turn-on as her standing in front of Lake Superior in a red satin bra and rose-covered long johns. God, he nearly got hard again thinking about it. Shocking, since he'd had about as much sex in the past twenty-four hours as he'd had in the last ten years.

But this gesture—taking her hand from him when she sensed they were at the site—tore at his heart and made him realize just how hard and fast he was falling for Deni Casparich.

And surprisingly, it didn't scare the shit out of him.

WHEN THEY WERE NEARING CALUMET, Sawyer said, "Are you in a rush to get back to Hancock? Would you like to stop at Tootie's for a beer?"

"Yes, I'd like that," she answered. He hadn't said much of anything since they'd turned in Copper Harbor, and she'd tried to give him his space, such as it was in a truck cab. But Deni didn't want the weekend to end with the pall of Molly's accident freshly hanging over them.

Sawyer let Lucy out of the truck with them when they parked in front of the bar. She thought it was to just let Lucy do her business, but Sawyer walked up to the window of Tootie's, looked in, and said to his dog, "Shorty's bartending," which made Lucy wag her tail and give a bark.

"Your dog knows the bartenders at Tootie's?"

He shrugged and held the door open for them, Lucy bounding in the bar first. "She knows that Shorty lets her in the bar and feeds her beef jerky."

"I guess I'd wag my tail for Shorty, too," she said, and they both laughed. Sawyer swung an arm around her shoulder, and they walked into the bar together.

Lucy, however, had bypassed her bartender friend, who had shouted a greeting to the lab, and beelined for a man at the end of the bar who could only be Sawyer's brother.

"Oh, shit," Sawyer said, not quite under his breath.

"Twain or Huck?" she asked.

Sawyer chuckled, sliding his arm from around her. She felt a moment's disappointment until he took her hand in his and started leading them to the far end of the long, narrow bar. He said a few hellos to some of the people drinking at the bar but didn't stop.

"Twain. Do we really look that much alike?"

As they neared the man who had squatted down to scratch Lucy's neck, Deni realized that up close there were not as many similarities as she'd first thought.

Twain was much larger than Sawyer, for one thing. Like, Petey Ryan larger. And his hair was a few shades darker than Sawyer's, more of a light black than deep brown.

Twain looked up from Lucy as they approached. Deni saw his eyes dart from Sawyer to Deni to their clasped hands and then back to Deni with an assessing look.

Same shrewd, green eyes as Sawyer. And same sexy-as-hell, but troubling, look of world-weariness on his face and around those beautiful green eyes.

"I thought you had Matt this weekend?" Sawyer asked as they reached his brother.

"He's not feeling good. Flu, Liv thinks. So she kept him at home with her."

"Sorry to hear that," Sawyer said. He dislodged his hand from hers and placed it at the small of her back. "Twain Beck,

Deni Casparich."

She stuck out her hand, which Twain shook. His hand was huge and rough and swallowed hers up.

"Great to meet you, Deni. What are you drinking?"

"You too. Um…how about a Sam Adams?"

"Make it two," Sawyer added, pulling a stool down to join the empty one next to Twain, which he waved her to sit on. Twain pulled the stool he'd vacated out a little from the bar so he could see Sawyer on the other side of Deni, then sat back down.

"Shorty, two Sam Adams," Twain called out, then turned his attention to them. The beers were in front of them before Twain finished saying, "So, Deni Casparich, tell me everything about yourself."

Lucy left them then to visit her buddy Shorty, who had come out from the end of the bar with some kind of treat for the dog.

"Um…not much to tell, really."

"Is that because you're *soooo* young?"

"Ha ha," Sawyer said on her left. Twain gave his brother a grin that Deni recognized from Sawyer. It seemed more natural on Twain, as if he smiled, and grinned, with more ease.

"Born and raised in the Detroit area, went to Tech, fell in love with the area, work at Summers and Beck," she said.

Twain gave her a wink and said, "You're right. Not much to tell."

She laughed as Sawyer gave his brother a stern look. "So, you're the charmer in the family, I take it? I thought the middle child was supposed to be the quiet, shy one?"

"Well, we Bad Luck Beck Brothers never really did things in the right order," Twain said, and she saw Sawyer cringe out of the corner of her eye.

"Bad Luck Beck Brothers? People call you that? Seriously?"

"Oh, yeah," Twain said, almost with some pride. Sawyer's large sigh confirmed it.

"Well, not to our faces," Sawyer said.

"Well, not *sober* to our faces," Twain clarified. "And not if they want to keep their teeth."

Deni laughed again and took a drink from her beer.

"So, from the scent of Irish Spring wafting from the both of you and your still-wet hair, Deni, I'd guess you're both freshly sauna-ed?"

She nodded, feeling a flush crawl up her face. "Is that a verb? Sauna-ed?"

He shrugged. "If it isn't, it should be." He took a swing from his beer bottle and then set it on the bar. "So, this sauna…was at…." He looked at Sawyer pointedly.

"The ice cube," Sawyer said, causing Twain to grin again.

"Really? So a female has breached the glass walls? Interesting."

"Can it, Twain," Sawyer said in what was obviously his big-brother voice.

Twain gave a taunting laugh and wiggled his eyebrows in what was obviously a little-brother move.

Deni had the brothers to know all the moves.

Twain regaled her with stories of the Beck brothers as kids, told her about his own son, Matt, and just generally endeared himself to Deni in a very brotherly way.

"You didn't feel it necessary to carry on the Mark Twain obsession with your son?"

"Hell no. And even if I had, Liv would have had the good sense to shut that down."

She took another sip and looked around. She was having a beer with her boyfriend and his brother in a neighborhood bar on a late Sunday afternoon…and all was right with the world.

Twain left first, saying he wanted to go check on his son. He gave Deni a kiss on the cheek and whispered in her ear, "Stay with it. He's worth all the bullshit." She could only nod at him, her chest suddenly tight.

He hugged his brother and said in a fake whisper, "Don't fuck it up, bro. She's a keeper."

Deni and Sawyer stayed for another drink, though Sawyer switched to Coke at that point.

He also moved his stool closer to Deni, threaded his legs between hers, and cupped under her knee with one of his hands, just like he had last Monday when they'd been here.

Only one short week ago when she'd laid it on the line and told him she'd wanted more than a snack.

And here they were after a weekend feast.

Yes, all was right with the world.

"So, what does Twain do?"

"He's a logger."

"Ah, that explains the rough hands."

Sawyer nodded and absently looked at his own hands. "He played hockey. Was pretty good."

"Better than you?"

Sawyer chuckled. "Oh, yeah. A fact he never lets me forget."

She rubbed her hand on his knee and kept it there. After last night's gut-wrenching story about Molly's death, it felt good to be just a normal couple enjoying the day together.

"He actually played at Tech with Petey Ryan. They're about the same age."

"Oh, did he get his degree in forestry, then?" Besides engineering, Tech's forestry department was top-notch.

"No. He dropped out after his second year. That's when he and Liv got married. Matty was born a few months after the wedding."

"Ah. But they're not still together?" she said with sadness in her voice.

"Nah, Twain fucked up. Well, I mean, they were both young and stupid, with a lot of pressure on them. They made it eight years but just couldn't make it work."

"That's sad."

"Yeah, it is. But Matt's great. Turning sixteen this year," he said with obvious pride.

"Do you see him much?" There was skepticism in her voice, which he picked up on.

"What? Hermits aren't allowed to visit their nephews?"

She giggled. "Well, it does kind of defeat the purpose of being a hermit."

"I wasn't totally cut off the last ten years. I saw family. I built the ice cube with my brothers. I'd have dinner at Liv and Twain's once a month or so when they were still together. I just didn't want to deal with the business—which I'd spent too much time on and not been available for Molly—"

She started to interrupt him on that, but he held up his hand. "Or that's how it felt at the time."

She nodded at that—you couldn't change the way someone felt ten years ago.

"You said you and Molly had a house in Houghton?" He nodded. "But not anymore?"

"No. I sold that place after she died."

"And you obviously don't live in the ice cube full-time."

"Don't think I could rough it like we've been doing on a full-time basis?"

"Yeah, you probably could, but there was too much fresh snow on the tracks for that to be the case."

He leaned over and kissed her quickly. "My little logical engineer."

She pushed on his chest a little, but secretly preened. "So, *where* do you live?"

A last-ditch effort of her Rumplestiltskin image played through her mind.

"Laurium."

So, no small man prancing around a hidden cottage after all.

"Laurium? Like across the highway from here?"

"Yep. Good ol' Laurium. Neighbor to Calumet. Home of George Gipp."

"Who?"

"George Gipp. The Gipper."

She shook her head, still not getting it.

"You know…'Win one for the Gipper.'"

"I've heard of that…I think."

He let out an exaggerated sigh. "Good God, how young *are* you? Never mind, don't answer that. I'm feeling creaky enough today after our workout this weekend."

She took a drink of her beer and grinned at him.

"We'll have to rent *Knute Rockne, All American* so you can see who George Gipp was."

"Now you're showing your age, old man. You don't rent anymore. You stream."

"Whatever. Ronald Reagan played the Gipper."

"Who's Ronald Reagan?" she teased.

"Ha ha, you're so funny.

"So, since you live so close, are you going to take me to see your house before you bring me back to Hancock?"

"No way. It's a disaster zone right now. Basically just a mattress in one room and all my shit piled in another."

"Why?"

"I haven't been in this one very long, and I don't really unpack much more than my tools and some clothes, anyway.

"When I sold the house Molly and I lived in, I gave all the furniture to Liv for her and Matt's new house—she and Twain had been renting an apartment before that. The good stuff that I didn't want to sell or give away, like photos and some wedding gifts, is in storage."

"Again, why? I mean, I get selling the home you and Molly were going to have a family in, but why all the moving?"

"I kind of buy places cheap and fix them up. Then I want to find a new one."

"You flip houses?"

He chuckled and took a drink of his pop, a look of chagrin on his face. "Well, not exactly. Flippers usually *make* money. And they're certainly quick about their renovations."

"Well…yeah. That's kind of the whole point."

"But it's not *my* point. I live in a place for a while, take my time, move from one project to another, and then change my mind. I use materials and finishes that price houses out of the market, so I end up underpricing them just so I can get rid of it when I'm done. I get to a point where I need to move on to a new one. So, yes, technically I'm a flipper—I'm just not very good at it."

"I'd love to see one of the houses you've finished sometime."

"There are a couple that are now owned by people who'd be cool with me bringing you by, if I gave them a little notice."

"But I don't get to see the one you're in now?"

"I'm not holding out on you. There's literally nothing to see. It's gutted right now with just a bare bones kitchen and bath."

She sat back on the stool and took the last drink of her beer.

He paid the tab and they rose to leave. Before she could move away from the stool, he leaned into her space. Leaned into her. "Besides," he whispered in her ear as he gently kissed her neck, "I've already taken you to the place where I *really* live."

She wrapped her arms around her and kissed him right there at the end of Tootie's bar with the stained-glass canopy behind them and the catcalls of the other patrons in her ears.

Twenty-Two

SHE INVITED HIM IN WHEN HE DROPPED HER OFF, BUT he told her he needed to be at his house early the next morning because flooring was going to be delivered.

So instead, they made out like teenagers in his truck before she finally pulled away, patted Lucy goodbye, and went into her home. Leaving him horny as hell for the drive back to Laurium.

The flooring was delivered and unloaded Monday morning. Typically Sawyer would dive right in on a large, mindless project like laying hardwood flooring.

But instead, he found himself showering up, putting on khakis and a work shirt, and loading Lucy in the truck.

"Wanna go for a ride, girl?" Lucy barked, wagged her tail once, and then began to curl up in her designated area in the backseat. "Wanna go see Deni?" Lucy sat up, putting her snout on the back of Sawyer's seat, barking madly with her tail wagging wildly.

"Yeah, I know what you mean," he said as he put the truck in gear.

ANDY WAS SURPRISED TO SEE HIM and even more shocked when Sawyer asked about his old office.

"I've been telling you for a long time—it was yours anytime."

"Yeah, I know. I think…" He looked his partner, his oldest friend, in the eye and said, "I think it's 'anytime.'"

It was all Andy could do not to hug him, Sawyer could tell, so he quickly shook hands with him and made his way to his old office with Andy following in his wake. Not knowing what the future held, he'd spent the last week working out of the conference room.

"We've kept the equipment up to date. Sometimes we use it if somebody's machine is down or something, but you should be able to connect with the network. Yeah, there we go." Andy had stepped behind Sawyer's old work area and booted up the laptop and the three larger screens that were in a semicircle on the sleek walnut desk.

"What do you want to look at first?" he asked, stepping back so Sawyer could sit in the cushy leather chair, which he did. "Here's the open projects list. And on this server is status updates for each one. And here's the instant messaging system that came with our last upgrade. And—"

"Andy, slow down. Let me just get used to sitting at a desk first," he said, giving his partner a stern look.

Which didn't deter Andy at all, and he continued for another ten minutes, then left Sawyer and Lucy alone, the door open— though the walls were glass anyway.

He looked down at his dog sniffing around the unfamiliar room. It was as if she knew she was going to be spending some time here, so she tried to find the optimum place to snooze.

Sawyer called up the instant messaging software Andy had showed him. Icons for the entire staff came up with their statuses showing in different colors and messages. There was a yellow diamond next to Deni's name. When he hovered over it, the message came up "away from my desk." Well, duh. It'd been the first thing he'd noticed walking down the row of cubes to Andy's office. Okay, like a lovesick schoolgirl he'd been dying to catch a glimpse of her. He would have seen her if she'd entered the main work area in the fifteen minutes or so since he'd been here.

Where the hell was Deni?

DENI WAS IN THE LADIES' ROOM on her cell, talking her mom out of hopping in her car and making the ten-hour drive from Detroit to Houghton.

"I'm telling you, I'm fine. I've just been really busy at work this past week. We had a big new project that had a quick-turnaround deadline."

"You couldn't have answered an email?"

"Mom, I barely had time to eat or sleep last week. I didn't answer *anybody's* emails."

"They're working you too hard there," her mother said, concern in her voice.

Okay, walking a bit of a tightrope here. "No, it was just some late nights during the week. We turned it in on Friday." Letting her know that her job was not too much for her, and yet opening herself to….

"So, you had the weekend off? But didn't return any of my calls? I tried your cell half a dozen times."

The other side of the coin.

"I was away for the weekend. And where I was didn't have cell coverage. I didn't get back into town until late yesterday, and since I was tired from the long week, I went right to bed."

There was silence on the other end as her mother digested this all. Deni knew her mother worried about her. And had worried even more these past months since the SAD hit her. But it was well past time to define her boundaries. See, she'd even picked up shrink talk from Alison.

"Mom," she said in a calm, adult voice, "I know you're concerned. But there will be times when I can't get back to you right away. Because I'm busy, or away, or just generally living my own life. You need to respect those times and try not to worry. I know that's hard. I know you love me. I love you too, very much. But it's time to let go, Mom."

More silence. Deni feared she'd hurt the woman who, yes, drove her crazy at times, but whom she deeply loved.

"Well," her mother began hesitantly, "you're right, of course."

Deni waited for the "but," which never came.

"I'll let you get back to work now, honey. I was concerned because I couldn't reach you over the weekend, but…did you have a nice time? Wherever you went?"

"It was up past Copper Harbor. And yes, it was a great time." She tried to keep her tone even, not to gush. First, she wasn't a gusher by nature. Second, she didn't want to talk about Sawyer to her mom. Not yet.

"That's nice. Okay, honey. I'll let you go."

That seemed a little too easy, but Deni took it. "Bye, Mom. Love you."

She hung up and started to leave the women's room when her phone rang again. Alison's number popped up. Happy that she'd decided to take her mom's call in the privacy of the seldom-used women's room, Deni propped herself back against the counter and answered.

"Hi, Alison."

"Hi, Deni. Do you have a second? And are you able to talk freely?"

"Yes. And yes. I'm in a private room right now."

And until Sue needed to use the bathroom, it would be all hers.

"Great. Listen, a quick trip to Detroit has suddenly come up, and I'm going to be leaving Friday morning. I'm calling to reschedule."

"Oh, okay."

"How does Thursday look for you?"

She thought her schedule was pretty clear, but said, "Look, I'm okay just skipping this week, if you are. We don't have to try to reschedule. I'll just see you the following Friday, regular time."

"Are you sure? I'm happy to get you in. I can be here any evening too, if that would fit better into your schedule."

Very nice of her, but Deni didn't want to put Alison out. Besides….

"Actually I'm feeling pretty good right now, so I'm okay with skipping a week."

"I'm glad you're feeling better. As we've talked about before, moods play a big part in SAD. So being in a good mood is its own therapy, in a way. Have you been continuing on with the light box? Do you think that has played a part?"

If they'd been in Alison's office, sitting in the comfy chairs, she probably would have told her therapist that a big part of it was from getting laid—repeatedly—over the weekend. But being in the women's room at work?

"I'm sure that's part of it."

"And the irritability?"

Even Snide Randy didn't bother her this morning. She actually didn't want to punch his face when she'd walked by him on her way to her cube. "Not bad. Better, in fact."

"Well, good. Then we'll see each other the following Friday, if you're sure."

"Yes, that's good."

"Okay. And Deni, feel free to call if you want. This number gets you my service when I'm not available, and they can reach me. But…" Deni could feel the hesitation in Alison's voice and wondered if they weren't at the edge of the therapist-to-friend line. "I'm going to text you my cell number. Call that if you need to talk. I mean it."

"Okay. Thanks, Alison. But I'm sure I'll be fine. Have a good trip."

"Thanks, bye."

Deni left the bathroom and made her way back to her cubicle. Sitting at her desk, she noticed her office IM blinking, which was unusual. Usually Charlie just popped over to her cube to talk. Were they to this point, then? That he'd be IM'ing her instead of dropping by? And was that probably for the best?

But no, the IM wasn't from Charlie. It was from…Sawyer?

She read the message and smiled.

"How about lunch? This office life is killing me."

SHE TURNED HIM DOWN FOR LUNCH. But she did invite him to her house for dinner, which he quickly accepted, even telling her he'd bring over takeout.

This was all done via IM, and he took his cue from her and didn't approach her cube to talk specifically with her. Or drop to his knees and put his head under her skirt and get her off, as he really wanted to do.

Yeah, he'd been gone from the office for a while.

Throughout the course of the day, pretty much everyone stopped by his office to talk with him. Some were welcoming him and some feeling him out. He wasn't really sure what to tell them. He wasn't really sure himself what he was doing here.

Charlie didn't stop by, though, and he supposed that was just as well.

And neither did Deni. But that was okay, too. It just built the anticipation that had begun the minute he'd dropped her off last night.

God, it'd been so long since he felt like this…it was so foreign to him and yet was so natural.

Around three, he turned off his laptop and decided to call it a day. Lucy wasn't in his office. He hadn't noticed when she'd left, but he wasn't too concerned. His dog never strayed too far from him, and she always came back.

Yeah, his brother Twain could be an asshole at times, and he'd been completely pissed when Twain had shown up with puppy Lucy, but it was one of the best things that had happened to Sawyer.

Well, behind meeting and loving two incredible women at different times—and different phases—of his life.

The thought was so overwhelming, he almost stumbled as he walked. And then…and then it wasn't.

Yes, he had loved Molly. With all his heart. And there would always be guilt that he couldn't have helped in some way. But there was also joy when he thought of their life together, short as it was.

And yes, he did love Deni. Was in love with her. It was fast, and they didn't know each other all that well—and yet they did. His love for Deni was different than what he'd shared with Molly. He and Molly had been young, just out of high school when they met, and had grown into adulthood together, learning their way.

He loved Deni with more maturity, with an open eye, and, yes, an open heart, which he honestly never thought possible again.

"Hey, I'm heading out," he told Andy from the doorway to Andy's office. Andy waved him in and motioned for Sawyer to close the door behind him, which he did.

"So, how does it feel?" Andy asked him.

Thoughts of admitting to himself that he loved Deni were still running through his mind. "Scary as hell," he said, not really to his friend. "But really, really good, too."

"That's great, Sawyer. And, you know, take your time. Ease into it."

Sawyer figured in about two hours he'd be easing into it—easing into Deni. "Oh, I will."

"But here's the thing," Andy said, leaning forward, his forearms on his desk. "We probably don't want to confuse the group, you know? I mean, you come in for a few days, maybe a week, and then they don't see you for another ten years."

Sawyer was about to say that wasn't going to happen, but he kept quiet.

"I would love for you to be back full time. The business would be much stronger for it, and I would have my partner back." Andy's voice caught at the end.

Not for the first time, Sawyer realized that he'd been incredibly selfish with his grief, leaving the business for Andy to run on his own.

"And if you want to continue on as silent partner, I'm okay with that too. But, for the staff, I'm asking you to think about this. Only come back if you're back. If you're ready. If you're truly committed."

He nodded to his friend and then started to open the door. "I will, Andy. I'll think about it. But right now?" He looked down the row of cubes and saw Lucy's hindquarters sticking out of Deni's work area. "I'm ready to commit."

Twenty-Three

—꩜—

FINALLY SHE PULLED UP IN FRONT OF HER HOUSE. SAWYER looked at the clock on the dash of his truck—five-fifteen. Okay, so she'd come home straight from work. It wasn't her fault that he'd been parked at her curb for nearly an hour.

When he'd left the office, he'd driven by Liv and Matt's house to see if his nephew was feeling any better. No one was home, so Matty must have been well enough to go to school and thus Liv could head to Tech, where she worked as an admin to one of the deans.

He then went to the Commodore and had a beer at the bar while they made him a pizza to go.

A pizza that was surely cold by now. He hadn't timed that very well, he thought. But seeing Deni leave her garage after pulling her Subaru in, her ponytail squashed down and under her knit hat, Sawyer was suddenly not nearly as hungry as he had been.

"How long have you been waiting here?" she asked as he and Lucy approached her.

"Umm…not long."

She quirked an eyebrow at him and then raised the lid of the pizza box. The pizza was definitely past its prime, the cheese congealed.

"Well, maybe a *little* while," he admitted. "I was anxious to see you." He leaned in and kissed her, but the damn pizza box got in the way of any real action.

"Come here," she said, and turned back to the small one-car garage. He followed as she went to a shelf that ran the length of the building and lifted an old, dust-covered terra cotta flowerpot. "I keep a spare key here." She pointed to the regular entrance door on the opposite side of the garage from the large door where her car entered. "That door is unlocked all the time, since there's nothing valuable in here."

"Except the spare key to your house."

She shrugged. "It's the Copper Country. And no one knows about this key. Thieves would be looking closer to the house, around that door." She breezed past him through the main door and then pressed the button to close it once Sawyer had followed her out. "Just in case you beat me here again, I wanted you to know about the key. And tell you that you could let yourself in."

"Thanks."

"You're welcome. Sorry I didn't think of it earlier."

"You didn't know I'd have time to kill."

She looked over her shoulder at him once she made it to the bottom of the hillside stairs. "No, I didn't. Not all of us can waltz in and out of the office when we feel like it," she teased, flashing that dimple as she smiled. When she got to the door, she started to unlock it, but stopped.

"You know, I wasn't sure when I'd see you again for sure. And I was sure shocked to see Lucy at the office."

"Yeah. Lucy got your affection, but there was none for me."

"Not in the office, that's right. Your little arm around my shoulder last week is going to be all I share with that group about what we do privately. Is that clear?"

"Yes."

"Good. But, what I meant was, I wasn't expecting you to be here. And…umm…I'm not the greatest housekeeper in the best of times."

"What's different about *these* times?"

She shook her head, waved a hand. "Nothing. Nothing. I mean, I have no idea if my house is…guy ready."

"Oh, shit, Deni. Do you think I care about that kind of stuff? I'm sleeping on a mattress in a gutted house right now. Do you have a bed that's on a frame?"

"Yes."

"And an actual matching sheet set? 'Cause if so, you're way ahead of me, and this will be a huge step up." He took her keys from her, opened the door, and stepped back for her to enter.

"Yes, but I'm sure the bed is unmade, and I can't testify to how clean the sheets are."

She walked past him, as did Lucy. They were in the foyer, stairs ahead of them. The living room was to his right and what looked like a dining room and then kitchen—which he couldn't see fully—was to his left.

She took her keys from him and placed them on a side table that held a glass bowl and some other knick-knacks. Then she peeled off her coat and hat, hanging her coat on one of the hooks she'd installed, and kicked off her boots. Another turtleneck, cardigan, wool skirt, and tights combination. At least this time the skirt had a plaid pattern.

The vision of her in red satin bra and panties flashed through his mind. As did the mind-bending blowjob in the sauna, and going down on her in front of the glass wall.

He threw the pizza box on the table and started pawing at the zipper on his parka, quickly taking it off as he too kicked off his boots.

"I don't care about clean sheets," he said as he walked the two steps to her and pulled her close. He kissed her, longer and deeper, with nothing in his way. She wrapped her arms around his neck and shimmied her leg up the outside of his thigh.

"And having the bed unmade just saves time," he said after pulling his mouth from hers. He held her face in his hands. "I'm not in the mood for pizza," he said, and then kissed her again.

"I'm not even hungry," she said—gasped—as he put his arms under her thighs and lifted her up. She instinctively put her legs around his waist—hitting his growing cock at a very pleasurable angle—and he started carrying her up the stairs. Each step he took brought them into closer contact, and she moaned his name, rubbing herself against him.

Reaching the top of the stairs (too fucking many and yet too fucking few), he knew he couldn't even take another step without being inside her. He backed down two steps and then leaned forward so that he could lay her down on the floor at the top of the stairs. There was a small stained-glass window and the dwindling light shone through, casting jewel-toned colors against her black sweater and across her face.

"Jesus, you're beautiful," he said, sliding her skirt up her long legs. Bunching it around her waist, he pulled the black tights down, mesmerized as they gave way to her pale skin. Black cotton panties today, but right now they seemed as sexy as the red satin… and just as dispensable.

"Sawyer," she said, her hips starting to move. "Hurry."

"I know, I know. I'm sorry, I can't wait."

"I don't want you to," she said, her voice as breathless as he felt.

He fumbled with his belt and then the fly to the khakis. Damn, where were his easy jeans when he needed them? She was pulling her panties off herself, lifting her ass up and peeling them down and off one leg. They stayed wrapped around one ankle, even as she moved her feet to the curve of the last step, her knees bent and in the air, legs spread.

"This is going to be fast. I'm sorry. Next time—"

"Will you stop apologizing and just do it?" she said with both teasing and pleading in her voice.

He pushed down his pants and briefs together, just barely to his knees, but it was enough. Cock in hand, he opened Deni's folds, getting even harder seeing how wet this was making her. Being two steps below her put him at exactly the right angle to—

"Oh my God," she moaned as he pushed, none too gently, into her.

"Too much?" he asked, but she was shaking her head, which

quickly became a thrashing of her head as he started pumping into her hard and fast.

"Never too much," she gasped.

The glass reflection was putting patterns of reds and purples across her thighs. He rubbed his hands down them and then palmed the back of her thighs. He pushed them up, bringing her knees to her chest and him that much deeper.

"Yes," she moaned.

Needing to see her tits while he pounded into her, he tore at the buttons of her cardigan. Mid-thrust, he gave up and ripped the damn thing apart. Then he pulled up her turtleneck so it bunched around her shoulders, much like her skirt did at her waist.

Unable to keep fucking her and undo her bra while she lay on her back, he just pulled the cups down, freeing her luscious globes. Leaning forward, which in turn pushed her legs even farther back, he held one breast and brought his mouth to it. He sucked on the pebbled nipple as his other hand slid around to her ass, holding her in place as he continued to stroke.

"Sawyer." His name came out on a sigh. He felt her tense around him in that moment just before—

"Oh, Sawyer," she moaned again as she came. He sucked her other nipple hard and then gave it a gentle bite, which sent another convulsion through her. Her pussy muscles clenched him tightly, and he gave over to the intense feelings as he came with one last thrust.

It seemed to go on and on as she milked every last bit out of him.

At some point, he regained his senses. Enough to realize that he had Deni pinned to the carpet. He had to be careful so he didn't fall backward down a long flight of stairs.

And yet he still didn't want to pull out of her. Being inside Deni's body gave him a peace he'd forgotten existed.

He scooped her up, trying to keep his balance, and climbed the last two stairs carefully. When he was at the top, his pants fell to his ankles and he still wouldn't put her down.

"Which is the bedroom?" he said as he duck-walked down the hallway.

"First one on the left," she said in a dreamy voice, her arms around his shoulders, her mouth burrowing into his neck, gently kissing him.

He entered the room and turned the light on with his elbow. She'd been right; the bed was unmade and seemed to have an inordinate amount of layers on it. He counted a comforter and at least two blankets. He knew these older homes had a lot of character but were heating challenged. Hers must be particularly bad.

He sat on the bed with her still wrapped around him. Her knees hit the mattress on either side of his thighs as she straddled him.

"I've wanted you back in this position since that afternoon in Iron Mountain," he said as he peeled the hanging cardigan from her and lifted the turtleneck over her head, throwing both in the general direction of an overflowing laundry basket along the wall. Reaching behind her, he unhooked her bra and removed that as well. She moved away from him to allow him to unzip her skirt and pull it over her head, but then quickly re-wrapped herself around him, her mouth seeking his.

They kissed and kissed. Gentle, exhausted kisses while he kicked his pants, briefs, and socks off. Deep, tongue-tangling kisses as he stroked his hands all over her naked body. Urgent, straining kisses as her trembling hands unbuttoned his work shirt and pulled it from him. She lifted his tee-shirt, their kisses interrupted as the cotton to slide over his head.

And finally tender, sweet kisses as he turned them, rolled her under him, and made love to her again.

DENI WOKE IN THE MIDDLE of the night. Well, it was only midnight, but for her that was the middle of the night. She reached for Sawyer, but found the bed empty. The light in the bedroom was out, which hadn't been the case as she'd drifted off to sleep in Sawyer's arms.

She saw a glow coming from down the hallway and got out of bed. She wrapped her oversized fleece robe around herself, slipped on her fuzzy slippers, and went down the hall to her workroom where the light shone.

"Sawyer? Are you okay?" she said as she entered the room.

"Hmmm? Yeah, I'm good. I needed to feed Lucy and let her out." He had his back to her and didn't turn around as he spoke. Lucy lay in the corner. She raised her head at Deni, as if in greeting, then laid it back down. She looked settled in, so Sawyer had obviously been in here a while. In his hand was one of her sketches. There were many strewn all over the office area. Lots were pinned to the corkboard-covered walls. Some were of real projects, past and perhaps future. Most were close-up sketches of particular elements she found fascinating. A rung of a wooden balustrade with an elegant flourish. The archway of an entryway. The shape of a window.

"These are amazing," he said, finally turning around to face her. "I mean, I knew you could draw, because I'd seen your sketches of the driving range. But these...." He held up the papers in his hand, then circled his arm around the room. He'd put his pants back on. And his shirt, but it was unbuttoned and open so she could see his bare chest and long torso. With his rumpled hair and the top button of his khakis undone, he looked sexy as hell. She walked toward him, wondering if three times in one night was too much for a forty-year-old man.

"All of these. It's like art. You should seriously consider framing them. They'd look great going up your staircase. With the light from the stained glass hitting them...." He was shaking his head as his thought finished, looking once again at the sketches in his hand.

She stopped in her tracks, the breath leaving her body. In that moment, she felt that same sense of rightness that she'd felt that long-ago day on Brockway Mountain. The feeling she'd tried to describe to Alison.

Treasured.

If she'd been three quarters of the way in love with Sawyer Beck in the glass house, she'd just plunged over the last quarter.

"That was exactly my intention. To frame some and put them up the staircase wall," she said.

"Why haven't you?" he asked.

"I wanted to crop some in ways that fit the sketch. I realized I'd probably need to do some custom framing."

He was nodding. He went to the wall and took down one of the sketches she particularly loved. "This one for sure. So, yeah, custom frames…."

"And then I thought that maybe it'd be cool to design the frames myself. And find a local woodworker or something."

"Great idea," he said, taking another one down from the wall and starting a pile. They definitely shared the same taste; he was gathering all the ones she'd planned on framing.

Until the SAD hit her last fall, and the whole project seemed so huge, so insurmountable that the sketches sat.

While Deni slept.

"Who are you working with? I know some guys who'd probably do a good job for you."

"I haven't gotten that far, yet. That's the next step," she semi-lied. He didn't know that the small step of sketching a frame design and calling a guy about making them for her was just beyond what she was capable of this winter. Making it to work each day, going to therapy, and seeing to very basic grocery and laundry needs maxed her out.

"Let me know if you need any names," he said, still making his pile of her sketches.

"I will," she said.

"Whoa, what's this one?" he asked. She looked at the one he'd put in a different spot, not in the pile.

She smiled; she hadn't seen that sketch in a long time. It must have been buried beneath the more recent ones she'd done. This particular one was at least eight years old, maybe more.

"Is that the view from Brockway Mountain?" he asked.

She stepped behind him and reached out to pull down the framed photo of her father and herself on top of Brockway that day twenty years ago. It was of their backs, she on the concrete pedestal at the "View-Master" and her father beside her, his hand on her shoulder. Deni's mother had taken it, unbeknownst to them at the time. She'd given the framed photo to Deni on her high school graduation to take with her when she entered Tech.

Deni held the photo in front of Sawyer, but stayed behind him, resting her cheek on his back and sliding her other hand around his waist.

"Yep. The sketch is of what I wanted to see on this day. What I saw in my mind."

"The hermit's shack? Seriously?"

"Uh-huh. I've had a fascination with that legend since I was eight years old." He started to turn around, but she clutched him tighter and dug her face deeper into his back, stopping his movement. "I so badly wanted to believe in him. For years, I drew floor plans and sketches of what I thought his hut looked like. It may be the reason I became an engineer."

He held up her sketch in one hand. It was a dwelling of intricacy that blended in with the surrounding area, and yet was very much a pleasant place to live.

"I saw Bill's shack before they tore it down. It didn't look like this. It was—"

"Shhh," she said. "I don't want to know. I want to keep my memory of the hermit alive. I want to think that he lived in this place." She kissed his back between his shoulder blades, feeling the warmth of his skin through his shirt. "And I want to believe that there's a reason I'm dating the man who had been jokingly called the hermit."

She placed the photo down on the table in front of him and turned to walk to the doorway. "Sawyer," she said, looking over her shoulder at him.

"Hmm?" He was still looking at the sketch in his hand, but

his head finally picked up when he heard the whoosh of her robe dropping.

"Race you back to bed," she said and ran, bare-ass naked out of the room.

He beat her back to the bed.

Twenty-Four

"WHAT'S THAT?" SAWYER ASKED HER WHEN SHE ENTERED her kitchen the next morning. He was dressed exactly like he'd been when she found him in her office—pants slung low, shirt undone, and chest bare. He was drinking a mug of coffee and looking suspiciously at her light box.

Time to face the SAD music.

"Oh, that," she said breezily, like big light boxes often took up half her kitchen table. "That's a light box. You know, to get the effects of the sun during the winter."

"Yeah, I know what a light box is."

Irritability started to crawl over her skin. She kept her voice even as she said, "Then why did you ask?" She got a mug out of the cupboard and poured herself some coffee. She'd been drinking tea most of the winter, trying to take in less caffeine, but coffee sounded good this morning. "Thanks for making this, by the way."

"Sure thing. I'm not the one who has to be to the office by eight."

"Nope, that's for us worker bees," she said. She retrieved her purse from the foyer where she'd dropped it last night—right before Sawyer had hoisted her in his arms and taken her at the top of the steps. Back in the kitchen, she rummaged in the fridge and pulled out a yogurt that she'd take with her. She'd barely make it in time as it was. Sawyer had pulled her back into bed when she'd tried to get up and she was now—happily—going to work with hair still wet from her shower.

"I *mean*, why do *you* have a light box on your kitchen table?"

"Listen, I'm running late. I'm very happy for the reason why"—she gave him a quick kiss as she passed him—"but can we have this discussion—"

"Deni," he said, grabbing her arm, stopping her. "What's going on? Talk to me."

She looked at the looming white machine, then at Sawyer. "Last October I started sleeping a lot more than normal, had a lack of energy, and some other things."

The look of suspicion on his face slowly turned to disbelief. "Are you shitting me? You're only telling me this *now*?"

"It's not major depression, Sawyer," she explained, putting her hand on the hand that still held her arm. "It's SAD. Seasonal affect—"

"I know what SAD is," he said a little harshly.

"Then you know that it's seasonal and will go away when the days get longer. And, I also have a very mild case of it. Nothing to worry about."

"Christ. 'Nothing to worry about,' she says." He released her arm and turned away from her, setting his mug on the counter.

The slivers of irritability were digging in now, as if little shards of glass were right on the surface of her skin.

"That's right. Nothing to worry about. I'm sleeping a little more than normal, and I put some activities on hold, but it hasn't affected my work—"

He whirled around at that. "Your work? You think I give a flying fuck about you taking a sick day or two? Or ten or twenty?" He grasped her upper arms in his hands and gently tugged her closer to him. "I don't give a shit about work. I care about *you*."

She placed her hands on his bare chest. The same chest she'd used for balance late last night as she had ridden him. This time she soothed him with her hands.

"I know you do. Sawyer, this isn't Molly all over again."

She felt his chest stiffen beneath her hands, but she knew that was where his mind was going. "This is not clinical depression. I mean, technically it's a diagnostic subtype of depression, or what they call a sub-threshold. But there are absolutely no suicidal thoughts. I'm just really tired and bitchy all the time. It's mild and it's seasonal. It may never even appear again, but Alison says now that we know about it, we can do the light therapy next October when the time change starts."

"So, Alison knows."

She nodded. "That's when I started seeing her. It hasn't even gotten bad enough that we've felt I needed to try anti-depressants."

"So, what? Just seeing Alison and the light box?"

She nodded. "Yes, those things seem to be making a big difference."

"Who else knows? Does Andy know? Should we have something in place at the office for you? A light box somewhere?"

Always the fixer, Sawyer. "Not necessary. I do it first thing in the morning for a half-hour and that's it. And no, Andy doesn't know and doesn't need to. Charlie knows. And my mother. Alison, of course, and now you."

"Charlie knows? You've told Charlie and not me?" There was just a tiny touch of petulance in his voice that wavered between making her happy and pissing her off.

"Charlie has been my best friend for a lot of years. I've known you two weeks," she said in as much of a matter-of-fact voice as she could muster. "Listen, I've got to go. Now I'm running late." She moved her hands up his chest and placed them against his face. She could see the confusion, pain, and a little fear in his beautiful green eyes. After gently kissing his lips, she whispered, "Besides, being in a good mood does almost as much for SAD as therapy and the light box. And Sawyer?" She kissed him again. "You put me in a very good mood."

HE TRUSTED THAT DENI had told him the truth about the severity—or non-severity—of her disorder. He really did.

Still, as he sat at her kitchen table after she'd left for work, he eyed the light box warily.

The day he'd found out about Molly's depression—to have it diagnosed and with an actual name—came flooding back to him. He'd been unable to help her, had felt so useless. It was something he'd never felt with her.

Had never felt useless, period. At least not since his father had left, making Sawyer the man of the house.

He turned the light on, moving to the chair Deni must sit in each morning. He drank his coffee as the light blazed at him. As if it shone a bright light onto his biggest failure—his inability to save his wife. He leaned over and shut it off.

He knew everything Deni said was true, that it was different from Molly's case. And yet, that same sinking feeling he had when Molly was in a spiral crept over him.

He rose from his chair and took his mug to the sink, where he washed it out. Lucy rose from where she'd been in a corner of the kitchen and slowly walked over to him.

Last night when he'd let Lucy out, he'd brought in some dog food and the dog dish for her that he always kept in his truck. He'd fed her there, just putting the bowl in the foyer and not even going into the kitchen. This morning while Deni showered, he'd fed his dog again, but this time he got a bowl from Deni's kitchen and filled it with water. That was when he'd seen the light box.

"Come on, girl," he said to Lucy after he'd unplugged and washed out the coffee pot. "Let's go home and get some fresh clothes. Then we'll go back to the office. You liked it there, didn't you? Didn't you, girl." Lucy barked her approval of his plan.

He wasn't sure what all he'd do at the office on day two, but he knew he'd spend a fair amount of time Googling seasonal affective disorder.

BY THE END OF THE WORKDAY, he was both more reassured and more freaked out about Deni and SAD.

He hadn't spent the entire day surfing the net. Andy had

given him a file of projects that he'd heard wind of across the U.P. and in Wisconsin but hadn't pursued.

"I haven't had a chance to look at them to see if they're anything viable, or even if we'd want to bid on anything. I'm sure some of them are well past deadline."

"I'm not a numbers guy," he told Andy. "I can't tell you whether we should bid on these or not."

"Just see if you find any of them interesting. If you'd want to take on any of them yourself. Then we'll worry about if we could competitively bid it or not."

He figured Andy had probably handed him the equivalent of a junk drawer—full of odds and ends that nobody cared about or had time to sort.

He spent the rest of the day weeding through the files, putting the dead ones in a different pile and going online to check on a few. Before he knew it, Deni was standing in his doorway.

"Um…I'm heading home now. I just wanted to say good night."

Holy wah, was it five already? He looked at the clock on his laptop. Nearly six. Yes, most of the lights in the office behind Deni were out.

He got up from his chair quickly. "I had no idea it was so late. Were you working on something in particular?"

She shrugged. "No, not really."

He reached for his coat. Lucy rose from the doggie bed he'd brought down with him from the house and stretched. "What do you feel like? Pizza? We never did get to eat it last night. Or how about Chinese?" he asked as he neared the doorway.

He saw her body relax, and he realized she wasn't sure… what? Sure about him? About them? After telling him about her SAD, did she think he'd dump her? That he couldn't handle it?

He slung his arm around her. "I know, I know. No PDA at the office. But everyone's gone."

She didn't balk at his arm around her; instead she slid hers around his waist and walked with him until they reached her cubicle where she disengaged herself to pull on her coat.

"Chinese sounds good," she said, flashing him that dimple.

Twenty-Five

HE SPENT THE NIGHT AT HER PLACE. THEY ALSO HAD dinner Wednesday night after work, and then made love on the foyer floor, not making it to the bedroom, or even the stairs.

When she got up and started for the bedroom, he told her he needed to spend the night in Laurium.

"I told Andy as I was leaving that I'm going to stay at home tomorrow and Friday. With the weekend, I can get the floor laid in the house."

"Three days in the office and you're already chomping at the bit to get out of there?" she asked. She'd thought he was enjoying being back, but maybe he'd spent too much time alone to truly be happy in office life again.

As if knowing what she was thinking, he took her in his arms right there in the foyer with his pants undone and her skirt wrinkled, panties and tights still lying on the floor.

"Relax. I *want* to be back at work. In fact, I think I may have found my next project. And if that's the case, I want to get this house in Laurium finished, pronto. No taking my time on this one. It's going to be on the market within a month."

She made sure her voice was perfectly calm when she said, "And then what?"

He took a step back, sliding his hands down her arms and clasping her hands in his. "Well, we have a couple of options. I really like this place, and you've put a lot of work into it."

"I have."

"But it's a rental, you said, right?"

She nodded.

"Once the house in Laurium is done, we can figure out what makes sense."

"What are you thinking?"

He shrugged. "I could keep the house in Laurium, not even put it on the market, and you move in there. Or, I can sell it and move in here, and we can talk to the owner about selling. Or, we can find something totally different, maybe another fixer-upper and do it together, just like we'd want it."

She took a deep breath, stunned.

"What? Too fast? Does the idea of living together freak you out?"

The idea of living with a man she'd only known a few weeks *should* freak her out. But it was Sawyer, and she shook her head. "No. Not really. It doesn't feel fast to you?"

He leaned over and kissed her cheek. "It's been ten years since I've felt like this about anybody." He kissed her lips. "I'd say it's moving too slow."

He left soon after, with a determination to have most of the flooring laid by the time she came up to see the house on Friday night after work.

So she was surprised to see him walk into the office at three on Thursday afternoon. Apparently so was Andy, who came out of his office upon seeing Sawyer.

"I thought you were taking today and tomorrow off."

"So did I. You mean he didn't call you, too?" Sawyer asked Andy as he walked down the row of cubes. He peeked in Deni's as he passed, but she was at one of the collaboration tables at the end of the room, near Andy.

"Hey," he said softly to her.

"Hey," she said back, and then put her head down to try to hide the flush that was no doubt turning her face red.

"Who didn't call me?" Andy asked him, ignoring the look

that had passed between her and Sawyer.

"Pete Ryan. He called me an hour ago and said he needed to see us right away. Told me to meet him here at three."

"Well, that doesn't sound good. He didn't say anything else?"

"No. I tried to get more from him, but he said he was leaving for Detroit at four and needed to take a meeting first."

"Well, shit."

"Why shit?" Deni asked. Others were starting to gather around them now. At hearing Petey's name, Charlie and Mac had come over and were giving her a questioning look, which she returned with a shrug.

"If he's heading out of town, he's probably going to tell us they're not going to do the project. Hell, maybe he's moving back to Detroit after all."

Deni had seen the looks that had passed between Alison and Petey—he wasn't going too far away from her.

"Well, we'll know soon enough," Mac said from near the window. "He just pulled up."

When the hulking figure entered the office area and then broke into a grin and lifted high a bottle of champagne in each of his hands, the whole group broke into laughter and applause.

His smile stayed on as he walked the length of the building toward them.

"Let's build this fucker."

An hour later, with the initial agreement signed and the champagne gone, Petey Ryan left the building with as much pomp as he'd entered.

"We're back late on Sunday. I'll call you guys Monday morning to start rolling."

Lots of handshakes all around, and then he was gone.

They'd been awarded a lot of jobs at Summers and Beck, most much larger than an indoor driving range, but Deni didn't remember having such elation before.

"Why don't we all call it a day," Andy said. "Nobody's going to get any more work done, anyway." He clapped his hand on

Sawyer's shoulder and said, "Let me buy you a drink, partner. Just like we used to when we got a job."

She saw the hesitation on Sawyer's face. But then his expression relaxed. "Yeah, that'd be good. I'd like that."

"Let me get my coat," Andy said, returning to his office, leaving Deni and Sawyer alone in the conference room where they'd moved the celebration.

"Hey, this should only take a couple of hours. How about if I swing by after we're done and we have our own celebration?"

"What about the floors?"

He waved a hand in the air and then bent over to where she was sitting. "Screw the floor, it'll be there tomorrow. I can't see you and then not...*see* you, you know?"

Oh yes, she definitely knew.

"I'd like that," she said. He smiled and started to lean in, but she gave him a warning look.

He sighed, but stood back up. "Later," he whispered, his eyes dropping to her mouth.

"Yes," she softly said, but he was already out the door.

She decided to pick up some champagne for when he came over, so she swung by the store. She put two bottles in her cart and slowly made her way down the aisle, lost in thought.

And then she realized she wasn't lost in thought but mired in the fog. It had closed in around her, and her brain was fuzzy and unfocused. Her arms could barely lift to the cart handle, and she started to move to the front of the store. She looked around her and saw she was in the section with the ready-made mashed potatoes. Oh, they looked so good to her. She threw a package into the cart. Then she took three more and placed them in, too. She turned and went back to the deli area to get a tub of the homemade mac and cheese. At the checkout area, she looked away as the woman at the register rang up her odd collection.

Just get home, just get home.

It was an effort to lift her arms to the steering wheel, and when she made it home, she almost left her two bags of groceries in the car, as the thought of carrying them down the steps suddenly seemed so daunting.

But the promise of warm mashed potatoes with butter generously applied made her summon up her strength, and she made it from the garage, down the stairs, into the house, and to the kitchen. She put one of the packages of potatoes in the microwave and the rest of the items in the refrigerator. The champagne seemed foreign and unnecessary to her puzzled mind. And then she remembered Sawyer would be there soon.

She was still in her coat and boots. She was dripping melted snow all over her kitchen floor, but that seemed inconsequential. Pulling her phone out of her bag, she put it on speaker and dialed Sawyer as she moved to the microwave. She took the potatoes out, peeled back the plastic, and stirred them up. Then she put them back for another two minutes—which seemed like a lifetime to her.

"Hey." Sawyer's voice came through the air to her. "I'm sorry. We're just finishing up and then I'll be—"

"No," she said, perhaps a little shrilly. She couldn't really seem to hear her voice very well. "That's why I called. I'm beat. Why don't you just stay with Andy and grab some dinner with him? I'll see you tomorrow night like we planned."

"Really, we're settling the check right now."

"It's okay, I'm not mad, really. I just got tired all of a sudden. I think the late nights last week...the weekend...and then the adrenaline of this afternoon just caught up with me. I'm going to make an early night of it and catch up on some sleep."

"Are you sure?"

"Yep. Have fun with Andy. Get going on those floors tomorrow, and I'll see you tomorrow night. I'll call you when I'm done with work and see what I can bring us for dinner."

"Okay. Deni, are you okay? I mean—"

"Everything's fine, Sawyer. Enjoy the night, and I'll see you tomorrow."

"Okay. Good night."

"Good night," she said quickly, and disconnected just as the bell on the microwave sounded.

HER ALARM PULLED HER out of deep sleep the next morning. Or, maybe it hadn't, because when she sat up and really looked at her alarm, she realized she must have been hitting the snooze button for the last hour without really waking up.

Already ten minutes late for work, she made her way to the bathroom, staring down the crusty bowl of mashed potato dregs as she passed her bedside table.

She'd lost her tights somewhere along the line last night, but otherwise she was still wearing what she'd worn to work yesterday.

After using the bathroom and brushing her teeth, she turned on the shower and started peeling off her clothes, letting them fall to the floor in a heap. She leaned against the bathroom counter waiting for the shower to heat up, still wearing her bra and panties.

And suddenly, it all just seemed like too much. Taking off her undergarments, getting wet, drying herself, and then having to—what? Put clothes back on again?

No, she couldn't do it. Not today.

She turned the shower off and left the bathroom, her clothes still on the floor. Back in her bedroom, she found her comfiest sweats and pulled them on along with an old Tech sweatshirt. Then she wrapped her robe around herself and crawled back into bed.

Her cell was on the nightstand—apparently she'd brought it up with her last night out of habit—and she called the office.

"Sue," she said when the older woman answered. "It's Deni. I'm taking a sick day today."

"Too much celebrating last night? That's good, honey, you deserved it. Great job on the driving range."

"Thanks. And I *wish* I were just hung over. But I've got some kind of bug or something. Didn't even get to celebrate last night."

"Oh, you poor thing," Sue said sympathetically, and Deni almost started to cry. "Well, you take care of yourself. Do you need anything taken care of here?"

"No. Nothing that can't wait until Monday."

"Okay. Can somebody bring something over to you? Medicine or soup or anything? I'm sure Charlie would be happy—"

"No, that's okay. I've got stuff here. I'm good." She thought of the packages of potatoes and mac and cheese. And, more importantly, whether she'd be willing to leave her bed to go downstairs and heat them up.

Would she even be able to?

"Okay, Deni, take care," Sue said. Deni answered with another thanks, and they both hung up.

With Herculean effort, she made her way to the kitchen, where she deposited last night's bowl in the sink and microwaved a new batch of potatoes, adding an extra spoonful of butter.

She'd sit at the light box and eat the potatoes and let the magic do its trick. Then she'd shower, and as long as she'd already called in sick, she'd get some stuff done around the house. Like tackling that good-sized pile of laundry.

Then she'd go up to Laurium and meet Sawyer this evening like they'd planned.

She took her new bowl of potatoes to the table, but sitting there, even to get the much-needed light rush, instead of lying in her bed seemed so tiring that she bypassed the table and light box altogether and made her way back upstairs.

The pile of laundry mocked her from the corner of her room as she wrapped herself up in her comforter and inhaled the potatoes. Ah, such smooth, creamy goodness that seemed to melt on her tongue and warm her insides.

Okay, change of plans. Instead of showering and getting stuff done, she'd just take a little nap. *Really* catch up on her sleep (apparently the fifteen-plus hours last night didn't quite do the trick), and then shower and go meet Sawyer.

The laundry—and other chores—could wait another day.

She set the now-empty bowl on the nightstand, burrowed

into her pile of blankets, and slept.

Again.

Twenty-Six

—ᴍ—

WHEN SAWYER'S PHONE RANG AT SIX, HE'D JUST finished showering and dressing after a long, dirty day of installing flooring. Seeing Deni's name on the caller ID, he answered with a quick "Are you running late? 'Cause so am I, so don't—"

"No, it's not that," she said. Her voice sounded odd, like maybe she'd just woken up or something. "Well, yes, I'm running late. But…I need to cancel, Sawyer."

A shiver ran through him. Two nights in a row she was canceling on him. One—okay she was tired and it'd been a long week. But two? And a Friday night at that?

"What's going on, Deni?" he asked in his best "cut the bullshit" voice.

"Nothing. I'm just tired—"

"You were tired last night. Didn't you get any sleep?"

He heard what sounded like a small snort on her end. "Yeah, I did," she said.

And then he remembered the SAD. "But you're still tired?" Understanding now.

"A little," she said, her voice sounding small and frail. Not like the Deni he knew.

"Were you really busy at the office today? Did that wear you out?"

"I called in sick this morning."

Shit. If he'd been in the office, he'd have known that. Instead, he'd wanted to get the flooring laid so he'd be that much closer to finishing this house and getting back to the office on a regular basis.

And back to Deni.

"And are you sick? I mean…umm…like a flu or something?"

"No, it's not that. I kind of hit a wall."

"Metaphorically speaking?" Visions of her actually hitting a wall—perhaps in a car—quickly drifted through his head. But no, she was calling him herself and was obviously okay.

She chuckled. "Yes, metaphorically. Although my body kind of feels like it's been thrown around a little. Alison warned me that this might happen. That there might be a day or two where I'd just kind of shut down. There's nothing to be worried about. I just kind of have to sleep it off."

"Sounds like you went on a bender or something."

"You know, that's kind of what it feels like. Like one big, fuzzy hangover. Except I didn't get the party beforehand."

"We'll have our party. It'll just be after the hangover."

"Thanks, Sawyer. And sorry about tonight. I really wanted to see the house you're working on."

"Don't worry about that. But what I can do? Shall I bring you some soup? Or would something more solid be better?" He looked at his watch. "I'll be about a half-hour and—"

"No, don't come tonight, Sawyer. Really."

Again a chill ran through him. "But I'd like to help, Deni."

"I know, but there's… You know what? Why don't you come tomorrow? Not early morning, but sometime tomorrow morning. I'm sure I'll be feeling much better and we can go grab an early lunch or something. I'd like that."

"Really? Not until then?"

"Really. Tomorrow. I'll be looking forward to it."

"Okay. Well…get some rest, and I'll see you tomorrow."

"Okay. Thanks for understanding. And, oh, probably just use the key from the garage and let yourself in tomorrow."

"Okay, will do."

"Okay, good night," she said.

"Deni?"

"Yes?"

"This is just a small wall, right? You'd tell me if it was something larger?" he said with some hesitation.

"Yes, Sawyer, I'd tell you. Good night," she said softly, and disconnected.

Sawyer put the phone down on what was left of the kitchen counters and then found his way to the one comfortable chair he'd moved into the house when he'd bought it.

He sat down, and Lucy made her way over to him, sensing his need for company. Leaning over to pet his dog, he buried his face in Lucy's neck, trying to gain some sense of control in a situation he couldn't control at all.

"It's not happening again, is it, Luce?" he whispered.

He knew on an intellectual level that what Deni was going through was different than what Molly had gone through. But on an emotional level? On a punched-in-the-gut level?

It hurt. And scared the living shit out of him.

He leaned back in the chair. Lucy lay down right on top of his feet, as if protecting him.

But could she?

Could anything protect him from going through this all over again?

DENI HEARD THE DOOR opening the next morning and pulled herself out of her haze.

Crap, it was Sawyer. And she'd planned on being showered and dressed and ready to go out for some lunch.

And she was still in bed, still in the sweats and sweatshirt she'd donned yesterday morning. *Was that only yesterday?*

"Deni? You home? You awake?" Sawyer called from downstairs. Except it wasn't exactly his voice.

"It's Twain," came the voice. "Are you here?"

"Twain?" she called.

"Yeah. Are you upstairs? Is it okay to come up?"

Why was Twain here? Had something happened to Sawyer? "Yes, come up," she shouted, then started unwinding herself from her cocoon of covers. "Is Sawyer okay?" she called out, but Twain was already in her doorway. Taking up the whole doorway.

"He's fine. How are you doing?" he asked gently, then slowly moved into the room. She saw his eyes wander the room...the messy, much-slept-in bed, the pile of laundry in the corner, even the ever-present bowl of crusty potatoes on the bedside table. *Or was it mac and cheese last time?*

She should feel shame, but she didn't have the energy.

"I don't understand," she said, while shaking her head as if she could knock the fog loose. "Sawyer's okay?"

"Yeah, he's fine," Twain said, taking another step in the room. "A total dickhead, but fine" she thought she heard him say under his breath.

And then she got it.

"He's not coming, is he?" At Twain's sheepish look, she knew she'd nailed it. "And he sent you in his place."

A short nod from Twain.

Emotions whirled through her. Yes, she'd bailed on Sawyer the last two nights, but this was different. At least, it felt different to her. She was terribly hurt, and that hurt would normally make her sad. But maybe she was pulling out of her funk, because instead of sadness, the hurt quickly turned to anger. "What a douche," she spat out.

Twain snorted. "You'll get no argument from me." He was to the bed now, and he gestured to the spot beside her. She nodded, and he sat down next to her.

"So, what? He called you and asked you to come over here? To check up on me?"

"Something like that."

"Told you where I kept the spare key?"

The big man nodded. "Hide it somewhere else now...just so you feel better."

She waved that suggestion away. She really didn't care that Twain Beck knew where she hid her spare key. She cared more that her "boyfriend" had bailed on her and sent his brother instead.

"I can't believe this," she said, burying her face in her knees.

"Yeah, I know. But, hey, Deni…." He waited until she looked up at him, which she reluctantly did. "Forget about that for a minute. How are *you* doing?"

"I'm okay," she answered.

"Yeah? 'Cause you don't look okay."

"No, I am. I just needed to rest for a bit."

"Going on two days from what I understand."

"Whatever."

"Listen, why don't you hop in the shower and then we'll go get something to eat."

"I was supposed to do that with Sawyer," she said. Even she could hear the pout in her tone.

"Well, his loss is my gain." He started to pull the covers from her and something in her—almost a panic—started to rise. She held on to the comforter.

"Come on, Deni, let's get you to the shower."

"No, I'm okay. I think I'd just like to take a nap now. Thanks for stopping by, Twain. You can tell Sawyer you saw me and I was fine." *Then tell him to go fuck himself.*

"I'd feel better about telling him that if you'd take a shower and put some fresh clothes on."

"No, I'm good, but thanks." She pulled the covers away from him and started to tuck herself back in.

The bedding was ripped from her hands and torn off of her, leaving her naked. Well, okay. She had sweats and a sweatshirt, socks and underwear…but she *felt* naked without the heavy bedding.

"Hey!"

Twain scooped her up in his arms and carried her out of the bedroom and down the hall. Finding the bathroom, he set her on her feet in the middle of the small room. Then he reached over and turned the shower on. He left for a moment, taking the clothes that were still on the floor from Thursday night. Deni stood in place, not daring to move. She heard him rummaging around in the hall linen closet and then he deposited two clean towels and a washcloth on the vanity.

He turned to her and took her shoulders in his big hands.

"Deni, you stink. Literally." She flinched and started to pull back, but he hung tight. "Now, I'm going to step out of the room. If those clothes you're wearing aren't thrown out into the hallway for me in twenty seconds, and you in the shower, I'm coming back in to put you there myself."

She stared at him, stunned, her mouth open, but nothing coming out.

"I know you've sauna-ed with one Beck brother, but if you don't get your cute fanny in gear, you're about to shower with a different one." He let her go and left the bathroom, shutting the door softly behind him.

Slowly, she started peeling off the sweatshirt. Twain was right, she did stink.

"I'm waiting," came his voice through the door. "And I know how to use a loofa."

She started yanking off clothes much more quickly.

Twenty-Seven

—⚏—

SHE HADN'T THOUGHT she'd been in the shower that long—though it had felt good and she'd let the hot water pound on her shoulders for what could have been a good, long while. When she went back to her bedroom, wrapped in a towel and hoping Twain was downstairs—or better yet, gone completely—she realized she must have been in the bathroom longer than she'd realized.

The overflowing laundry basket was gone, as was her bedding. It had been replaced with crisp, clean sheets that Twain must have taken from the linen closet.

The effort—the gesture—touched her deeply. She moved to the edge of the bed and sat down, becoming emotional.

God, what if she started crying over how sweet Twain was being to her and never stopped?

The thought that it was her boyfriend's brother who had done this for her, and not her boyfriend, changed the oncoming tears to irritation.

"Deni?" Twain called from downstairs. "Need any help?"

"No," she answered, rising from the bed, her pissiness at Sawyer driving her to the dresser to pull out some clean undergarments. "I'll be right down."

He took her to lunch at the Sisu café. Just as they settled in and started looking at the menu, Twain got a text. He read it and quickly put the phone back in his pocket.

"Was that Sawyer?" she asked, then wished she hadn't.

"Hmmm," he said, not committing. He studied the menu. "How about a steak? Or a burger?"

"A steak? For lunch?" She shook her head. "They do breakfast all day. I'm thinking pancakes."

"Really? Doesn't a burger sound good?" he asked.

"So have a burger."

He put his menu down and placed a hand on hers, gently taking her menu and placing it with his. "You should have some protein. Probably not so many carbs right now."

"What do… Wait. Was that what that text said? That I should eat protein? Are you kidding me? He won't show his face, but he's going to tell me what to eat?"

Well, the fog was gone, which was nice. But it was replaced by irritability like she hadn't felt in a long time.

Or maybe she was just good old-fashioned pissed.

"Sort of. But the protein thing isn't coming from him."

"That wasn't him who texted you just now?"

"Well, yeah, but…."

"Twain, what the hell is going on?"

"Sawyer called Alison Jukuri to see if there was anything that he could do to help. She suggested that some protein might help. Especially if you'd been carb loading."

She ducked her head, embarrassed. Of course Twain had seen the bowl of potatoes. It had been gone from her bedroom. And her kitchen had been straightened when she'd gone downstairs— so he'd disposed of the empty containers.

Their waitress came and Deni almost ordered the pancakes, but then the thought of cutting off her nose to spite her SAD face got the best of her, and she ordered steak and eggs. "Hold the hash browns. Hold the toast," she added. Twain ordered the same and then sat back in the booth, putting his long arms across the back. It was as if he was preparing for the barrage Deni was going to throw at him.

Which she dearly wanted to, but she knew she had the wrong Beck brother in front of her.

"Listen," she said after taking a long drink of coffee. It was strong and hot and seemed to give her a tiny bit of clarity. "I'm still kind of muddled emotionally right now."

"Sure, okay."

"Which is hard for me, because I'm not typically very emotional. I'm an engineer. I think in terms of logic, equations… right angles, for God's sake," she said, her voice full of emotion.

"Totally unemotional. Got it," he answered, a grin creeping across his face.

"And while I realize what Sawyer has gone through—and I sympathize, I really do—it was still pretty shitty of him to send you in his place."

Twain leaned forward and held one of her hands in his. They were rough and warm and brought her comfort. But again… wrong Beck brother.

"It was, you're right. And honestly, I'm not going to defend his actions. But I do know he was pretty freaked when he called me, Deni."

"When was this exactly? I talked to him last night and he seemed okay."

"This morning. I don't think he slept, which isn't unusual. He called pretty early, and I know he'd already talked to Alison, so I'm not sure when he called her."

Deni took her hand from Twain's and put her head in her hands. "Jesus, how am I going to face her?"

"You have no problem with Alison…it's Sawyer who will have to face her."

That was true.

"Besides, Alison's pretty cool. She'll be glad he called her."

Also true.

"You said you weren't going to defend him…but you kind of are."

Their food arrived then, and Deni admitted that the steak and eggs did look good.

"Yeah, I know. He can be a dick, that's for sure, but he's my brother and I love him."

That was the problem. So did she.

AFTER LUNCH, TWAIN TOOK HER to the ski hill. "The only place I know where the deck is open this time of year and you can get some rays—even if they come with a minus-ten-degree wind-chill factor."

He got her settled on the outdoor deck, a blanket from his truck wrapped around her in addition to her parka, then went inside the chalet. When he came back, he handed her a hot chocolate and then sat on the same side of the picnic table as she, both facing the hill.

They sipped their drinks, she mindlessly watching the skiers coming down the hill, Twain more avidly watching.

"See the kid in the yellow ski jacket? The one with the red hat?" he said, pointing to a group on the east side of the hill.

Deni nodded, picking out the skier.

"That's my son, Matty."

"Oh," she said, and watched the boy ski the hill with grace and skill. "He's good."

"Not bad. We're all still kind of in shock that he'd rather ski than play hockey, but we're dealing with it." The pride in Twain's voice contradicted his words.

"Do you have him today? Am I keeping you from time with your son?"

"Nah. Yes, I have him this weekend, but he wanted to be dropped off here first thing, and I'm not supposed to pick him up until five. He's at that age now where it's all about his friends. And skiing." Wistfulness was in Twain's voice.

"And yet here we are, watching him. Well before five."

Twain shrugged. "I thought it'd be good for you to be outside." He smiled at her. "And yes, I wanted to watch him."

When he took her home, he sat her in front of the light box while he put another load of her laundry in and brought the load he'd done earlier up to her room.

"Okay, I've got to go pick up Matty at the hill, but I can drop him off at home and bring you back some dinner or something," he said, entering the kitchen as she turned off the light box.

"No, but thank you. I've got some chicken breasts in the freezer I'll thaw out."

He seemed hesitant to leave. She walked to the big man and kissed his cheek.

"Thank you for today," she said quietly. "It helped a lot."

"Good, I'm glad," he said. He kissed the top of her head and headed to the foyer. She followed him and watched as he put on his coat and boots.

"Please let me know if you need anything," he added as he stood in the doorway. "I'll be here in a second."

Again, the right words came from the wrong damn Beck.

Twenty-Eight

—⁓—

LATE SUNDAY AFTERNOON, SAWYER PUT HIS PHONE down on the counter. Again.

Christ, why wouldn't Twain answer his damn phone?

Nothing since the one short text from him last night: "She's fine, and you're a dick." Which did make him feel better—well, not the dick part. But he already knew that.

He knew it down to his soul, but the vision of lifting Molly's mitten from the snow and seeing all the blood had played through his mind on a never-ending loop since Friday night when Deni had called.

And he knew he just couldn't go through it all again. He needed to distance himself, or this time he surely would go mad.

And he knew how to distance himself. He'd done it after Molly's death, pulling away from the business that, with Andy, they'd grown together. Extracting himself from his family. He knew all about distance.

But he loved Deni and needed to at least know that she was okay. Thus the calls to Twain and Alison.

Sawyer hadn't heard from Twain since the "dick" text, neither by text nor by picking up when Sawyer had called him. Numerous times.

Shit, anything could have happened since Twain saw Deni yesterday.

His gut twisted, his breathing grew labored, but he heaved

himself from his chair. "Come on, Luce. We need to go see Deni," he said, and his dog rose excitedly from the floor.

Three sharp barks from Lucy were the only notice Sawyer had before Twain burst through his door, looked wildly around the room. Seeing Sawyer, he charged and pushed him up against a wall.

Sawyer hadn't seen his fun-loving brother act like this in a lot of years, not since he and Liv had first started having problems. Why would he—

"What happened to her? What happened to Deni?" Sawyer yelled at his little brother, grabbing the front of his coat, much like Twain held him.

Twain pushed him harder into the wall—not the little brother any longer. "Nothing's wrong. She's good. Matty and I just had dinner with her before I dropped Matty off."

Sawyer relaxed, his grip on Twain loosening, until Twain once again pushed him into the wall, this time pinning him there.

"You, on the other hand, are a complete and total *asshole.*"

Sawyer pushed back, which was like pushing against a brick wall. "You think I don't know that? You think I haven't spent every waking moment—and they've *all* been waking, believe me—thinking about what a dick I'm being? How the woman I love needs me and because I just can't go through it again, I leave her hanging?" His hands full of Twain's coat, he pushed again.

Twain pushed right back, the framing on the unfinished wall behind him digging into Sawyer's shoulders. "You love her? You seriously love her?"

"Yeah, so?" Push.

"Then you're an even bigger asshole than I thought. I could kind of see you not wanting to do the heavy lifting with a chick you've only been on a few dates with, if that's all it's going to be."

"That's not all it's going to be," Sawyer responded. "Not with her."

Push. "That's not what I'd say after seeing her yesterday and today. I'd say she's done with your sorry ass."

Which was Sawyer's worst fear, and one he'd been obsessing about all day. He took that fear out on Twain, pushing even harder—hard enough to have his own back finally away from the wall.

"What the fuck do you know about relationships? How would you even be able to tell? Liv kicked your cheating ass out the door eight years ago." He saw his brother flinch, and Sawyer knew he'd hit below the belt. But he felt like he'd been sucker-punched, too, and couldn't help but share the pain. "I'll tell you about relationships. I never wanted to be a pussy-chasing hound like you, Twain." Push. "I *wanted* to be a husband, a partner, a best friend to the woman I loved. And I was." Push. "But I also wanted to grow old with her, to have a family with her. To be a father to a little girl who had her mother's eyes and her father's curiosity. And I'm not." The fire went out of him then, and he dropped his hands from Twain's coat. "And I'm not," he whispered this time. Meeting his brother's eyes, knowing Twain could see the pain Sawyer felt.

Twain's grip on him loosened, but he gave Sawyer one last shake. "But you could be, Sawyer. You *could* be." He let go of him, turned, and sat in Sawyer's only chair. He pulled off his coat. Sawyer went out to the empty kitchen, grabbed two beers from the mini fridge he'd bought for the interim, and handed one to Twain when he returned to the living room. He took his and sat his ass on the newly laid floor. At least he'd put his panic to good use yesterday.

He took a drink of his beer, then looked at his brother. "What is it about me, Twain? Why do I fall in love with women who…who…are in pain? Women I can't help?"

Twain took a swig of beer, then held a hand up in a "stop" motion. "I saw Molly at her worst, remember? Deni is not Molly. This is not the same, Soy Sauce."

The old childhood nickname, one his brother hadn't called him in at least twenty-five years, made a small smile rise from Sawyer.

"I know that, I really do. And yet the fear is the same, Twain. The feeling of helplessness is the same. I can't help her…and I can't stand to watch her in pain."

"But you're going to have to, if you want to be with her." Twain took another drink of beer and then leaned forward, his elbows on his knees. "It's time to man up, Soy."

"Christ, this isn't about just doing the right thing. This is about keeping my sanity. I just about lost it last time, you know that. And you know what? I'd do it. I'd be willing to lose my fucking mind if it would help. But I know it won't."

Twain nodded, understanding, knowing. "But you've got to ask yourself this: Is living without fear, without the feeling of helplessness at times, better than living without Deni?"

He got up from the chair, walked over to Sawyer, tousled his hair—much like Sawyer had done to him when they'd been little kids—and then let himself out.

Leaving Sawyer on his ass in an empty house…alone.

SAWYER WASN'T IN THEIR Monday morning status meeting. Andy didn't mention him at all, but as they were finishing up, one of the guys asked if Sawyer was now back full time.

"It's still being worked out," Andy said. "Though I do expect him in later today."

So, she would see him today after all. She'd spent yesterday thinking about what she'd say to him when she saw him.

Funny how her Sundays were going lately. Two weeks ago she had done some deep thinking about what she wanted out of a relationship—out of Sawyer. And boldly told him the next day at Tootie's.

Last Sunday, they'd been having sex in the sauna in the morning and beers with Twain at Tootie's in the afternoon. With Deni knowing on some level that she was already in love with him.

And yesterday, she had a late dinner with Twain and his son and thought about how she could go about falling out of love with Sawyer Beck.

No protractor or CAD drawing or any other feat of engineering was going to help with that one.

Alison had called her to check in yesterday—apparently while she and Petey were driving back from Detroit—and Deni assured her that she felt much better. She relayed to her therapist that she'd gotten out of bed at a normal time (for a Sunday, so like ten), had showered (even without the threat of Twain on the other side of the door), had done the light box, and was going to meet a friend and his son for dinner later (a last-minute decision when Twain had called her and asked).

She'd enjoyed meeting Twain's son, Matt, and it was nice to see the deep bond between father and son. But it only drove home to her that she was in love with the wrong damn Beck brother.

But loving Sawyer wasn't enough.

Sawyer came in around two. Lucy stopped at Deni's cube for some affection, but Sawyer did not. No IMs. Nothing.

He was making it a lot easier on her, that's for sure, she thought, her irritation starting to rise. And yes, in a way he was just following her edict not to draw attention to their relationship in the office. But still.

She worked late, catching up on things from missing work on Friday, but also hoping Sawyer would stay, too, so she could say her piece and go home.

And start falling out of love with him. More mashed potatoes would definitely be needed. Like, Idaho quantities.

Sawyer did stay late, and by six-thirty, they were the only two people in the building. She IM'd him "Can I see you in the conference room?" and got an almost-immediate and affirmative response.

Taking a deep breath and straightening her shoulders, she walked into the room and turned the light on, then leaned against the table, waiting.

"Why in here?" Sawyer asked when he entered the room. He eyed a chair but in the end stayed standing. "Why didn't you just come to my office?"

She shrugged. "Neutral turf."

He moved to the wall nearest the corner of the table where she was and leaned against it. "So, we need turfs? It's going to be that bad?"

She relaxed her shoulders a little. "Remember that first day at Tootie's? When I told you I needed more than a snack?"

"Yes."

"You seemed to appreciate that I was being honest with you. That I came out and told you what I needed and what my expectations were."

"I was. It was refreshing. And I liked knowing where I stood."

"Well, good, 'cause you're about to get a big dose of honest."

He moved from the wall. "Deni, wait. Before you—"

She held a hand up, stopping his words as well as his movements. "No, Sawyer. I have to get this out."

He stopped, standing halfway between Deni and the wall. He motioned for her to go on.

"I'm not pissed any more about you not showing up or that you sent Twain instead—who has been absolutely lovely, by the way."

There was just enough of a flare from him at the mention of Twain to give her hope—if he still cared enough to get a teensy bit jealous…could he…?

"I *was* pissed. Really pissed. But I do understand what you were going through. What you *have* gone through. I can only imagine what was running through your mind."

He took another step, "Deni, you have no—" She held the hand up again, and he stopped.

"But I'm not Molly. My…*disorder* is mild, and it's temporary."

"I know that. I get that."

She nodded, knowing that he did on an intellectual level. But she also knew that the emotional level was a whole different ball game.

"And you need to come to terms with the fact that you can't

fix me. *I* can't fix me. And, quite frankly, the ten pounds and lost winter aside, I don't really want to be fixed—I like how I am."

His face gentled and his voice was soft when he said, "So do I."

"But what I want—no, what I *need*—is someone who is going to fight for me—for us. I need someone who will hold my hand when it needs holding and who will leave me alone when I need that. Someone who will carry me to the shower and make me get in when I don't want to." His eyes narrowed at that. "And who will wait for me to get over the humps that need to be gotten over. And I'm not just talking about the SAD humps. I'm talking about all the stuff that life throws you on any given day."

"I...I...." He took a step closer.

Say you can do that. Please, please, say you can do that. Some part of her was desperately holding out hope that this conversation was going have a different outcome than she'd calculated.

He didn't take another step.

Please, please, please. Be the guy I know you can be.

"I don't know if I can do it, Deni," he said, regret in his voice.

She wasn't mad, and she couldn't blame him for being honest when she'd been so honest with him. In a way, he'd saved them the couple of years, probably, before they would have realized it wasn't going to work.

And perhaps a whole lot of heartbreak, although she wasn't sure heartbreak a few years down the road would be any less painful than it was now.

"Thank you for being honest," she said, then rose from the table. She'd have to walk past him, smell that pine-tree scent, and she wasn't sure she could bear it, so she waited for him to leave first.

"I want to, Deni. God, how I want to. But I don't know if I can do it."

"Only you can decide that, Sawyer. I believe you could, and I could fight for that—fight for you to realize it." She sighed, wishing she'd just sucked it up and walked past him. "But I'm tired, and I don't want to have to fight for love." She took a deep breath and walked past him. Screw his lovely, outdoorsy scent. And even though she knew it probably wasn't true, but only how she felt right now, she said as she passed, "And, quite frankly, I'm not sure you're worth fighting for."

Twenty-Nine

"HE PROBABLY IS, YOU KNOW," ALISON SAID AT THEIR Friday session. "Worth fighting for. He's one of the good guys. But you were wise to know you didn't want to take that on."

"Hmmm. I'm not feeling real wise right about now."

Alison shrugged. "Wisdom and people in love don't always go hand in hand."

"I'm finding that out."

"Still, though…pretty good parting line," Alison said.

Deni smiled. "Yeah, I thought so, too."

"And how has the rest of the week gone?"

Deni shrugged. "Well, I haven't barricaded myself in my bedroom with nothing but carbs and dirty bedding."

"So, you've got that going for you," Alison teased, making Deni smile.

She shrugged. "It's been okay. Andy sent an email out on Tuesday that Sawyer would be working the afternoons for the foreseeable future until he had some personal projects cleaned up. I'm assuming that meant making the house in Laurium sellable."

"And after that? Back full time?"

"The email didn't say. So, I see him come in for the afternoons. I usually leave before he does. His office is in the back of the building. We really don't even see each other. His dog comes and takes a nap in my cube but always goes back to him when I leave." Still, it had been a small balm to her heartache to have

Lucy literally underfoot.

"And the others in the office?"

"Charlie could tell something was up. And he's offered to take me out for a beer so I can cry on his shoulder, but I haven't taken him up on it. Yet." She didn't want to take advantage of Charlie, but she might just need that shoulder soon. "I think everyone else in the office just thought we'd been flirting around, a couple of dates, and it didn't work out—no big deal. I don't think they understood that...."

"You'd fallen in love?"

"Yes," she whispered, and for the first time since talking with Sawyer on Monday, Deni started to cry. She didn't need to hold out for Charlie's shoulder after all.

Alison waited patiently while Deni cried it out. Not big, gasping sobs, just quiet tears that streamed down her face until Alison handed her a box of tissues.

They sat like that, not saying a word, until what was surely well after Deni's time was up. Finally, she cleared her throat, wiped the last of her tears away, and said, "I'll be okay."

Alison nodded. "Yes, *I* know you will be. I'm glad you do, too."

"It just sucks right now, you know?"

"I know. It's going to suck for a long time. And then it won't."

"Promise?"

Alison smiled. "No."

Deni laughed, and a last half-sob caught as a hiccup.

"But I *think* so, I really do," Alison added. "And I truly believe that if two people are supposed to be together, they find their way back to each other."

"And if they're not? Supposed to be together?"

Alison shrugged. "I don't know. I think I told you once that I sucked at guy stuff on a personal level, right?"

Deni laughed again.

They went through the regular assessment questions. When it came time for an "assignment," Alison waved it away.

"I think you've been out of your comfort zone enough for a while. Be gentle with yourself this next week. And call if you need me."

SHE COULDN'T GO BACK to the office. She just couldn't see Sawyer after crying about him for over an hour. She pulled out her phone and called Sue.

"Sue, I know it's last minute, but I'm going to take the afternoon off as vacation time."

"Oh, tell me you had a three-martini lunch and are in no shape to come back to the office. I've always wanted to do that."

Deni laughed, her throat aching from the crying jag. "Nope, though that sounds tempting. Maybe I'll have a three-martini Friday afternoon."

"Okay, Deni, you enjoy it. We'll see you Monday."

"Thanks, Sue."

She thought about calling Charlie and having him meet her for lunch somewhere, but decided against it, preferring to just go home.

When she pulled onto her street, she saw Sawyer's truck parked in front of her house. She couldn't imagine what he was doing there; he knew she spent her lunch hour on Fridays at Alison's. There was no way he could know she wasn't at the office.

Why would he be at her house when he thought she was at the office? Damn. She should have listened to Twain and changed the hiding place of her spare key.

She didn't bother with the garage, just pulled to the curb behind his truck. She peeked inside looking for Lucy, thinking that if perhaps Sawyer was just running into her house for a moment—like, maybe he remembered something he'd left at her place?—he'd leave Lucy in the truck. No Lucy.

Uncertainty filled her as she made her way down the steps. She opened the door, and as she stepped into the foyer, Lucy bounded around the corner from the kitchen to greet her. She knelt down to pet the dog, and that was when she saw Sawyer. Or, more accurately, Sawyer's legs. He was balanced on some kind of portable scaffolding three quarters of the way up her stairs.

She stayed kneeling by Lucy, watching Sawyer's jeans until he slowly crouched and looked at her. "What are you doing here?" he asked.

"Um…isn't that *my* line?"

She rose from her knees, took off her coat, hung it up, and walked past the entryway and fully into the foyer, where she could see the entire staircase. "What are you…." The words trailed off as she took in the display Sawyer was completing.

It was her sketches, framed and staggered up the tall wall of the staircase—just as she had imagined them. Except not.

"Those frames? They're…." She stood on the second step, able to get up close to one of the sketches at the bottom. "Are those…?" She looked up at him. He'd moved from a squat to sitting on the base of the scaffolding, his legs hanging over the side. "No. Really?"

He rubbed his hands up and down his denim-clad thighs. "Do you like them? 'Cause I can take them down if you don't. I didn't cut the sketches. They can easily come out."

"I love it. I love them." Her sketches, the ones she'd done of unique views of interesting bits of architecture, had been placed in glass frames that were hollow on the sides and filled with stones. Hundreds of beautiful stones. They were subtle and didn't overpower the sketches. Instead, they added just a touch of warmth and texture, offsetting her black and white drawings all the more.

"I knew you didn't come home for lunch on Fridays. I wanted to have it all done and be gone by the time you got home. Although it's nice to see that you like them."

She just nodded, taking another step up and looking at the designs he'd created with the stones, different on each frame. "You must have used that whole container."

He chuckled. "Yep. In fact, I ran out on the last one. The one I want to put right there." He pointed to a spot high on the wall, almost to the wall of the landing. "I thought the stained glass would really play off the glass of the frames." Then he held up the drawing that was to go in that coveted spot. It was the one she'd done of her imagined hermit's hut.

A lump rose in her throat and she had to wait a moment before she could say "This is amazing, Sawyer. Thank you."

He swung down from the scaffolding, landing on the stair above her. He took two steps down so that their eyes were level. "You're welcome. I thought a lot about what I could do. Take you back to the glass house. Something at Tootie's. Find a miniature of the stained-glass canopy. But then I thought of this. It was a lot simpler than I wanted, but I thought you'd appreciate it just as much."

"I don't understand. Why were you trying to think of things to do for me?"

He shrugged and looked away, embarrassed. "You know, some kind of grand gesture. Something that would get your attention so you'd...I don't know...stick around long enough to hear me out."

"Grand gesture?"

"Yeah, I know. Stupid, right? Because then I thought, 'Deni's not the grand-gesture kind of girl,' and it all seemed hokey."

She didn't know whether to be insulted or proud. "Oh, I don't know. I think every girl appreciates a grand gesture...." She almost finished with "from the man she loves," but didn't. The frames, and the thoughtfulness—and practicality—of them touched her. Deeply. But that didn't negate anything she'd said to him on Monday.

"Yes, but Deni, while you might *appreciate* a grand gesture, you don't *need* one. There's a difference. And that's one of the many reasons why I love you."

"You do? Love me?"

"Yes, Deni. I love you."

God, she wanted to wrap her arms around him, tell him she loved him back, and ride off into the sunset. But she didn't.

"Here's the thing," he said before she could. "I was happy to use up the stones on these frames. And if you want more, I would love to go stone hunting with you next summer."

She started to break in, but he gently put a finger on her mouth. His eyes dropped there for a moment before returning his intense gaze to hers. "But I won't be collecting anymore. At least not alone. Or, at least, not in the semi-conscious trance I'd be in before." His finger moved from her mouth, his hand cupping her face. "No more long walks that I don't remember. If I'm hurting, I'll hurt. I won't hide anymore."

"Sawyer, what exactly are you saying?" she whispered. She laid her hands on his chest. His other hand moved to her face, gently cradling it as he moved even closer.

"I'm saying you were right. I'm not worth fighting for. At least not in the state I've lived in the past ten years.

"But, Deni, *you're* worth fighting for. *We're* worth fighting for. And I think I can be the kind of man that *is* worth fighting for. And if you give me the chance, I won't let you down again."

Her mind buzzed, but it wasn't the fog that enveloped her. It was hope. And love.

"I love you," she said, and he kissed her lips tenderly, just the tiniest whisper of a touch.

"I love you, too, Deni. And I'm not saying you might not have to kick me in the ass from time to time and let me know what you need from me—even if it's to leave you alone...."

"I can do that," she said, her voice raw and those damn tears starting to fall again.

He swiped at them with his thumbs, then kissed her eyelids. "Oh, baby, don't cry. It's going to be okay. We'll figure it out as we go along."

She was nodding, unable to speak.

"But I have to tell you," he added, stepping back. He dropped his hands and instead took her in his arms and pulled her close. "I'm a pretty old dog. It might take you a while to teach me some new tricks."

"How long?" she asked, nuzzling into him. The smell of outdoors wafted over her, making her hug him all the tighter.

"Oh, I'm thinking forever." He kissed her, then looked at her with a smile. "Yeah. Definitely forever."

~*~

Author's Note

Okay, I took MAJOR creative license with the whole indoor driving range project. I did some research, and it would pose some problems in an area with as much snowfall as the Copper Country. I can't say that wind power would be feasible, but I'd like to think that whatever the solution would be, my engineering masterminds—the crew at Summers and Beck—would figure it out.

To all my Michigan Tech engineering friends who are surely rolling their eyes, I say this…it was all in the name of romance!

The Worth Series continues with

TOTALLY WORTH CHRISTMAS
THE WORTH SERIES BOOK 4.5
A HOLIDAY NOVELLA

—∽—

WORTH THE PRICE
THE WORTH SERIES BOOK 5

—∽—

WORTH THE LIES
THE WORTH SERIES BOOK 6

—∽—

WORTH THE FLIGHT
THE WORTH SERIES BOOK 7

Try Mara's Freshman Roommates Series

IN TOO DEEP
FRESHMAN ROOMMATES TRILOGY, BOOK 1

IN TOO FAST
FRESHMAN ROOMMATES TRILOGY, BOOK 2

IN TOO HARD
FRESHMAN ROOMMATES TRILOGY, BOOK 3

—∽—

Mara Jacobs is the *New York Times* and *USA Today* bestselling author of The Worth Series

After graduating from Michigan State University with a degree in advertising, Mara spent several years working at daily newspapers in advertising sales and production. This certainly prepared her for the world of deadlines!

She writes mysteries with romance, thrillers with romance, and romances with...well, you get it.

Forever a Yooper (someone who hails from Michigan's glorious Upper Peninsula), Mara now splits her time between the Copper Country, Las Vegas, and East Lansing, where she is better able to root on her beloved Spartans.

You can find out more about Mara's books at
www.marajacobs.com

Mara loves to hear from readers. Contact her at
mara@marajacobs.com